NINE YEARS

Beneath the Clouds
Series

JESSICA LEED

ISBN: 978-0-6486797-0-7 (eBook)
ISBN: 978-0-6486797-1-4 (Paperback)
ISBN: 978-0-6486797-2-1 (Hardcover)

Printed in Australia
First Edition, 2019
www.jessleed.com

One

IT WAS A perfect afternoon to be out.

The sun was shining, the autumn leaves were falling, and the air was warm. Sienna took a moment to breathe in, allowing the country air to fill her lungs before taking the four steps to the door and gave the little silver bell a ring.

It was a new day—she had to remind herself that. A day she had been looking forward to for weeks, months even; her niece's second birthday. A good enough reason to be with her family in old Aringdale to celebrate it.

She swayed side to side on the heels of her black leather boots, unable to still herself. She exhaled a drawn-out sigh. It didn't matter that her fiancé wasn't by her side. In fact, part of her was relieved.

It wasn't long before she heard footsteps approach the front door. Her heart raced with the unknown. How long had it been since they had been under one roof together? It must have been before her niece, Bailey was born. Surely no longer than two years? She shuddered at the thought. It would have been longer than that. Maybe as far back to when they were newly engaged, four or five years ago. How could she have let so much time pass? A familiar pain of regret swept through her body, commanding her dancing feet to stop.

Her thoughts were interrupted as the door opened. Her sister embraced her with a smile as though all had been forgiven for not having returned her eleven calls over the past month. There was no bitterness in her expression, just a genuine joy to see her. Her heart was replaced with a glow of warmth at the very sight.

A feeling she barely recognised these days.

'You're here!' She threw her arms around Sienna, locking her in an embrace reserved for a sister.

Sienna accepted it graciously, latching onto her long dark hair as it tickled her neck. She pulled back and tugged it gently from either side. 'Your hair! It's grown!' she gasped. It only felt like yesterday where it sat above her shoulders, and now fell half way down her back.

Mia laughed lightheartedly as she took hold of her locks and tossed them over her shoulder. 'I know, so long now! I'm reminded every day the way Bailey latches onto it. I need to cut it before she rips it all out on me!'

Sienna managed a giggle. Oh, how her heart soared at the very mention of her little niece. She not only missed her so much, but had missed so much. Why hadn't she made the time to come up more often? Aringdale was only a couple of hours drive away. She couldn't think of a single reason why she hadn't made time for her own family. The same way she couldn't think of a single reason why she hadn't packed her bags and …

'Where's Patrick today?'

The question strangely took her off guard even though it was a copied and pasted line at every family get together.

She fiddled with the straps of her handbag, gripping tightly onto the handles at the mention of his name. The concern in her sister's eyes didn't match the resentment in her tone. A tone that always held a sharpness whenever she turned up at events like these without the man who was supposed to be her other half. Just because they weren't glued to each other one hundred percent of the time didn't mean he deserved such a harsh verdict. They were two people, leading two very busy lives.

If anything, they should be commended for being individuals with an independence to do things on their own.

Yet the look in her sister's eyes told her that she thought differently. Mia had always questioned Patrick, finding reasons to slam him down from the day she basically met him.

She shouldn't be so affected by it, but she couldn't help it as she caught herself inhaling deeper than normal. She had become tired of having to defend him all the time. What would she tell her? That he was home hungover yet again, burying his head in the sand? Stuck in a bottomless pit he had been digging for himself for the past four years? Obviously, she wouldn't say such things about the man she was going to marry. She wouldn't give her family another reason to hold a grudge over the man she loved. Besides, he had been through so much, even if it had been years since the accident. She didn't need their judgement, too.

'He got called into work. You know how things have been since his promotion. He's biting off more than he can chew.' She smiled, pretending she wasn't bothered in the slightest.

The lies, so many of them. When would they stop?

Mia nodded slowly as she processed, then waved her inside. 'Yeah, ok. Shame he can't be here … again.' She pursed her lips in a hard line on the last word. 'Anyway, come on in, everyone's here and lunch isn't too far off.'

Before she could work out if her sister's disappointment was sincere or not, she found herself being ushered down the corridor.

Her parents were in the living area, pecking away at a table filled with fruit, cheese and various slices. As soon as they heard the sound of her boots pattering along the floorboards, their heads turned.

Sienna smiled tentatively, before a real one took over at the gentle tug on her jeans. 'Bailey!' She reached down and scooped her niece into her arms, planting a thousand kisses on her forehead. She had grown so much over the few months she had seen her last.

Bailey's lips parted, revealing an adorable tooth gapped smile, her deep brown eyes glistening at her with a love that made her heart want to explode. 'You have grown so big,' she whispered and swung her little body to her hip. She finally had the nerve to exchange eye contact with her parents whose had been focused on hers the entire time.

Her mother was first to come forward. 'Sienna, darling! How was the drive?' She popped the last of the slice in her mouth, dusted her hands on her blazer jacket and presented her with wide stretched arms. It felt strangely unnatural as her mother's arms closed over her, squeezing onto her waist. 'Have you been eating?' She leaned back and observed her, scanning her body like a security wand checking for explosives at an airport.

Before Sienna had a chance to defend herself, her father came to the rescue. Unlike her mother, his eyes were beaming without all the burning questions behind them. 'It's good to see you baby girl.' He leaned in giving her a kiss on the cheek. There was a sadness in his voice that knotted her heart with the same web of pain she was caught in earlier.

She couldn't blame him.

It had been over eight months since she had spent any sort of quality time with either of them. She hadn't even made it home for Christmas that summer. How things had gravitated that way over the years, she had no idea. She was sure Mia would run her mouth with an explanation, blaming Patrick for the countless times he had pushed her away from her own family.

But she knew she has no one to blame, but herself.

'How are things, sweetheart?' He placed his arm on her shoulder and peered into her eyes with a concern that validated just how much he had missed her. She had missed him too. She had missed everyone. It was enough to make her suddenly feel all thick in the throat. She gave Bailey another kiss and lowered her wiggly legs down onto a free space of carpet that wasn't submerged with toys. Her big dark brown eyes were looking up at her as if she too, was waiting for an answer.

'Things are fine. Busy, but fine. The semester is drawing to a close so report writing and parent teacher interviews are just around the corner.' She forced a stiff smile and spotted the bottle of wine on the counter. She took a few unnatural strides towards it and poured herself a glass for the first time in years. A glass she didn't even want. The stuff had already caused enough destruction in her life. 'Looking forward to the break to be honest,' she muttered and inhaled a giant sip.

Lately, she found herself questioning whether her career choice as a teacher had been the right move. Maybe she just wasn't cut out for the job. It wasn't the hours, the obsessive parents or the challenging students as such. It was everything else she hadn't signed up for. The rivalry between her work colleagues, or to be more accurate—the war between her and them. They despised her that much. Not to mention the principal at top of the chain who would date her tomorrow if she gave him the all clear. That was what it truly felt like, a food chain. Where she was at the bottom being mulled alive by everyone above her.

And then there was Patrick, her fiancé.

If you would even call him that.

She was beginning to doubt if she would ever walk down the aisle. But that was another story. One she now wasn't sure would have a happy ending as she once imagined. Every suppressed emotion bubbled to the surface in a blur. She could no longer pinpoint the moment where everything in her life became such a … mess.

'Lunch is served! Hope you're all hungry because I think I over calculated this one!' sung Lance, Mia's husband, as he burst through the kitchen with trays piled high with steak, chicken, sausages, onion and tomatoes.

Sienna's stomach grumbled as the sizzling aroma of a good Aussie BBQ filled the room in an instant. Bailey let out an excited squeal and everyone raptured into laughter as they took their seat at the family table, just like old times.

THE AFTERNOON PLAYED out in a flash and to Sienna's surprise, a little too quickly than she hoped it would. Lance cooked the meat to perfection, his recent passion and hidden talent for cooking failing to go unnoticed as compliments flew around the room as many times as her mother eyed her plate. She had only dropped a couple of kilos over the months, she didn't know what her problem was as she watched her every chew.

The mood seemed to lift as soon as Mia brought out the cake she had spent the entire previous afternoon working on. It looked like something a professional would put together. She had managed to create the perfect owl, decorated with pastel coloured icing, using chocolate buttons and licorice to detail the features of the bird.

The animated look on Bailey's face was priceless as it was lowered onto the table, her eyes growing wider by the second. Her excitement only escalated when everyone started singing happy birthday before taking five or six slobbery attempts of blowing the candles out. Sienna smiled savoring the moment. A warmth filled the width of her heart, comforting her like a blanket. She had almost forgotten what it felt like to have her family all together under the one roof. It felt, well ... like home.

SHE WAS IN the kitchen, helping with the clean up when her sister came in carrying what was left of the bird. It looked a little disturbing with its limbs missing after all of that effort.

Lance came whizzing up behind her, wrapping his arms around her waist and planted a kiss at the top of her forehead. She couldn't help but feel a little bit jealous with all the affection.

'Sweetie, you completely nailed that cake.' He curled his finger into the icing that hung from the side.

Mia slapped his hand away playfully. 'Hey! Get out of there!' she laughed spiritedly, resisting him as he pulled her in closer.

He grinned and in slow motion, placed his finger to his mouth and licked it. Sienna watched, admiring her sister and brother in law who were clearly still so in love, even after a decade. They giggled as they maneuvered around the kitchen together, tidying up like a perfect team. They looked like two teenagers flirting with one another, even after all this time. She couldn't help but smile, grateful her sister had found a love that hadn't wavered in the eleven years they had been together.

When was the last time she and Patrick had laughed like that? She quickly filtered through the memories. There were many times, surely? There was that time where they…

'Here you go S, a slice for Patrick to take back with you.' Lance placed a clear plastic container down on the bench beside her.

She laughed at the generous serving of cake inside. It was pretty much three slices thick. 'He'll love that, thanks.' She smoothed her hand over the container, hoping Patrick would actually appreciate the gesture. He probably wouldn't even think twice, if she was honest.

It wasn't until Lance joined the others in the other room where Mia jumped in on their time alone and begun the familiar conversation. 'Talk to me, what's going on with you?'

Sienna squirmed, knowing confrontation was just around the corner. It was something she didn't do well, especially with her sister who never seemed to give up. She knew exactly where this was all heading. She tilted her head to the side, planting a vacant expression as though she had no idea what she was talking about. 'What do you mean?'

Mia rested her hand on her hip, clearly irritated at the game they continued to play. 'Ok … what is your plan? You and Patrick? When's this wedding going to happen? It's been how long now? Six years?'

She was bringing out the big guns today. This was her sister in full force, and it looked like there was going to be no holding back. Why wouldn't she leave it alone?

Everyone else had.

'Five, actually,' she snapped, not meaning to respond as sharply as she did. 'We'll get around to it. Like I said, he has a lot going on at the moment. Work's busy, we are at a stage in our careers where we don't want to be asking for time off for a honeymoon and the craziness that comes with planning a wedding.' It wasn't what she truly felt, but these days, it was the best she had.

Mia shook her head, clearly not believing a word. Sienna studied her, not knowing if her sister was frustrated at the scripted response or was at a loss as much as she was. The problem was, Mia had been questioning every detail about their relationship for *years*. It wasn't the first time they have had a conversation that went down this path. It carried out the same way every time, despite never having reached a different outcome.

So really, why did they have to go down this road again? Couldn't they enjoy an afternoon together without devouring into something that clearly upset her?

'Don't you think this is dragging out far enough? When are you going to make a stand?'

Clearly not.

It looked like they were back there again. Sienna sighed, feeling the weight of her body slump against the bench. 'Make a stand? Come on, let's not start, please. I didn't ask for you to open all this up again.'

Mia sighed heavily. 'Come on S, you aren't seriously making excuses for him still, are you? Is it him putting the planning off? Because the sister I know had the whole thing planned out since she was ten. Every single detail.'

And there was that lump again. Why did she have to bring her past into it like that? Damn her for pulling on her heart strings this way. They had been pulled hard enough already. Yet, the comment had a way of taking her mind right back.

Growing up she had taken advantage of their long, narrow, lounge room—it having been the perfect aisle as she pretended it was her wedding day. Every time she put on the ugly, stained, silk dress that lived in the family's old dress ups box, it would transform into the most beautiful dress in the world. Throughout her teenage years, she had envisioned the gown she would wear, the music that would be played and the choreography of the dance she would share with her future husband. Even before she was engaged, she had created a Pinterest board for inspiration, documenting all of her ideas.

'It's in our future, it will happen eventually. We just need to find the time to look at venues to find what we want.' It didn't matter that she had already researched over a hundred at the time, narrowing the list down to a top ten. A list she has put forward to Patrick on numerous occasions. Every time he would say the same thing.

'This weekend is no good for me babe, next week.'

But they never actually set a time to make it happen. Soon enough the weeks rolled into years. Before long, so much time had passed to the point where it was almost out of context to bring it up a single time more.

He had accused her of nagging him, pressuring him whenever it was gently brought up in conversation. 'Leave it alone S. You pushing this is making me not want to go.'

After five years of being patient, she had given up.

Then when the accident happened, she kept silent. The wedding would just have to take a back seat.

'As long as you're happy to keep on waiting.' Mia sighed again and filled her glass with water from the soda stream.

The defeat clouded in her eyes was obvious as she inhaled deeply— and Sienna could understand why. They both knew she wasn't happy. Well, not really anyway. But they also both knew the conversation wouldn't move forward to a place where it was safe to uncover her true feelings. She wished she had the courage to openly speak her heart. If only she could tell her sister everything that was going on then maybe the burden would ease, even slightly.

But she couldn't.

It wasn't that she didn't trust her. She knew she could, they used to tell each other everything once upon a time. But time had hardened her, and now she was too stubborn, even if she couldn't admit it out loud.

Of course she was happy.

For the most part, anyway.

She shouldn't be so quick to write it off. She had so much to be thankful for, today being a perfect example. It only felt like yesterday when her heart was bursting in those early years when she found the person she believed would make her happy forever.

She was only young when she first met Patrick, a skinny blonde with legs for days. It was her twenty-first birthday and she had been out for dinner with a group of her closest girlfriends. He had been a waiter back then, working part time whilst completing his business degree. She couldn't remember who noticed who first, but she did remember that their chemistry was instant. He was not only easy on the eyes with his chiseled jaw line and piercing blue eyes, but a gentleman too.

Throughout the course of the night he hovered around their table, offering to pour what must have been ten glasses of wine in the space of an hour. He had ignored the fact that each time their glasses were more than half full, but Sienna liked the attention so much and hadn't minded in the slightest.

'That guy is keeeeeeen,' her best friend Jacqueline said, smirking every time his eyes darted back towards them.

They really did lock on Sienna like a spell.

She had waved off her friend's remark casually. 'Nah, not a chance. He's just polite and efficient at his job. In fact,'—she reached into her purse—'I think he deserves a tip girls, what do you think?'

They had all laughed. This wasn't the United States of America. A tip was hardly necessary. At this stage Patrick had lingered around their table yet again with another wine bottle in his hands. Her friends had looked on in with anticipation at what crazy remark would fly from her lips. She was witty like that. Or at least had been back then.

She had spiritedly tossed her long blonde hair over her shoulder as she built up the courage to look at the beautiful man in the eyes for the first time. Oh, how her heart swelled as butterflies spasmed in her abdomen when their eyes finally locked. She cleared her throat. 'So Mr… um, waiter, Sir. On behalf of my girlfriends and myself, we would like to formally extend a token of our appreciation for your outstanding service tonight.'

The girls burst into laughter at the formality of her approach. With slightly quivering hands, she handed a twenty-dollar note towards the tall handsome man that stood beaming over her.

'Why thank you, Miss. Although regretfully, I have to decline your generous gesture.' He was smirking as he placed his hand over hers, sending the money back into her palm, and closed it.

Sienna bit her bottom lip and frowned, pretending to be offended. 'You should never deny a woman who's kindly extending her token of appreciation, sir.'

Patrick titled his head with a mesmerised look on his face, unable to whip the smile from his face.

Some would have found the level of smitten comical.

'I can do one better.' That was when he reached into his pocket and took out a piece of paper from his note pad and scribbled something down on it.

Her eyes glanced down and there it was, his name and mobile number. She was impressed at his boldness.

'What about this? What would you say if I were to ask you out one evening where you can enjoy a beautiful meal without a bothersome waiter harassing you every ten seconds?' His crystal blue eyes captivated her, sending her stomach into a collection of knots.

She had admired his confidence. And those high cheek bones and perfect face. No way she could have said no. She would have been crazy to.

So, she didn't.

One date soon turned into another and before long, they were inseparable. She clearly remembered the first time he told her that he loved her. It had come just shy of their two-month anniversary. They had been sitting in a park on a warm summer's day with a bag of skittles, grouping the colours as they often did with any packet of candy. He began to fiddle with them arranging them into patterns as she had run down to the Mr Whippy truck. When she returned with two chocolate coated ice-creams, she discovered that he had arranged the skittles into the three beautiful words every human soul longed to hear. She remembered staring at them for a while, wondering and hoping that she was reading them correctly before he took her hands in his, and squeezed them.

'I love you Sienna Henderson, more than anything.' He kissed her then. A tender, passionate kiss that confirmed all that he felt for her.

'I love you too, Patrick Daley.'

The months carried on in a blur after that. They had laughed often, vowing to never be one of those boring couples.

And they weren't.

Their friends and family could barely keep up with them. Their relationship was colourful, filled with the type of adventures people would be lucky to experience in a life time.

'I'm going to marry you one day, you know that?' he said as they reached the top of Mount Murdock after a strenuous and sweaty bike ride to the top.

It was like something from a movie the way he had whispered it in her ear as the sun set around them in golden tones. She had used the last of her energy to jump up and wrap her legs around him.

They were engaged not long after that, at the tender age of twenty-two. On their one-year anniversary on a still summer's night, Patrick had set an array of tea light candles along their favourite beach on the Morning Peninsula. Hand in hand, he had guided her through the sand dunes that led to a heart, outlined by red petals where the ultimate question was presented in giant letters in the sand. She remembered the whirlwind of emotions that overcame her as he knelt down on one knee. Dizziness, anticipation and sheer excitement, all mixed in one. It all seemed to have taken place in slow motion, exactly the way she wanted it to carry out. She had wanted the moment to last forever if it could.

But it didn't.

And neither had all the wonderful feelings she had felt that night. If only she knew how much would change. How much he would change.

Because now, she no longer recognised the man she fell in love with.

Two

IT WAS ALMOST midnight by the time she returned home.

She unlocked her phone as she stepped from her car, checking to see if he had responded to any of the messages she had left throughout the day.

There were none.

An apology would have been nice for not getting out of bed when he had committed to going, but who was she kidding to think she would get one?

She dragged her feet up the single flight of stairs to their apartment, slowing as she neared the door. As she fiddled with the keys she felt a familiar unease make its way to the pit of her stomach. It was a feeling that overruled any inkling of happiness she felt just hours ago. The afternoon had served as an escape in that way. Nothing really compared to the unfailing love a family could bring, and its way of making every problem just drift away.

Even if she did feel miles away from her own family.

She turned the key and returned to her reality.

Through the reflection in the mirror and the light that luminated from the TV, she spotted him sprawled out on the couch. He appeared to be fast asleep, not flinching in the slightest.

Tiptoeing into the kitchen, a frustration took root at the sight of the pile of dirty dishes stacked up in the sink. A pet hate of hers. One he was well and truly aware of, having caused far too many arguments to count. She took a deep breath and let it pass. She slipped off her shoes and quietly made her way down the hall to the bedroom.

'S, is that you?' came a muffled murmur from the lounge room.

She managed a stiff smile and tip toed back up and took a seat on the edge of the couch beside her man. 'I didn't wake you, did I?' She gently reached out her hand to stroke his sandy blonde hair.

He took hold of it and sent it back to her lap.

'Sorry,' she whispered, staring down at her hands that longed to be held.

He prompted himself up on his elbows and yawned. 'How was the birthday thing?' He was on his phone now, refreshing his Instagram.

'Yeah, it was really nice.' She sank down next to him and hugged her legs to her chest, keeping her eyes on his even though his hadn't met hers once. 'Everyone missed you today. They were asking about you.' She paused, 'Anyway, I've brought back some cake.'

'Nice.' He was still scrolling through his phone as though he couldn't care less. 'Did you tell them I'm sorry I couldn't be there?'

The frustration was back.

'I didn't tell them that you were hung over, if that's what you mean.' She knew her words were sharp, but in that moment, she didn't care.

He looked up at her, his eyes quickly filling with anger. 'Don't even think about using that tone with me,' he hissed.

She inhaled a defeated breath. 'Sorry, I guess I just really wanted you there with me today. It's been a long time since we've been all together.' She didn't dare look at him. With teary eyes, she flickered her eyes around the room taking in the cans of beer scattered across the coffee table. So much for being hungover. He was probably still drunk. She has no doubt he had been drinking all day.

Yet again.

'I don't like seeing you like this,' she whispered as she studied the room.

He stood up and abruptly extended the remote towards the TV, sending the room into complete darkness. 'I'm really not in the mood to be doing this again with you,' he said coldly. He stood to his feet, leaving her in the dark looking helplessly back at him.

For every second she sat there, she felt her heart grow heavier, starving for affection from the man who once gave it to her so freely. She switched the lamp on beside her and slowly peeled herself off the couch. Ignoring the tears that had made their way down her face, she began cleaning up the mess, one can at a time.

PATRICK NEVER USED to be a big drinker. His addiction to alcohol was like a disease, destroying him slowly one day at a time. When Charlie was killed in a car accident, he not only lost his friend, but seemed to have lost his entire purpose for living. The day they lost Charlie marked the beginning where everything took a turn for the worst. A tragedy in which to this day Patrick still hadn't worked through, their strained relationship being a daily reminder of that. But she couldn't blame the loss of his friend for the turmoil of their relationship.

That wouldn't be fair.

The truth was, red flags had presented themselves far back, shortly after their engagement years ago. When Patrick began his new job at Cortex Consulting, he had made it very clear that his new manager position would be his first priority—and that was exactly what happened. For months, she watched him strive with a tunneled focus on his career, pursuing her less and less. Soon the adventures, the spontaneous dates, the laughter and joy that once coloured their relationship, became a shadow of the past.

And just like that, Patrick began to change.

After she completed her degree and went through the rounds of grueling interviews, she was accepted to teach a grade three class at Kings Cross College; A competitive private school she had been extremely fortunate to have landed a job at. In the beginning he had been supportive, helping her with the constant laminating and marking, even offering his creative insight with her classroom displays. But soon he became 'too busy' or 'too tired' on the evenings that saw her up late, drowning in work. The man who had once been her rock and unfailing support, no longer saw her as a priority.

Through the stress of a new job and feelings of abandonment, she had still tried to do everything she could to bring the spark back into their relationship. She booked countless dinner and movie dates and purchased the latest gaming consoles even if it meant that he never left the study as he locked himself away for hours to play them. She spent many evenings slaving it out in the kitchen, preparing all his favourite meals just so they could sit down together for ten minutes without a sulk on his face. She even organised day trips to spa resorts, mini golf courses and escape rooms, encouraging them to find a hobby together. But every thoughtful gesture only seemed to push him away even more.

'I don't need you to keep guilt tripping me, Sienna.'

Clearly her efforts had been taken in a different light.

'I just want to feel like us again.'

'Well, that's not going to happen if you're going to keep forcing things,' he snapped.

It had all been for nothing.

It was only a short time after when the call came through. A year after they were engaged.

She remembered it as though it was yesterday. He had been hiding out in the study as usual whilst she had been at the kitchen table buried in papers when the frightening sound of his fists slammed onto the table. The sound had startled her but it wasn't until she heard the hysteric wailing where the blood drained from her body. She found him curled over his desk, face buried in his hands, his body trembling violently. It had scared the life out of her. She had wrapped her arms around him, dragging him off the chair and into her lap onto floor. He had aggressively shaken her off then, fighting to free himself from her embrace before he scrabbled himself into a huddle tight against the wall. They sat there in separate corners for what felt like an eternity as she spoke whatever comforting words she could find over him. The more she tried to comfort him, the more hostile he became, demanding her to leave the room. Failing to be strong for him she burst into tears, pained from rejection, longing more than anything to hold the man she loved.

It was more than her heart could bear.

The boys had been good friends since high school, having played soccer in the same league for over eight years. Their parents had been close friends growing up, even having holidayed together on occasion. Years of memories they thought they had only scratched the surface of. All it took was a single moment for a promising future to cease as his life was taken so abruptly.

A pedestrian car accident. Witnesses said he had run out onto the road in the middle of a major intersection. A couple of seconds was all it took for a car to come racing around the corner, swallowing him underneath.

He never made it to work that morning.

Patrick had taken it hard. It took two weeks before he even contemplated leaving the house. Despite her own grief over the inconsolable loss, she had done everything she could to look after him. Calling his work those countless mornings where he refused to get out of bed, compiling a lunch box of all his favourite things before she left for work every day to make sure he would eat. But he was motionless, angry, showing no sign of gratitude for any of it.

'I don't know what you're trying to do but I don't need you looking after me like I'm a child,' he said coldly.

Did he even realise that she too, was affected by the tragedy?

But someone had to hold it all together and that person would be her.

'I love you.' The tears brimmed her eyes had begun to feel familiar to her. 'I'll do everything I can for us to get through this difficult season Patrick, I have always promised you that.'

'Right.' He hadn't met her eyes. 'I don't need you feeling sorry for me all the time, it's that bloody obvious. I'm a big boy, I can look after myself.'

It was a side to him that had never come to light, until then.

Alcohol had become an escape mechanism, a stronghold over his daily existence. He would often drink himself to sleep, numbing the pain he neglected to confront. She would dread coming home in those first few weeks to find him in the same curled position on the couch with empty beer cans scattered around the living room. She never knew what state she would find him in each day she walked through that door, his emotions unpredictable. Sometimes he would be so drunk he would be happy to see her, buzzing with a fabricated energy before anger would take hold of him if she didn't respond with the same liveliness. It was like walking on egg shells. She couldn't do anything right.

'Why aren't you happy to see me? Don't you love me anymore?' He would ridicule her if she left his side for even a second, quickly becoming agitated at the way he began to emotionally manipulate her.

Maybe what frustrated her most wasn't his inconsistency, but rather her inability to find a strength to stand up to herself during these times. Was she scared? No, not really. She knew he would never hurt her. Well, not physically anyway. She wasn't sure why she never had the courage to tell him that a change needed to be made. Maybe she was afraid that he wouldn't be able to. Or maybe she was afraid they would never be able to find their way back if the words were spoken aloud.

THE WEATHER COULDN'T have been more unkind.

Her body rippled in shivers as she zipped her training jacket all the way to her chin and placed the hood over her wet, matted hair. She was soaked through. Her socks were drenched inside her shoes and her top kept clinging to her bra. Despite looking like a drowned rat, she was determined to hold a positive attitude for her grade three students who were about to run the eight hundred metre relay.

It was the school's annual athletics day and although the forecast made it clear the day should without doubt, be a write off, Damian was determined for it to still go ahead as planned.

'A bit of rain won't hurt anyone.' He laughed as he waffled on about the importance of carrying on through all conditions.

She had no problem tolerating the crappy weather, it was the beauty beneath those dreary clouds she was dying to see. And it was only a matter of time until her and Patrick would.

It was on the ever-growing bucket list.

So here they all were, a chilly fourteen degrees with heavy downpours slamming the track and field every ten minutes or so, delaying the events of the day with the constant stop starts.

'Do I have to run this, Miss Henderson?' Nolan Livingston's dark brown eyes flared with concern through his thick glasses as he watched his peers position themselves at the starting line.

She wondered if he would freak out at the last minute like this. Prior to the day he had won every practice race in his P.E class on the very same oval as the one before him, proving time and time again that he was the competitor to beat. But she knew whenever he was placed outside his comfort zone, fear and doubt would take over. Even then, she had her concerns there was more going on than what met the eye.

She kindly placed her hand on his bony shoulder and knelt down on the asphalt, immediately regretting her decision as her compression pants filled with water. 'Just pretend that this is just another practice race, buddy. Focus in on what you have to do and forget about everyone around you.'

He nervously eyed his classmates, holding the glance of one boy, who was pulling a face at him. Sienna followed his eyes and sent Jacob a stern look. He saw her warning and immediately turned. Nolan must have noticed and turned his eyes back on her. She flashed him a warm smile, showing him there was nothing to worry about.

'I suppose I can try and do that.' He nodded. 'I am a pretty fast runner, right?'

She grinned. 'Most definitely.' She leaned over. 'The fastest,' she whispered.

He smiled back, his big eyes gleaming as she watched him march over to his peers with a confidence that had sprung from nowhere. He found a place and begun a focused stretch, like a true athlete.

The sun suddenly appeared from the clouds, warming the track in an instant. What a bizarre day it was. One-minute freezing, then warm like a summer's day the next. She could feel herself overheating so unzipped her jacket and tied it around her waist as she made her way over to Jacob. He saw her coming and hung his head, knowing that a consequence wasn't far away.

'Miss Sienna!'

She hesitated, knowing exactly who the voice belonged to. The exact reason why she wanted to pretend she hadn't heard it at all. Surely enough, jogging up to her was Damian—the school principal.

He was a good-looking man; tall, dark and handsome with a thick British accent that seemed to be a selling point to the single mums who constantly hovered within a ten-metre radius of him. Especially at school events like these, where they willingly volunteered for the eye candy alone. She swore his muscles expanded a little more every day as they protruded from his athletic attire that was clearly too tight for him. She could only imagine how often he must work out to maintain a youthful figure when he had to be pushing late forties by now. How he found the time to fit what she imagined to be a very strict workout, she had no idea.

Anyway, she didn't want to think about it. She felt a swarm of eyes on her as he lunged into a deep hip flexor stretch right in front of her, as though he too was preparing to run the race.

He smirked at her. 'How are the little tackers coping today?'

Maybe this wouldn't be so painful.

'They've done really well, despite the conditions.' She studied the house points she had recorded for each event. Probably studying it a little too hard as Damian switched legs and deepened his lunge.

'They are in fine form. You have done well … but I'm really not surprised.'

She felt herself squirm, feeling her clothes cling tighter against her damp skin. It wasn't the comment itself that made her feel uneasy, it was conversation starters like these that almost always, crossed the line.

'You're looking fit these days,' he added.

Yep, and there it was.

Was he serious? The smirk on his face told her he was. She was disgusted to find his eyes wondering up and down her body as he stayed grounded in his stretch position, checking her out from below.

Maybe it was a strategic move, the creep.

Luckily the sound of the siren saved her just before she had the chance to respond.

'Go Nolan! Go Jacob!' she cheered, cupping her hand over her mouth, focusing on the students who whizzed by. She followed their every step from the side lines as they ran their little hearts out on the track. Just as she predicted, Nolan caught up, passing the others in no time, his legs powering towards the next team member whose hand was stretched out ready to receive the baton. She enjoyed watching one of her most timid students soar with a strength and confidence on the track she scarcely saw in the classroom.

'Come and find me before presentations so we can cross check the house points.'

There again was the voice she thought she had managed to escape as he had somehow caught up with her half way across the oval in the same space of time. It must have been those long legs of his, doubling her single stride.

He patted her shoulder three or four times and gave it a little squeeze. With that he gave her a deliberate wink before he strode off towards the stadium, his chest puffed out like a bluebird.

Cross check house points? It was the first time she had heard about this. It wasn't a responsibility she had been assigned to today. No doubt an attempt to spend some one on one time with her. She lifted her eyes to find one of her colleagues glaring at her from the other side of the track before turning to the woman beside her. They both laughed as their eyes looked back at Sienna.

She felt sick.

She never asked for this and hated all the negative attention she seemed to be attracting. It wasn't the first time Damian had shown an interest in her. It all began months ago when he transferred to the junior campus. For whatever reason, he was drawn to her. Sienna; the most introverted teacher at the school. The woman who always kept to herself.

He would always find ways to be in her company, rolling off little flirtatious comments that nested uncomfortably in her stomach. It wasn't like she gave him anything to work with, half the time too stunned to even form a response. She hated herself for not being assertive enough to make a stand. But what could she do? She didn't want to do or say anything that would put her job in jeopardy, fearful of damaging Damian's pride in the process.

What started off as playful comments thrown around by her colleagues whom she once thought were her friends, quickly turned to jealously. Damian began to make quite the effort to signal her out during staff meetings, praising her for her smallest efforts, most recently the comments he made about the 'astonishing' results her students achieved in their Naplan testing. Her work colleagues loathed her without even knowing her. The sad thing was, they didn't want to. According to the rumours, she was cheating on her fiancé with her boss to get to the top. It couldn't have been further from the truth. It simply wasn't the way she was wired. She would be stupid to anyway. And with Damian?

Not a chance.

Yes, the bloke was good looking but that was about all he had going for him.

Her thoughts were interrupted as the crowd broke out in a roar of applause as the final students crossed the finishing line. Their faces all puffy, with bodies hunched over from exhaustion. Within seconds Nolan ran up to her, his eyes larger than life, his cheeks red and swollen from exertion.

'We did it!'

She reached out her hand and he sprung into the air to high five it. 'I never doubted you for a moment!'

He missed her hand and stumbled around for a bit.

'Are you ok?' she asked, watching him struggle to find his footing again.

He nodded quickly and tried again, slamming his hand enthusiastically on hers this time. 'That was the best fun, ever.'

The uneasiness in her stomach settled. It was small victories like these that made her forget everything else. She inhaled and readjusted her clothing for about the twenty seventh time that afternoon. It was time to arrange her students into their groups for the final event. All she had to do was focus on the task at hand. As long as she kept her mind busy, she would make it through another day just fine.

On a side note, she couldn't wait to get home and change.

Three

IT HAD BEEN a busy morning organising student folios ready for the end of the semester.

Her students were tired, she could see that. She had recouped every last bit of energy to help push them through the last couple of weeks of the term that remained.

It was the second last period of the day and her class were out at music class. She decided to spend her release period inside her room accompanied by the dreaded piles of papers on her desk, waiting to be marked and sent home in their portfolios. She sighed as she stared down at them. There was no such thing as a spare moment as a teacher. It just didn't exist.

Silence.

All she could hear was the faint ticking sound of the clock on the wall as she released her breath. She stared blankly at the mountain of work in front of her, opened the draw and took out her phone for the first time that day. She groaned.

Three messages from Patrick.

> **Sorry babe, I lost track of time last night and
> didn't want to wake you. Hope you have a nice
> day.**

Her annoyance dissolved as she read over what seemed like a sincere apology. He had said he was sorry and had wished her a good day. It was a start, right? She opened the next message sent two hours after the first one.

> **I hope you're not mad at me? Let's go out for
> dinner tonight, you can choose.**

Her lips curled, feeling a swarm of butterflies make their way around her abdominal region. She couldn't remember the last time he had taken her out anywhere for that matter. It would have been almost five months ago for her birthday. He wasn't one for thinking ahead so she had taken the reins and booked them a table at a modern Japanese restaurant in the city. That was as good as taking her out, right? Thinking back, that would have been the last time they had been out together.

Then there was the last message where the butterflies vanished as quickly as they had appeared.

> **Have a team dinner tonight for work. Will
> have to take a raincheck on dinner.**

Without taking a moment to process her feelings, her fingers typed away.

> **That's ok babe, always next time. I'll see you
> home some stage tonight x**

She set her phone down a little too abruptly on the edge of her desk, took the first paper from the pile and began what would be hours of sorting and grouping. She came across Nolan's work, gritting her teeth with every cross she made against each answer. She had begun to worry about him.

In the last couple of months, his work had fallen behind. It wasn't that he was low academically. In fact, he was a bright child but had no confidence. He was always second guessing himself, laying low during any group activity and chosen last for any partner work. She had quickly noticed how isolated and withdrawn he had become which only made him more of a target to Jacob and Henley, who had somehow established themselves as the class 'jocks'.

She had noticed the bullying begin a couple of weeks ago while on yard duty one lunch time. He had been playing with an action man figurine on his own when they approached him, snatching it out of his hands. She addressed the situation as soon as they had mocked him for playing with 'Barbie dolls', calling him a baby. She hadn't seen him play with anything since. He now spent his lunch times inside the locker breezeway with his head in a book, where the popular boys couldn't hurt him.

She often hovered by him whenever she was on duty. He amazed her time after time with his knowledge from all the reading he was doing. As the weeks carried on, they spent hours discussing all types of facts where she would blindly quiz him and be astounded by his ability to recite every bit of information, and accurately too.

It wasn't long before a special bond was formed between them. He would be the first to arrive at school each morning where he would quietly take a seat, diving his nose in a book as she prepared for the day ahead. Very few words were exchanged between them, but she could sense that he felt safe in her company.

Perhaps the safest.

His love for books became a source of comfort, to the point where it became an effort to get him to put them away once class began. She would often catch him sneakily take out a book when he was meant to be doing another task. Although she was thrilled with his desire to learn, she had become growingly concerned at the quality of his work. It didn't help that she would often hear snickers from the children behind him as they teased him for this love of his, calling him a 'nerd' and 'four eyes' every time he took out his old fashioned, wide brimmed glasses.

SHE MET HIS mother once, but not in the way she imagined she would meet a parent for the first time. The woman had barged into the class one morning just minutes before being dismissed for recess, oblivious to the scene she was causing. Her erratic hand gestures complimented her scorning tone.

'Nolan, how many times do I have to tell you to take your lunch with you? I specifically left it on the bench for you, it's not hard,' she hissed aggressively, taking hold of his arm.

Nolan had lowered his head in embarrassment as he tried to shake off his mother's grip. A couple of words were exchanged that Sienna hadn't heard, but she had smiled politely at the woman even though it wasn't returned.

It hadn't been the most convenient moment to introduce herself as her son's teacher but being half way through the term, it needed to be done. She had met all the other parents within the first couple of weeks of school.

But not Nolan's parents.

In fact, she didn't know a thing about them other than the woman's name.

'Miranda,' she called gently, maneuvering her way past the students as they filtered their way out to recess.

The woman hesitated before turning around, noticeably annoyed with the hold up. She was a thin woman, dressed as though she was ready to hit a night club. She had worn a mini white skirt that barely covered the top of her thighs, not to mention a bright pink top leaving absolutely nothing to the imagination. To complete the picture, she wore the highest wedged shoes Sienna had ever seen. She had tilted her head and glared at her as Sienna presented her with a warm smile.

'I'm Sienna, it's lovely to meet you.' She shook the woman's long slender hand.

Miranda managed a half smile. 'Yeah, you too. It's about time I met Nolan's teacher, ay?' she asked dryly.

Sienna shook her head, smiling, not really knowing yet what she was in for. 'That's alright, I know exactly how busy life can be.' The woman's expression hadn't budged. 'Thank you for coming in and dropping off Nolan's lunch. I'm sure he's grateful for that,' she laughed lightheartedly.

'Doubt it.'

Sienna shifted unnervingly. 'Nolan is a great kid,' she changed the subject. 'He's very bright, a delight to have in my class.'

By this stage the woman was rummaging through her purse, barely paying any attention. She couldn't believe the lack of interest the woman seemed to have about her own son. An uncomfortable pit formed inside her stomach. She had had a feeling that Nolan's home life wasn't any rosier than his one at school. 'Speaking of Nolan, I would like to chat to you about his progress if you have some time.'

The woman looked up from her purse and stared squarely into Sienna's eyes. 'Is he in trouble?' her tone frantic.

It had been an odd reaction, but Sienna had assured her he was a beautiful child with incredible potential before informing her about the bullying she had noticed.

She had waved it off, dismissing the idea in an instant. 'I'm sure he's just overreacting for attention. He's completely oversensitive like that.'

Sienna couldn't believe the words as they sailed from the woman's mouth. 'I can assure you Miranda, that's not the case,' she said almost too abruptly.

'Well,'—Miranda flicked her dead straight black hair over her perfectly tanned shoulder—'I'll have to check with my husband and see if there's a time that works for him and let you know.'

A few more words were spoken before she flashed Sienna another fake smile, and left.

Miranda never got back to her. She had tried contacting her on numerous occasions but every time her calls reached message bank. Emails hadn't been successful either. The woman may not have been responsive, But Sienna wasn't going to sit back and watch Nolan come completely undone. There was little time in her schedule, especially with the curfew she felt tied to. But even that would have to take a back seat when she knew she had to do something.

Her heart sank as she watched Nolan sit by his usual spot by the locker breeze way each day, curled up against the cement wall with his head in a book. If only his parents saw him the way she did. All she needed was one conversation with them. But at this point she had every reason to believe that the conversation would never happen. They were simply not interested, so she made her mind up.

She would tutor him.

He was often one of the last kids to leave school each day anyway so she couldn't see how it wouldn't work. By now they had developed a bond strong enough for him to at least be open to it.

The bell rang at the end of the day and as usual, Nolan was the last to collect his belongings. Sometimes she wondered if it was deliberate, a thought-out plan to avoid running into the bullies. Or maybe he was just reluctant to go home. Either way, the thought was enough to make her heart crumple. She knew he caught the 792-bus home alone every day after school and had offered to walk him to the bus stop but he had always politely turned her down, reassuring her that it was good for 'developing his independence'. She was sure it was a line his parents had fed him. Eventually she stopped offering to walk him but she always kept an extra eye out.

She sat on the edge of his desk watching him as he threw on his blazer and adjusted the straps of his backpack, preparing himself for the chilly walk home.

'Have you got your spelling book, buddy?' she asked, spotting it sticking out of his tub.

He peered into his bag and looked up at her with a sheepish grin. 'Whoops!' he said a little too enthusiastically as he took it and jammed it into his bag.

She leant in and gently took the book from his hands. 'How are we going with them this week?' she asked, flicking to the page with the week's spelling words on them.

'Ok, I suppose.'

She took a look at the first word. 'Let's do some together now.'

He shifted uncomfortably but nodded and slowly sunk into his seat.

'Stripe.' She placed the book down and waited for him.

He grew quiet for a moment then opened his mouth. 'Stripe. S-t-r-i-p.' He knew he has it wrong, his face had turned red and he was shifting about in his chair again.

'Good try,' she encouraged him. 'Here.' She turned to a blank page in his book. 'Let's sound it out together.'

He sunk his head into his hands, staring down at the page in front of him 'S-t-r-i-pe,' he tried again.

Sienna nodded. 'Good! Let's have a look at what the silent "e" does to a word, that will help us understand the spelling a bit more.' She began to write out the word neatly. 'If we get rid of the e on this word, what does it become?' She covered the end letter of the word.

'Strip,' he answered correctly.

She smiled nodding, pleased at how well he was responding. 'Now, notice when you say "strip" and "stripe" out loud, notice how the only difference is the vowel sound in the middle. Both words end in the same sound because the "e" at the end of "stripe" is silent. The "e" becomes bossy—'

'Miss Henderson?' He stopped her before she had a chance to finish. She looked into his eyes to find an expression of confusion. 'Thank you for this, I promise I will work it at home.' He reached down and picked up his bag. She had never seen him so eager to leave, he was usually always so keen to draw out time for as long as he could. She closed the book and stood to her feet.

'I am always here for you Nolan, I hope you know that.' She was trying to meet his eyes but he was too busy focusing on the zip on his bag after stuffing the book inside. 'I thought that maybe we can work on a few things each week together after school for a little bit.'

He looked up then, and his eyes connected with hers. 'Like my spelling?'

She smiled. 'Yeah! Maybe we could take a look at some math too, like the fractions we worked on earlier in the week' she suggested, remembering all the crosses she made against his work that afternoon.

'I suppose we could do that.' He nodded. 'Thank you.'

'You're welcome, buddy,' she said gently. 'Do you have some time now?'

She knew that he did. He wasn't involved in any activities or sporting commitments outside of school. Already he had told her how rarely his parents were around, often arriving home late each night. In fact, most nights he was responsible for preparing his own dinner and putting himself to bed.

'I suppose I have a bit of time.' He placed his bag back down. 'But can we please maybe work on something else if that's okay?'

She smiled at his manners. It didn't bother her that he wanted to do something else, she was just glad he was open to it. She wanted him to slip back into feeling comfortable around her always, and knew what it would take to bring it back out.

'Let's have a look at the book you're reading.'

His eyes lit up as he unzipped his bag again and pulled out a giant, colourful book. He passed it over to her with a big grin, his big brown eyes dancing for the first time that day.

She laughed light heartedly and read the title aloud. 'One hundred most disgusting things on the planet.'

He nodded, his smile never leaving his face as he opened the book and flicked through the pages. 'It has the most repulsive things inside Miss Henderson …' he started.

She grinned. *Repulsive.* She didn't know any other grade three student whose vocabulary even contained the word.

'See here? Look how disgusting our body is!' He pointed to a page of the human body that was filled with images of snot, scabs, earwax and god knows what else.

She chuckled. 'What can you tell me about them?'

He lifted his head and cleared his throat. 'A scab forms when a clot dries up after you stop bleeding. Their job is to protect the cut by keeping germs and other stuff out and giving the skin cells underneath a chance to heal.'

She smiled at him, impressed at his knowledge. A frown appeared across his face.

'Am I correct?'

'You certainly are, Nolan,' she agreed, nodding. She snapped the book shut and held it to her chest as she quizzed him. 'What else can you tell me?'

He placed his hands on his hips and swayed back and forth, well aware of how impressed she was by him, and was lapping it up. He grinned at her and stood taller. 'Under the surface, all kinds of things are going on,' his tone composed, confident. 'New skin cells are being made to help repair the torn skin, damaged blood vessels are being fixed.'

She tilted her head in amazement and patted his shoulder. He looked at her with a big smile of accomplishment.

'Your parents must be very proud of you! Have you shared these facts with them?'

Instantly, his smile dissolved and he lowered his hands into his pockets. 'Nah,' his response came short.

She had a curiosity to dig deeper. She could sense things couldn't possibly be right at home, her single conversation with his mother had told her that much.

'Nolan,' she had to be careful how she worded this. 'How often do your parents listen to you read?'

His hands were still in his pockets, his eyes quickly focused on the floor.

She felt for the boy and a frustration built inside of her. How could any parent possibly show such little interest towards their son? Especially Nolan, who was bright, sharp, intelligent, kind. The thought alone was enough to make her blood boil.

'They're really busy.' He looked up and shrugged. 'They say stuff like if I'm doing well enough in school there's no reason to be doing any extra work at home.'

They say *what?*

She took a deep breath to try and tame the anger that had escalated inside of her. 'They don't think you are doing well at school?'

He shrugged and looked at the floor again. 'They say I wasn't blessed with "the smarts,"' he said, emphasising the words that had been spoken over him.

In the moment, all she wanted to do was drive Nolan home and wait as long as it took for his parents to arrive so she could serve them a piece of her mind. What type of parent manipulated their child's mindset like that?

She cleared her throat and placed a hand on his shoulder. 'Look at me Nolan,' her voice tender, but stern.

He met her eyes. There was a visible sadness behind them. 'Don't let anyone determine your worth, you hear me? You are an incredibly intelligent boy. You are capable of anything.'

The corner of his mouth curled into an encouraged smile. 'Ok … thanks,' he whispered.

THEY SPENT THE next hour in the classroom working through the various learning tasks from the week. They didn't discuss anything beyond the four walls of the classroom. After seeing the hurt in his eyes after their brief conversation, she thought it was best to leave his home life alone.

At least for now.

In the short time they spent together, she was reminded over again just how clever he was. With a little prompting, he was quick to grasp concepts and worked through them with a confidence she was yet to see in the classroom. Every morning he would be the first to arrive by a good twenty minutes, playing with the kinetic sand or lego as she wrote up the day's timetable on the whiteboard. A quiet assurance began to unravel, one that had been suppressed by a self-doubt she was determined to get to the bottom of. After spending another hour finishing off another pile of marking, she made her way home.

She was exhausted.

As she stepped into her deserted apartment that night, her body instantly relaxed. She reached into her handbag and took out the cheese and tomato sandwich she hadn't had the chance to eat. Her stomach rumbled as she bit into what was now two pieces of soggy bread. She finished it within seconds, she was that hungry.

She released a heavy breath, darting her eyes around the kitchen as she contemplated what to cook for herself as Patrick was out at a work dinner. She opened the fridge to discover a scarce array of condiments. She groaned not seeing potential in any of it and she shut the door. That was when the pizza magnet sitting at eye level took her attention.

It was exactly what she felt like.

She couldn't remember the last time she had eaten the stuff with it not being an option in their home. Which only made her question what it was doing on the fridge in the first place really.

Patrick was adamant about clean eating. He hadn't always been that way, but out of nowhere in the last couple of years had set a meal limit of three hundred and fifty calories. Her stomach began to growl more violently. She decided not to ponder the calorie thing too much and instead, took out her phone and tapped in the number.

Half an hour later her pizza arrived. Before she knew it, she devoured nearly the entire thing, leaving only one sad, sloppy piece behind. Minutes later a tightening feeling invaded her stomach.

She felt sick.

She wasn't used to greasy food, or the extra few hundred calories. If Patrick knew about her little binge, he wouldn't be impressed—he would be mad. Suddenly, the thought of his disapproval was more than she could handle, especially with how strained things have become between them lately. She was too exhausted to risk a fight over something as petty as her choice for dinner.

In a sudden panic, she took the pizza box and keys from the counter and jogged her way downstairs to the set of bins at the front of their apartment block. She nearly knocked him over on her way out of the security gate. His strong hands took hold of her waist, pulling her in as she nearly fell over him.

Talk about timing.

'Wooooah babe, slowdown,' his voice playful, surprising her.

Her body tensed up as she subtly tried to hide the box behind her. But this quickly failed as it fell open and the pizza sloshed down her leg, landing in a pile by her foot.

He stared at the slice she now wished she had eaten. 'Hiding the evidence, are we?' His response came somewhat light, yet she was no fool to detect a rising tension behind it.

She bent down, feeling his eyes on her as she sent it into the bin. She looked up at him and casually flung her arms around his neck. 'Let's be honest, I knew you wouldn't approve, but the cravings got the better of me tonight,' she laughed, uneasily.

He frowned as he took hold of her arms and lowered them to her side. 'You know how I feel about you eating shit like this.'

She smiled at him, hoping it wouldn't become a thing. Surely not?

He was in such good spirits just minutes before, wasn't he? The stern look in his eyes told her that his mood had changed.

She nodded slowly, knowing all too well what was coming. 'Yes, I do know.' She took a step back. She didn't have a witty comeback, or a response of any kind for that matter. She knew the battle was lost before it even begun.

She was yet to win one, and tonight wouldn't be the first.

What was the point? Any playful side of him was made extinct months ago. She hated that she always felt like she had to justify everything.

He took hold of her hand and with a strength, flung her around so her face mirrored his. 'Really? Are you really going to have an attitude about this when all I'm doing is looking out for you?' His eyes tapered, piercing hers like daggers.

Her heart did a flip flop as he inched his face closer to hers. She stared into his eyes, feeling his breath hard against hers.

He had been drinking again. She was certain of it.

There was no mistaking the familiar smell. Her defeat quickly turned to frustration.

'Have you been drinking again?' she asked firmly.

He raised his eyebrows and jerked his head back, noticeably peeved for having been questioned. He threw her hand away. She reached for it again, but he had already begun to make his way inside without her. 'Patrick, how much have you had? You were behind the wheel tonight!'

He kept walking ahead without her, throwing his hands up in the air in exasperation. 'Maybe sometimes I need to drink in order to tolerate you, have you ever thought about that?'

She caught up to him and reached desperately for his hand before he had a chance to go in without her. 'You don't mean that.' It came out more like a yelp than anything.

With his other hand positioned around the door knob he just stood there for a moment before turning to face her.

'Do you?' she whispered. Fresh tears welled in her eyes before she had a chance to stop them. How could he possibly think of her in this way? She was always so careful not to put a foot wrong, every day trying so hard to be the woman he wanted her to be.

He stared blankly back at her, his face unreadable. She inhaled shakily waiting for his response as she continued to search his eyes with her own. Slowly, they began to soften and he hung his head.

'No.'

There was an honesty behind his tone that allowed her to breathe again. She squeezed his hand even though he loosely held hers back. She longed for a sign of reassurance, a squeeze back. Anything.

But his eyes were down at his hand that hadn't moved an inch from the handle. She slipped her arm around his waist and they just stood there in silence. The wind picked up, sending a wave of shivers down her spine. She couldn't figure him out. She couldn't read him the way she used to. It used to be so easy. When had they become so disconnected? She hated not knowing what was going on inside his head.

'How was the team dinner?'

He looked at her with questioning eyes, then his face relaxed. He slowly nodded his head. 'Fine.'

Another one-worded answer.

She pursed her lips together, acknowledging the fact that he wasn't going to elaborate. Case closed.

It was time to go inside. With her hand in his they made their way up the flight of stairs together. She found herself needing to steady him as he struggled to find his balance, swaying with every stair they climbed. The thought of him driving home this drunk, scared her. But she enjoyed the rare moment of her hand in his too much to allow it to rattle her.

Even if it was all they had.

Four

SHE WOKE TO the buzzing sound of the washing machine.
It took a few moments to register what was going on as her weary
eyes fluttered their way open. She laid still on her back with
her focus towards the ceiling as her eyes adjusted to the light spilling
through the blinds. She turned her head, confused not to find Patrick
beside her as he was almost never up before her.

Then she remembered, it was Saturday.

Which still made no sense. She extended her arm out from the
warmth of the doona and reached for her phone on the bedside table.
She missed, knocking it as it slammed onto the floorboards with a
thud. With her eyes still foggy, she rolled over and squinted at the
clock to see it was only just after eight in the morning. She yawned, still
exhausted. It hadn't been a late night, but the weight of report writing,
folios, the Nolan issue and the stress of her relationship had taken a
toll on her.

By the time they went back inside, Patrick had gone straight to the
bedroom, flicked off his shoes and face planted it. It wasn't exactly the
form she liked to see him in, but over time she had adapted to it. A
small part of her was relieved as his unconsciousness meant that another
fight had been avoided. She hadn't had the energy for it. Besides, she

had wanted to finish the night the way it had, with his hand in hers. A sensation that had become rare these days.

So, she wanted to hold onto it.

'Babe, are you up?' He must have heard the slam of her phone on the floor.

She tucked the doona close to her chin and wiggled her body further down. She wasn't ready to get out yet, it was too warm. She heard his footsteps draw near. She shifted her eyes towards the door waiting in anticipation, wondering what mood she would be presented with this morning. But with the sound of the washing machine brewing away, she had a feeling it was going to be a good day.

To her surprise he was at the door, holding a tray of pancakes with a smile on his face that she hadn't seen in months. She sat up tall and returned a smile. A warmth radiated inside of her as he placed it down on the bedside table. He leant in for a kiss, sending her lips ablaze as they came together with hers.

'This is nice.' She took a minute to look into his eyes, detecting what she thought was a glimmer of remorse.

He lowered himself onto the edge of the bed, his smile slowly dwindled. 'Let's just call this a sorry for last night breakfast.'

She reached her arms out to him. He fell into them, wrapping his big hands around her little frame. His embrace felt comforting. The longer she held it, the more she felt her uneasiness slowly evaporate.

'It's ok, I shouldn't have ordered it,' she tested him.

He released his arms around her and positioned his hands on either side of her face. 'Well you won't be doing that again, will you.' He pressed his nose a little too firmly against hers.

She jerked her head back in discomfort. She didn't say anything, but it didn't seem to bother him as he was already on his feet.

'Thanks for breakfast babe, very thoughtful of you. You have the washing going too I can hear. Thanks.'

'I guess I'm not completely useless, am I?'

Ugh, really?

'I've never thought that of you.'

He shrugged and lowered his eyes to the floor. She didn't understand how he could be sincere one moment and then passive aggressive the next. Had she said something wrong while thanking him? And why wouldn't he look at her?

He gave her a weak smile. 'The washing's nearly done, and dishwasher is unstacked.'

She did her best to flash him a convincing one, even if it didn't mirror the condition of her heart.

She threw the doona back and lowered her feet to the floor and took his hand before he had the chance to escape her. His fingers eased their way between hers. She squeezed them gently. 'I love you.' They were three words she hadn't voiced in a while, but she still meant them.

His eyes darted back and forth, fighting against hers. It was almost although he didn't believe her. She kept her eyes on his, hoping he would look into her as deeply as he once had. But they were lost, more lost than they have never been. Yet, his smile made her question otherwise. 'You too,' his words came as a whisper. He didn't say it back but pulled her in closer. 'What would you like to do today?' He cradled her head as she nuzzled into him, enjoying feeling the steady rise and fall of his chest.

'Well, first of all I would love you to help me eat these amazing pancakes of yours, then maybe later we could go for a walk or go to Nancy Green's?'

He thought for a moment, then nodded. 'That sounds like a plan to me. Let's go to Nancy's. I want to see if their steak burger is as good as I remember.'

'I've heard it's still pretty amazing,' she said, squeezing him tighter.

'Well in that case I better reserve my appetite and leave all these pancakes to you.' He gently dug his fingers into her sides, sending her body in spasms as he tickled her. She shielded her arms around herself in protection as he playfully extended his arms, ready for more. She let out a squeal as he sent her back down onto the bed, knowing all too well how ticklish she was.

They continued that way for a few moments, enjoying each other's banter before he insisted she ate her pancakes before they got cold. She took the tray beside her and positioned it on her lap while he returned to the study. She took a look at the perfectly rounded pancake positioned perfectly on her plate and smiled. This had to be more than the calorie limit. It didn't matter that they were hard like cardboard, she just appreciated the effort he had made for her. His way of wanting to make things right stirred a hope inside of her. And for the first time in a long time, she was looking forward to their day together.

As she worked on getting them down, she noticed him enter the kitchen before quickly exiting with a beer in his hands. She noticed the conscious effort he made to hide the bottle behind his back, walking sideways like a crab back to the study. The thought of him sneaking around as he bribed her with pancakes was enough for any glimmer of hope to be completely squashed. How many had he had already this morning? The thought of him smashing down beers while she was sound asleep was enough for her to want to throw up. The pancakes suddenly became unbearably bland in her mouth, a chore to chew and swallow. Part of her wanted to go to him, but she knew if she did their conversation would quickly turn sour, the way it always did.

And then just like that, their plans for the day would be over.

She took a breath and focused on the sound of the gentle buzz of the washing machine to steady her soul. He had put in an effort this morning. She couldn't overlook that fact.

It was a small step forward.

It had been months since they had been to Nancy's but even so, not much had changed with the place. It was presented the same way with delicate fairy lights hanging from the roof in an enclosed tavern like setting. She reached for the door, setting off the bobble doorbell as it opened. Immediately the homely atmosphere calmed her like a remedy.

She scanned her eyes around, her nostrils responding to the blend of aromas around her. The tables filled with people of a variety of ages betrothed in laughter and conversation. Just being back brought upon a feeling of comfort.

Jeremy was quick to spot them from behind the counter. With open arms he cantered his way around the line of customers towards them. He was a short, stocky, middle aged man, with a personality that could light the darkest room. His love for people and attention to detail to produce fine, quality food had sparked quite a name for himself. If it wasn't for him there wouldn't be a carriage of customers waiting to be seated each day. The cafe simply wouldn't have the reputation it did without him.

'Look who it is! My favourite couple!' He stood between them, reaching his arms around them, drawing them in close. 'Where have you two been all my life?'

It was a fair question and it made her stall for a moment. She couldn't pinpoint the last time they were here. Was it a year ago? She honestly couldn't remember. 'It's our favourite man! And too long, I know!' She nestled in next to him, embracing the hug.

Patrick flashed one of his half smiles and observed the room. 'Looks like a full house today. Guess we'll have to take a seat out back, huh?'

Sienna felt herself frowning at his comment, agitated at his lack of acknowledgement towards the man who had always treated them like family. She thought she could sense a flicker of offence in Jeremy's eyes, but his bubbly personality made it too hard to know for sure.

'Ah, don't you worry, there is always room for you two!' He waved the comment off and led them down to a table in the far back corner. 'I know it's not your usual spot but the food tastes just as good here as it does from the other side of the room, I promise,' he joked. His eyes fixed on Patrick as he sat down grunting as though he was some sort of king being mistreated.

Sienna watched him too, embarrassed at the way he was behaving. She didn't know who he was anymore.

'Thanks mate,' his response short, but polite enough. At least he had found his manners.

'No problem-o.' He handed them menus, widened his stance and positioned his hands on his hips. His usual posture whenever he was up for a chat.

'I thought you guys must have eloped and whisked off to Hawaii or something, it's been that long since I have seen ya! Tell me, what's news in your world?'

She looked at her fiancé, hoping he had an answer up his sleeve to pull out. He was usually quick like that. But his eyes held no expression as he flipped open the menu and pretended to study it. Disappointment took root inside her. She wanted to snatch the menu off him and order the steak burger he already knew he was having.

She cleared her throat and presented Jeremy with one of her biggest smiles. 'It's a tempting thought!' If it meant that she would actually make it down the aisle, then she was all for it. 'This year has all been a bit crazy, you know how it is! Sorry we've been so slack to not have payed you a visit. Please forgive us!' It was all she had.

Jeremy nodded understandingly, and let out one of his booming laughs. 'I can only imagine! Wedding plans and all! Last time we spoke I think you guys were looking at a summer wedding. Is that still happening you slack buggers?'

It was the ultimate question, wasn't it?

The bulge in her stomach tightened. She should have known the question was coming but she hadn't given any thought about how she would answer. The question was enough for Patrick to look up. She was desperate for him to say something, anything. But instead he looked at her with an intrigued look, as if he too, was curious for an answer. She raked her hair behind her ears, her usual go to whenever she was anxious.

Jeremy must have noticed the silence and being intuitive as he was, waved it off. 'Whenever you guys get around to it, I am sure it will be perfect!' He turned to Patrick. 'Steak burger for you? I don't know what I was thinking giving you a menu honestly,' he laughed.

Patrick nodded with a smile so big, she couldn't help but glare at him from across the table. 'Yes please! The best steak burger in the history of mankind, how can I say no!'

She could see how relieved he was to have had the door shut on all the wedding talk. His enthusiasm was borderline pathetic.

Jeremy nodded. 'And the carbonara for you my sweetness?' He began to collect the menus.

She caught Patrick's frown and subtle shake of disapproval. Was he kidding?

'Someone's watching what she eats so she can fit into this wedding dress of hers,' he pitched in.

Okay, so, he wasn't kidding.

She stared at him, shocked at the blatant lie that slipped from his mouth with ease.

'Was it the warm chicken salad you were telling me about that you wanted to try, babe?' his tone gentle and all loving.

She pursed her lips together, feeling herself fume beneath.

There had been no such conversation.

She hated the control he seemed to have over her. And to have the nerve to be so manipulative when they were supposed to be enjoying a nice afternoon out together, made her even angrier. But with Jeremy watching she knew she had to go along with it.

'Sounds perfect,' she said, sarcastically.

Jeremy nodded slowly, obviously aware of the tension between them. 'Right! I better get back to it but catch me on ya way out, won't ya! Love you guys.'

They gave him a wave and he dashed off to help serve a flood of customers spewing from the doors. She positioned her eyes on Patrick as he casually took out his phone, his eyes making every attempt to avoid hers. 'Trying to watch my weight so I fit into my wedding dress, hey?' She couldn't help herself. It was time to speak up.

'It's never too late to start getting into shape. Especially after that pizza you devoured the other night.' He didn't look at her but his face held a smirk as he scrolled through his phone.

She couldn't understand it. For as long as she has known him, she had never had an issue with her weight. Maybe she didn't exercise enough according to his standards, but she was far from being out of shape. Some would say she was even too skinny. Sure, like anyone, she had her moments. In those moments of weakness, he had discovered her stashes of chocolate and, to this very day, ridiculed her for it. But that was the extent of it. She was always conscious of making healthy food choices, keeping to his strict calorie guideline set out for her. Maybe he didn't find her attractive anymore.

The very thought made her stomach clench.

'I would like to start looking for my dress soon. I have an idea what I like but until I try anything on, I can't be set on a style,' the words sailed from her mouth without thinking. She was tired of forever avoiding the topic when it was constantly sitting at the forefront of her mind.

He placed his phone down and settled himself into the chair. She had his attention. She inhaled, suddenly nervous. At least he appeared as though he was ready to talk about it. There was no reason why this has to be difficult, she was ready to try again.

'What are your thoughts on me taking a look at some of the bridal shops next weekend?' Her tone gentle, not daring to take her pleading eyes off him. She only hoped he could sense her energy.

He cleared his throat. 'Is that really something you feel you need to rush into?'

What?

'Rush into? Really?' She couldn't help but allow her voice jump up an octave. Before they knew it, it would be a bloody decade. Surely then they would hold some sort of record for the longest engagement in history.

He raised his eyes, and leaned in. 'Are we really going to do this now?' he hissed aggressively. She flickered her eyes around the room to see if anyone was looking in, but everyone was engaged in their own conversations. The laughter in the room mocked her, especially now, booming louder than ever.

'I just want us to be able to talk about it,' she said, defeated. When had a simple conversation become such an ordeal? She had no idea what he wanted from her anymore. Her mind was blank. She knew she had to ask the question that had been strewing in her mind for months now. 'When do you see us getting married?' She looked into his eyes, desperate to seek some sort of validation. But his eyes were absent.

They held nothing.

'Do you really think with the way things have been between us that we're ready to plan a wedding?'

The question completely threw her. It was obvious that their relationship was fragile, the years had only seemed to water down any strength that had once been there.

The truth was, he has hit the nail on the head. But even then, the answer was too painful to face.

A commitment had been made on that perfect night he proposed. No matter where they stood now, they were a team. It didn't matter they had been fighting the same storm for the past five years. Together they would find their way out of it.

She was sure of it.

She stretched out her hands out towards him, reluctantly he took them in his. 'I know things have been better between us.' She squeezed his fingers wanting to have some form of connection in this moment. 'And you're right. Until they are, the wedding stuff can wait. But can you be honest with me about something?' She felt herself struggling for oxygen in anticipation for his answer to the question she knew that needed to be ask.

'Of course.' His expression didn't flicker.

'Do you still want to marry me?' She wasn't sure if he had heard her. She could barely hear the words come from her mouth over the pounding of her own heart.

He dropped her hands and sent them into his lap as hers laid exposed on the table towards him. Her eyes began to well as he withdrew from her during a time where she needed his reassurance the most.

'I don't know what you're trying to do, manipulating me like this,' his words came harsh, impaling her.

She felt a trickle of cold liquid run through her. Why wouldn't he answer the bloody question?

'Do you?'

He picked up his phone again and started shaking his head. 'For fuck's sake, we are not going to do this here,' he responded, irritated.

She took in a sharp breath. 'When are we going to talk about it? I'm starting to think you don't want this anymore.' She felt a tear slither its way down her cheek, but she actually didn't care.

And so it seemed, neither did he.

'Not at the moment, I don't,' he hissed. 'Look at the attention you're drawing to yourself, it's ridiculous.' He continued to play on his phone, not seeming to care in the slightest that her heart was being shattered into a thousand pieces.

She knew she had to hold herself together. She was an ugly crier. She wouldn't have herself looking all blotchy by the time Jeremy returned. She considered asking him if he still loved her as she hadn't had the words reciprocated in months.

But she decided against it.

She knew if she raised such question he would probably walk out, leaving her stranded in a room full of people looking back at her sympathetically. The thought alone was enough for her to let it go. Besides, she was too scared to know the answer.

Instead she put on a brave face, poured herself a glass of water and smiled as she exchanged a little wave to the familiar customers nearby. She could hardly wait for their food to arrive so they could quickly eat what would be another silent meal together before heading home. The only thing was, home didn't feel like home anymore.

It had begun to feel a lot like a prison.

Five

JUST LIKE THAT, it was the final week of the semester and parent-teacher interviews were in full swing.

It had been another crazy week with preparations leading up to the night. So far, Sienna had managed to push through the first group of interviews smoothly, despite feeling delirious from sleep deprivation. As predicted, it had been yet another week of walking on egg shells. No further conversations about wedding plans had been mentioned since that hideous afternoon at Nancy Green's. She had held off visiting the bridal shops—they too would take a back seat. Although this didn't stop her from taking a stroll past the stores on several occasions, admiring the beautiful gowns that only seemed to glare at her from the window bays.

There had been many nights where Patrick would return home late from a night out with his mates or work colleagues, drunk as anything.

It was part of the routine now, one she had grown accustomed to.

But what she hadn't grown accustomed to, was the accumulating expense of Ubers. She would often willingly offer to pick him as she waited up for him at some ridiculous hour in the morning, but he would bluntly refuse, scorning her for being 'his mother'. It crossed her mind that he wasn't seeing friends at all, that maybe there was another woman in the picture, but she chose to hold those thoughts captive. There was no reason to be paranoid.

With holidays about to begin, she should have felt a weight lifted from her shoulders, but somehow the load only felt heavier. She liked routine. Especially with its way of distracting her from the daily ache inside her. She wasn't sure how she was going to fill her days. Yet, the thought of having nothing planned made her uneasy. She found it almost impossible to relax, especially when everything she did was never good enough.

Well, according to Patrick's standards anyway.

Back in the day she would spend the winter holidays in Aringdale, watching the local dance competitions for hours on end in the little old theatre in which they were held. She found herself smiling at the memories. It didn't feel that long ago where she was one of them, competing year in and out. It used to be the big event all the dance schools worked towards, preparing their students for an absurd number of routines, sending parents broke with ridiculous costume levies that came with it. Somewhere in her old room she still had cardboard boxes containing the countless trophies and medals from her days on the stage. She had gone out with a bang in her final year winning multiple championships, her face making the competition program for years following. She then spent the next three years living out her childhood dream before an injury struck, putting a stop to her career just as she landed her first contract with a major ballet company.

Posterior compartment syndrome in her calves.

The pain had been so excruciating, there were days she could barely walk. The daily battle of swollen legs and stabbing pains, robbed her from her contract as quickly as it came. And just like that, every dream she had of becoming a professional dancer, was over. It had left her devastated, broken and empty.

Over the years she had slowly disconnected from the dance world, to the point where she could no longer place her finger on the last time she had seen any sort of show. It hadn't been intentional. Well, not really. She had just changed over the years, and so had her interests.

Dance was a part of her past and she was content without it.

The thought crossed her mind to head back to Aringdale for a decent visit after all these years. Even though time had a way of standing still in the small country town, she knew that there would be a new generation of dancers she hadn't seen. Never mind the fatigue and exhaustion wrapped around her brain, she made the decision in that moment to go. Some time away from the city and Patrick would do her good.

It would do them both good.

Besides, she was sure he would be thankful to be left alone where he could drink freely, without her constant monitoring.

'Hiding out in the classroom, are we?'

There he was, standing at the classroom door posing like a mannequin in a bay window of a suit store. She wondered if Damian could ever be just, well … natural. Always staged, always posed, she didn't know how he had the energy to keep it up.

She glanced at her watch noticing that intermission was almost over. The second lot of interviews would begin in just ten minutes. She had gone over. She groaned, feeling her stomach react at the same time. She hadn't realised how hungry she was. It had been another one of those days where there had been no time to eat.

She smiled at him, yet careful in her expression. 'It appears that way!' She came out from behind her desk keen to make a dash to the staff room to grab whatever food remained. 'I need to learn to keep to a better time schedule.'

He grinned at her as he sifted his weight from the door frame and to her surprise, uncovered a plate from behind his back. He looked as smug as ever. 'In the short time I have known you Henderson, I have been quick to notice how little you eat.'

Sure enough, the plate was stacked full of snacks. She took it graciously, feeling her stomach rumbling as the smell of party pies and pastries coiled her hunger.

If only she could eat one of them.

She needed a healthier option. Maybe if she quickly went downstairs she could grab a piece of fruit or throw together a sandwich or something. She looked at the plate then up at him, she wouldn't be rude and refuse the gesture. She would just have to suck it up. She pushed away Patrick's controlling thoughts and sank her teeth into a meat pie. Nothing had ever tasted so good. She must look like some starving animal as she scoffed it down, any sense of self-consciousness going straight out the window. She didn't have time to care, yet Damian clearly found the sight amusing as a series of chuckles escaped his lips.

'If this is what it takes for you to eat then I'll happily bring something in for you every day of the week.'

She swallowed down hard on the cheese and ricotta puff she had hardly chewed.

It hurt.

'I'm not that bad.'

He rested himself on the edge of her desk, positioning himself at eye level with her. 'I'm starting to feel like your man doesn't look after you very well.'

Her entire body tensed up. Why did he always find a way to bring up her personal life?

'He looks after me. It's me not looking after myself, that's the problem,' she joked. She took another look at her watch. Five minutes until the next parent would arrive, with Nolan's parents scheduled for the last appointment for the night. She was actually praying that they will show up, although knowing they probably wouldn't.

'Well, you should probably do something about that before you fade away to nothing.'

She let out a grunt.

He tilted his head and let out a cheeky smile. 'Don't worry, you're still sexy.'

She stared at him.

How was she even supposed to respond to that?

'What do you two have planned for the break?' He situated his body almost horizontal on the table with only an elbow propping him up.

With nervous eyes she scanned the room, hoping her colleagues were nowhere near to misinterpret the scene.

She was in the all clear.

She took a cupcake and slowly peeled back the paper wrapper. 'No plans as yet. I'm thinking of heading back home to spend some time with the parents. What about yourself?'

He smiled at her, his eyes lingering on hers a little longer than usual. She gave him a blank look, ignoring the anxiety surfacing inside of her. He sank down even lower, releasing his elbow that had elevated him onto some kind of angle.

He was horizontal now.

'I'm sure they would love that. Will Patrick be joining you?'

She shook her head, sheltering her mouth with her hand as she chewed. He propped himself back up and she felt herself relax.

He leant over and studied the ring on her finger. 'And when is this finally happening?'

'We haven't set a date.' She shrugged. 'We're not in any rush.' It was a line she had used a million times by now. She would get married tomorrow if she had any say in it. But she wasn't about to tell him that. She really didn't want to encourage him.

He reached for her hand, tilting his head as he admired the solitaire diamond that still held its shine. 'It's a beautiful ring,' he said, smiling. 'If I met the woman of my dreams, I wouldn't be wasting any time!'

And off he went again.

She forced a little laugh and drew her hand in close to her body.

'I wouldn't call it time wasted.' She took another party pie and studied her watch a little too hard.

Three minutes to go.

'We are just enjoying being engaged for now.' It sounded convincing enough. He didn't know any details of their engagement anyway. And she planned to keep it that way.

He smirked. 'If you say so.'

Why did everyone seem to have the same opinion on this? It shouldn't have bothered her, especially coming from Damian, but the fact she had heard this too many times now.

She raised her eyebrows and let out an unintentional snort. 'You're not convinced.'

He shook his head a little too confidently side to side, propped himself back up and stood to his feet.

Thank god.

'Not at all,' he said, walking towards to the door. 'Do you know why?'

She tilted her head, her smile still intact.

'Your eyes don't light up the way an engaged woman's should.'

And just like that, he hit the nail on the head.

She lowered her head and took the empty plate. He barely knew her. How could he possibly draw that conclusion?

'Thanks for the food Damian.'

'You're welcome.' He adjusted his tie and lingered by the door for a moment. 'Keep me informed how your meeting goes with Miranda and Stuart,' his tone professional again. 'Something that could be worth looking into.'

'Will do, thank you.'

With a little wave, he left. She could already hear the flood of parents making their way up the stairs where they would soon disperse into different classrooms. She tossed the paper plate into the bin and looked at the list.

Nine more interviews to go, then she would be out.

She took in the naked blue walls of her classroom that had been coloured with an assortment of student work and displays over the semester. The chairs had been stacked neatly to the side, desks cleared from name tags and pencil pots. It was always the way at the end of the term, yet for the first time the emptiness of the room affected her. Sure, it was only a two-week break before she would return to a new term with her room decorated as buoyant as the last. Yet, the thought of facing another suddenly overwhelmed her. She loved her job, there was no doubt about that. So, what was making her feel this way? She put it down to being burnt out.

Yes, that was all it was.

'I'm glad I caught you!' It seemed to be a night for visitors. Allie, one of the newly graduate teachers popped her head through the door.

'Oh yeah? What's up?' She was surprised to see such enthusiasm when she really had no relationship with the girl. They hadn't even shared a conversation over the semester. Not that this was any different to any of the other relationships she had with her colleagues. No one seemed to want to get to know her.

Allie nodded quickly then pursed her lips together. 'We missed you at the curriculum brief,' she said condescendingly.

'Pardon?'

A frustrated look appeared on her face. 'You didn't get the email?'

Sienna hesitated and took a moment to think. Surely, she hadn't been so careless to have missed it. But then again, she hadn't checked her emails all day. But even so, why hadn't anyone let her know? And why was it scheduled on a day like this one where they already had enough on their plate?

'No?' Her eyebrows lifted, impatient at the delay.

'I'm so sorry, I must have missed it.' She started to fret. This was the last thing she needed. Another reason for everyone to despise her.

Allie stared blankly at her. 'I'll send you the minutes.' She disappeared out the door.

Sienna took a breath, exhaling heavily as she yanked her laptop open and refreshed the web page.

Two minutes to go, she barely had enough time.

The page loaded. Sure enough, there was an email. With a deflated sigh, she opened it and noticed the time it was sent. 4:47p.m.

She glanced at the clock, confused. It was now 5:58p.m. Meetings were never organised at such late notice. She squinted to see that Allie herself, had written it. She felt herself relax, relieved she hadn't missed anything formal as these meetings were always called by the curriculum coordinator. She clicked on the message and quickly scanned her eyes over the email.

Hey all,

While we are all together tonight, I thought that we could quickly take a look at human-ities unit on Indigenous Culture for next term. Keen to hear some of your ideas. Let's debrief during break.

So that was all it was. Surely there were others that had missed the memo too. Especially at such short notice. It didn't really concern her anyway. She already had her curriculum planner prepared, ready to go. She would share her ideas with them later.

With that, the bell went and it was time for her next interview. She took a couple of sips from her water bottle, closed her laptop and smiled at the parent who had arrived at the door.

SHE HAD BEEN waiting for over fifteen minutes for Nolan's parents to arrive. She hadn't expected them to have shown up but hadn't lost hope for it either.

It was 8:17 p.m.

Most staff had already finished up for the night and had gone home. She poked her head out of the class room and scanned her eyes around the empty hallway.

Silence.

She stood still contemplating what to do. She had done every-thing to communicate the importance of this night to them. She had tried calling, emailing, leaving notes in Nolan's diary for him to take home to read, but had been unsuccessful in every attempt. She couldn't understand how any parent could show so little interest in their child. Especially Nolan, who had quickly become so special to her. She knew she needed to talk to them about the tutoring she has begun with him too, and that was all going to be brought up tonight. If they had shown up.

The time her and Nolan shared became less about academics, and more a time where they would just sit and talk about anything he came to her with. Each time she was cautious of probing into his personal life, being mindful not to cross that line. It was challenging for her at times to hold back as deep under the surface, she had a feeling he was fighting a war. It was these suspicions that made her feel as though it would probably be best to pass him onto the school counsellor. But knew he wouldn't form a relationship with anyone else in the same way he had with her. He felt safe with her, this much was clear as day and night. She knew this by the way he spoke so freely with her, with a trust allowing him a freedom to do so. But even with all this in mind, she knew she had a responsibility to talk to Damian about it.

He would decide how things would proceed from there.

She made her way down the stairs for the first time that day, passing the staff room on her right before arriving at his door.

All the lights had been turned off, with only a single light from his office illuminating the hallway. She found him slouched against his leather chair, his feet casually resting on the edge of a desk, immersed in paper. His suit jacket was unbuttoned with his tie loosened. Clearly, he was ready for the day to be over as much as she was. She knocked on the door frame, his eyes instantly shot up.

'Look who has graced me with their presence,' he flirted, swiveling side to side on his chair.

'The Livingstons were a no show,' she stated bluntly, ignoring his playfulness.

'Right.' He paused and sat up straight. 'I will look into setting up a meeting with them,' his tone became more serious.

'And from there?'

'Let's hear your thoughts.' He gestured for her to sit down.

She took the seat opposite him. 'As you know, I've attempted to reach out to them on numerous occasions and they just haven't been responsive.'

It sounded like a script; her professional tone having a way of making her sound like some amateur actress. He must have thought so too as a smirk formed in the corner of his mouth. She felt her cheeks grow hot.

Why was he always this way around her?

'For the last couple of weeks Nolan has stayed back after school,' she continued, avoiding any eye contact with him. 'During this time, we have worked on different learning tasks from class and in a sense, I've begun tutoring him.' She gave in and positioned her eyes on his to find them smiling at her.

'You have a beautiful heart Sienna.'

'Excuse me?'

'The way you invest your time in your students, especially towards those who need that extra attention. This world is in need for more teachers like you.' He was back to swinging again on his chair, his eyes still fixed on hers, his smirk fully intact.

She exhaled deeply, suddenly agitated. 'I was wondering if Nolan would benefit with some sessions with Anita Moore,' she said ignoring his comment. The sooner she got to the point, the sooner she would be out of there.

'Counselling?'

'I think it's what he needs,' she agreed. 'There's only so much I can do. He's honestly struggling, and I have this feeling his home life is a contributor to that.'

He scribbled something down on a notepad. 'That can be arranged. Let me see what I can do.' He looked up. 'I will put it forward in a meeting I set up with them. But I'll need their consent first.'

Guilt washed over her. She felt as though she has just given up on the child, handballing him over to a complete stranger. Suddenly, she questioned her decision in saying anything at all. What if Nolan wasn't able to open up with Anita in the way he had with her? But then there was always the possibility his parents wouldn't be in favour of the suggestion, if they even showed up at the meeting. She wouldn't get ahead of herself with the hypothetical.

He must have noticed her concern and stretched his hand out towards her. She stared at it, not knowing what he wanted her to do. Fortunately, her hands were safely in her lap, behind the desk that separated them.

He pulled his hand back in and let out a sharp grunt. 'It will all get sorted.' He rose from the chair and stood beside her, placing his hand securely on her shoulder. 'You have done all you can Sienna.' He squeezed it and lowered himself onto the end of his desk. 'I will take it from here.'

Alarm bells went off inside her. She could feel his breath just inches from her. He was positioned too close.

Far too close.

The fact that there was a ripple of panic surging through her confirmed she had to get out, and fast.

'I appreciate that.' She slowly shuffled her feet under her, creating space she could between them.

He let out a loose laugh as he watched her. Her cheeks burnt from humiliation. How did she end up here like this? He placed his other hand on her other shoulder and positioned himself so his body was facing squarely with hers. She had no choice but to look at him.

'You're always so nervous around me,' he teased her.

Ok, it was well and truly time to get out.

'This is a bit close.' She eased herself up out of the chair. 'We don't want anyone getting the wrong idea,' her response came fast. She felt his breath against her, his cologne strong under her nose.

His brilliant smile remained whole. 'You're probably right.' Reluctantly he released his hands from her shoulders and rose to his feet. 'Enjoy the break Sienna.' He walked her over to the door, his hand hovering behind the small of her back with every step. 'Maybe when you're back you won't be so nervous around me,' he joked.

She gave him an awkward wave, feeling his eyes on her as she walked back down the corridor. Just as she was about to head back up the stairs and call it a day, Allie appeared from the staff room.

'A late-night trip to the principal's office hey,' she stated, syncing in step beside her.

Sienna felt her cheeks glow warm. How much had she seen? She mentally replayed the scene in the office, praying she hadn't seen his hands on her. The last thing she needed was for more rumours to be circling around the staff.

'Yeah, there was a student issue I needed to address with Damian,' her response civil.

Allie looked at her, her youthful green eyes glistening with a prospect of scandal. 'It's ok, I won't say anything.'

Sienna frowned. 'What do you mean?'

'I might be young, but I'm not stupid.'

Sienna's heart pounded profusely in her chest. Did she really think something was going on between them? If that was the case, how many others had she shared her thoughts with? This girl wasn't shy. It was fair to say Allie had a flare for the dramatic. She could only imagine the stories that could and would be created.

This wasn't good.

'I'm not sure what you mean by that, but like everyone else here, my relationship with Damian is strictly professional.'

The seriousness in her voice was enough for Allie to scrunch her face. 'I saw his hands on you just now,' she alleged bluntly.

She saw *what?*

Sienna felt sick. This was bad. Very bad.

'Well, it's not what you think,' the words flew from her mouth without realising how pathetic they sounded.

Her colleague must have thought so too and let out a snort.

'Yeah, ok.' She didn't sound convinced. Not even a little bit. Sienna struggled to find the words that could possibly save her from another layer of gossip formed against her. But she was too tired to defend herself. She had given up. She was dog-tired, defeated and desperate to go home. At this point, even the perfect response wouldn't save her. Her identity had already been sealed in this place.

'Maybe if you spent less time flirting with our boss then maybe you would have made the meeting earlier, like everyone else.' She slowed her pace and turned. 'I guess that was a little vague of me.' She puckered her lips together like she had it all figured out. 'I saw you two earlier as well.' She quickened her pace, leaving Sienna staring vacuously after her.

She must be one of the few people left by now. Classrooms were empty and the few remaining lights had been switched off.

Just like that there was a silence once more. A silence that screamed at her. She clasped her dainty hand over the cold hand rail and took a moment to inhale, her lungs closing in on her with every attempt for air. With shallow breaths, she dragged her tired legs up the last of the stairs, and into darkness. Darkness; her life resembled this to a tee.

A pit of darkness she couldn't seem to escape from.

Six

SHE ALWAYS IMAGINED she would be at her peak, her physical best by the time she completed her three years of intensive training at the National State Ballet. For as long as she could remember she had imagined walking into her first company audition with her head held high, her muscles fine-tuned, mentally prepared to tackle anything that was thrown at her. She had never been naive to think that it would be easy, or arrogant to believe she would be exactly what the directors were looking for. She was well aware of the standard she was up against. She knew the ballet world was ruthless, that she would have to audition for twenty jobs to have the chance of landing one. Even then, she never quite had the confidence in herself to even believe that.

When she stepped into her audition for the National Premier Ballet, her twenty-year-old body felt as though it was eighty. She couldn't understand why the last few months her legs had decided to shut down on her, especially when she was doing everything she was told to manage them. Massaging, rolling, magnesium salt baths, stretching, plenty of rest and sleep. Yet, none of these things eased the squeezing sensation as though there was something constantly tackling her to the ground. There would be an agonising pain every time she extended her leg, making it almost impossible to point her foot. After sending her body through hell and back, she managed to finish her audition with what she had hoped had been delivered with ease, strength and grace. It had taken every ounce of energy to make her movements appear effortless, working three times harder than usual to be able to portray exactly that.

By the time she walked out of the studio there was no feeling in her legs. Her calves had swollen up to hard balloons, her selection of foam rollers failed to release the giant knot they had become. It had terrified her as she looked down at a pair of legs she no longer recognised. After spending an hour practically paralyzed, she had worked herself up in such a state. After some time she somehow pulled herself off the floor, hobbled to the toilet, and threw up.

She must have danced well, somehow bringing something to the panel that was unique or special. It was a miracle when she was notified of her success in obtaining a position as a company artist at one of the country's most elite ballet companies. She had never imagined that she would have had such luck after just one audition. She had convinced herself she would have to travel overseas and do the rounds there. She never imagined that she would have to turn down the chance of a life time. It was only days after where she had been diagnosed with severe compartment syndrome in her legs, giving her no choice but to step away from the contract she had worked almost her entire life for. And just like that, fifteen years and quite literally thousands of hours of working her ass off, had been wasted.

She had never heard of such condition before. Medical specialists constantly commented how rare it was for dancers to acquire it, having been more common in runners, cyclists and footballers. An overuse injury one had said, caused by excessive exercise and repetitive motion. It made sense, considering she had been dancing sixty hours a week. The condition was described as an increase of pressure, causing bleeding in the muscle. Unfortunately for Sienna, her latest symptoms of swelling and numbing was caused by decreased blood supply, resulting in nerve damage in her calves. She hadn't accepted the first doctor's opinion of course. Instead, she put herself through a series of excruciating tests to be absolutely certain.

Blood tests were undertaken in search for chemical markers of muscle injury, where needles were inserted into the muscle compartment for pressure monitoring. Those doctors whom had been optimistic suggested a fasciotomy, an operation where the thick, fibrous bands that line the muscles are filleted open, allowing the muscles to swell, relieving the pressure within the compartment. Although most prognoses indicated that such operation wouldn't be successful as complications of acute compartment syndrome in most cases, were irreversible. In her case, muscle scarring and nerve damage had already been caused as the condition had been left untreated for too long.

Her final couple of months of training saw her away from the ballet school and at countless doctor and physio appointments, hooked up to a Tens machine, or submerged in ice therapy. Her audition had marked the last time she would tie a pair of point shoes on her feet. While her peers spent hours on the tip of their toes, she would either be in the next studio attempting Pilates, or taking notes for a rehearsal she knew she would never have the chance to put to practice. She was looked upon with pity every time she walked into the studio as she positioned a stool next to the pianist. With the music echoing in her ears she would watch with envy at the way everyone else's legs worked perfectly as hers curled beneath her chair. Until then, she hadn't realised what a gift it had been to be able to move freely. She had spent half her dance career time wishing to be 'normal,' wanting to enjoy a normal life such as going out for dinner, shopping with friends or seeing a movie. On the contrary, she had been abused and screamed at in an environment where she was expected to be perfect every single day. If only she knew she would be sitting on the sidelines, watching her competition get a head start, day in day out, she wouldn't have taken it all for granted.

Even though they pitied her, she knew there were times where they wished they were her. She certainly knew there had been days where she wished to be in their position when everything seemed too much. Times where she had questioned what the hell she was doing with her life as she stared at herself in the mirror all day like some self-absorbed robot. Maybe some of the girls really did wish they had been in her position, but the pity they presented her with had all been an act. If anything, they were relieved. One less dancer in the world to compete against. One less component in the running for the scarce array of contracts that were up for grabs. Even though they were yet to learn she had secured one. That was the reality of the ballet world. No wonder she often longed for a normal life, when the bubble she had been in was exactly the opposite of that.

But as soon as the one thing she had dreamed about forever was taken from her, she felt starved for oxygen and left without purpose. She never really had a back-up plan. She didn't expect she would actually need one. She had sacrificed everything to see her dream become a reality. The number of parties, road trips, holidays she had passed up to perfect her technique had been too many to count. She was left devastated, crushed, and empty. But worst of all, there was no one who could relate to all she was feeling. Her parents had never been for her choosing to pursue a career in ballet. She came from a very academic driven family with an emphasis on status and financial stability. If the dream didn't earn above a certain figure, it should be ruled out.

As anticipated, they took the whole injury as a blessing. In her father's eyes, it had added years onto her life, putting her on a pathway he had hoped for her. A pathway to University, leading to a stable life with everything that a secure life offers. Investments, shares, a mortgage for a home. A chance to put away for the future, ready for a family one day. A life she had been reassured time and time again that the ballet world would never give her. A life he had told her she would be foolish to neglect, one that she would regret when she hit sixty-five with no real savings behind her, struggling through life as a pensioner. Every time a situation challenged her to question her decision to follow her heart, these comments filled her head. Comments that played over, eventually turned to fears, stripping every ounce of confidence and mocking her for pursuing such a far-fetched dream. It wasn't that they weren't proud of her or failed to acknowledge that she had talent. They just wanted her to live an abundant life, convinced the dance world would rob that from her. They had some understanding of the toxic environment and the constant stress she had constantly been under to be 'perfect', along with the statistics of dancers that actually made it. But what they didn't understand was how dance had become her identity, her livelihood. The way it made her feel alive, her need to dance. Despite the odds, they didn't believe she would find fulfillment in it, that it was a healthy life choice, nor would it ever give her a balance she needed in order to be happy.

But as soon as she turned down the contract and hung up the point shoes once and for all, she didn't feel the freedom her parents assured her she would feel. She enrolled in a Bachelor of Education after being bribed that all her expenses would be fully taken care of. She was pretty much depressed for the first year, even though she really did try to enjoy 'College life'.

She really did try.

She hung out with her class mates in the cafeteria, the library between classes, spending many of her free blocks at quirky cafes before returning to campus with the best coffee everyone talked about, warm in her hands. It was the 'normal' life she had dreamed about during the days where pebbles of sweat streamed down her back into her already soaked leotard. Being able to be outside with the sun streaming down her face had been her biggest fantasy during the times she had been screamed at by her director. But as soon as she was tasting the life she had once longed for, she wanted nothing more than to be back in the studio doing what she knew how to do best. The one thing that made her feel something.

Dancing.

By her second the year the ache slowly dulled and her drive to give the university thing her best became her focus. She defriended all her dancing 'friends'—well—the ones who had contracts and were now living out their dream the way she imagined she would be. She hadn't wanted to witness their happiness and success pop up all over her news feed on social media. She didn't need the reminder.

It was simply time to move on.

Her grades sky rocketed to high distinctions, and to her parents' delight, she spent her evenings with her nose in the books. She barely had the time to talk whenever they called. She hadn't stepped into a dance class since her diagnosis but had been encouraged to engage in low impact exercise such as swimming and Pilates.

So, that was what she did.

Her legs were doing much better. There were times where she would walk the stairs at Uni and feel them tighten and begin to throb. But she knew what she needed to do to release the pain and was back to walking normally within record time. For the first time in her life, she actually had time to work and picked up a job as a check out chick at the local supermarket just two blocks down from her studio apartment in St Kilda. It was nice to earn her own money. Up until that point her parents had completely supported her finances. She only worked eleven or twelve hours a week but enjoyed the cash flow and the freedom to buy new things without feeling guilty of spending her parents' money. She felt a boost of confidence as she began to dress in nice clothes instead of the sloppy, old, active gear she lived in travelling to and from the Academy. There was no point buying nice things back then. There had been literally zero time to wear them anyway as she arrived at the studio before the sun got up, leaving well after it went down.

With her rent being paid for, a new wardrobe of clothes, a part time job and good grades—life was looking a lot brighter for Sienna. She had formed friendships with a couple of nice girls and enjoyed the night life of delicious dinners, cute bars, night markets and festivals. There was always something on at night, a comedy show, a movie, a musical. Even the ballet. Her friends at the time had suggested to see 'Giselle' performed by the National Premier Ballet as it premiered in Melbourne that year, but she had somehow talked her way out of it. She hated the sudden rise of passion surface whenever the word 'ballet' was brought up. She hadn't told them about her past as a dancer, she had somehow kept that gigantic part of her life a secret. There was no way she would put herself through the agony of reminiscing the contract she had scored with the same ballet company performing that season. It should have been her dancing that ballet on that stage. It was all she could think about as she stared out at the giant billboard they passed that night.

It simply wasn't fair.

It was in the same year when she met Patrick. It wasn't like her to have struck a conversation with him the way she had that night. Maybe it was the amount of alcohol she consumed, the way life was finally falling into place for her, that allowed her to tap into the playful, quirky Sienna that had been in hibernation since high school. She blamed the ballet world for killing off any sense of personality.

He came from a similar background, and like herself, was at College for all the same reasons. His father dreamed for him to own his own company one day, and a business degree would best prepare him to do just that. But unlike her, he didn't have much of a relationship with his family. Although he didn't say so, Sienna assumed it was due to the pressures they placed on him to be successful like his older brother, who was a lawyer in one of the top firms in the country. Because of his strained relationship with his parents, he never really made the effort to build one with hers. And so, she never really got to know them even though they lived in the same city. She had met them only a handful of times over the space of five years, every encounter being rather awkward and distant no matter how hard she tried to get to know them on a deeper level.

Although he loathed his parents, their expectations steered him like a bit in a horse's mouth as he worked himself into the ground, determined to make them proud. She had somewhat hoped he would have been more sensitive about her past as an aspiring dancer in those early days where they wanted to know every detail about each other's lives. But instead of talking it over, he brushed the whole thing aside like it was nothing other than a petty, childhood dream. Instead, he went on to talk about what things needed to be in place for a future together. As soon as he brought her into the equation, using words like 'we' and 'us', the niggling feelings she felt in that lost conversation were all forgotten as she fell in love with the prospect of a possible future with a man who would provide her a safe and comfortable life.

In the five years they had been together, ballet never made its way back into conversation. Not once had they stopped to re-evaluate where the other stood on anything that had once rattled their emotions and struck their heart strings. As time went on it became easier to keep it that way. To keep the door firmly shut on anything that could throw a spanner in the works, interfering with what had become a mind-numbing path together that once seemed exciting and filled with adventure. A path that now appeared narrow and empty, stripped of any sort of potential. Maybe one day that path would open up again. Maybe one day it would create a space where they could explore their passions and discover something that made their heart soar.

When that time would be, she didn't know.

For now, they had to keep on working hard, finding ways to keep their bank balances up. Adventure would just have to take a back seat; the fun stuff would come in time. And maybe when that time came, she would find something that held her heart the way ballet once had. The longer they stayed on this path, the more determined they were to see it through.

But the question was, would they?

For every step they climbed, they never seemed closer to reaching the top, wherever that was. Would they find anything that made it all worth it if they did?

Her decision to spend some time in Aringdale had come at a good time. It would give her a chance to rejuvenate and find the focus she once had when they first decided to set out on this path together. The only thing was, nothing about their journey so far filled her with an adrenaline than the thought of stepping back into her home town.

The town where all her dreams began.

Seven

SHE WAS HOME.
Even after all of these years, Aringdale still had a way of feeling like home to her.

As she stepped into the foyer bright and early that bitter cold Saturday morning, she was filled with a blend of the familiar smells from her competition days—sequins, eyelash glue, hairspray and coffee. She hugged her jacket close to her slender body as the piercing draught followed her in. She closed the door behind her, scanned the foyer and weaved herself through a swarm of parents to the administrative table. Being a small community, the committee generally consisted of volunteering parents across a range of dance schools that united for the event. As soon as she reached the front table, she realised just how apparent it was that after all of these years, very little had changed. In front of her were the same two ladies handing out coloured wrist bands for entry to the morning session.

And there she was, smack-bang centre on the cover of the program booklet.

She tilted her head to take a closer look as it was passed to the customer in front of her. There she was, dressed in a lilac tutu, holding an arabesque position on pointe, her twiggy leg extended long behind her. The photo must have been a decade old by now. A winning performance that had clearly still left its mark, even after all this time.

'It couldn't be!'

Her eyes were drawn to the voice of the mother of her former dance teacher.

'Valarie!' She flashed the woman her warmest smile. 'It has been a long time!' She reached over the small fold out table that separated them and closed her arms around the woman who had been one of her biggest supporters since she was a little girl. Even after all this time she hadn't aged a day; her black hair perfectly intact, held in a tight knot at the back of head. Her skin was still flawless like porcelain.

The woman squeezed her tightly, rubbing her ice-cold hands up and down her back. 'My dear, it has been too long! What are you doing with yourself? Are you dancing?' Her eyes were beaming like a kid at Christmas. 'Please tell me you still are?' She stepped back and ran her eyes over her. 'You certainly still look like a ballerina.'

'I'm afraid I'm not!' Sienna managed a stiff laugh, handing over the money and secured the blue band around her wrist. 'I had a good run though! It will always be part of me.'

It wasn't entirely a lie. She was drawn here for a reason, right? That had to count for something.

Valarie nodded slowly then gave her head a deliberate shake. 'Such a shame. You were such a wonderful talent.' She handed the program to her. 'You should come back here and teach for us sometime. You're still an inspiration to many young dancers here.'

There was a sadness behind her cheery tone and Sienna knew why. Although the woman hadn't personally coached her, but without fail, had always believed in her. A current of sorrow passed through her as the memories hit her like a tidal wave. It was a chunk of her life she forced to neglect.

Until now.

Being back in the theatre where her love for dance was planted had a way of making it impossible to run any further. Whether or not she liked it, her emotions sent her back to the year 2010 in one big sweeping movement.

She weaved her way through the crowd into the auditorium, feeling countless sets of eyes on her and the whispers that followed. She wasn't one to enjoy such attention, especially when all the attention she seemed to attract these days was negative.

But this was different.

After years away from the small community of Aringdale, she almost felt special that people still recognised her face. She couldn't help but smile as teenagers tapped their mothers' shoulders, pointing at her with starry eyes. Yet, part of her felt like a fraud. Did they even realise she never achieved a career in dance despite everyone's predictions that she would? That she didn't actually achieve anything beyond her full-time training? She was hardly a success.

In fact, she had let everyone down.

She was one of the few dancers that had been closely looked at from the beginning of time. She had thrived in all her ballet exams, competitions and performances, having made the local paper on numerous occasions. She was talked about as the next rising ballerina but had fallen short.

She had failed.

She took a seat at the back of the theatre, safely hidden from prying eyes. She wrapped her jacket tighter again as the cold air sent another penetrating chill down her spine.

Not much had changed, the lack of heating in the theatre being one of them.

She opened the program and turned to the morning session and ran her eyes over the list of competitors. Just as expected, she didn't recognise any names. Probably because they were starting off with the under ten-year-old song and tap solos.

Her body spasmed with more shivers as she settled further in her seat and took her mobile from her hand bag. No messages from Patrick. She wasn't surprised. He was more than likely passed out after a big night of drinking. She could only presume so anyway, not that she heard from him the night before either. Gone were the days where he would message her to see if she had arrived anywhere safely or sent her a text goodnight on the days they were apart. It had bothered her in the beginning, but not anymore. She had made the conclusion that every relationship reached a stage where these types of messages died out. She missed the early days where she would feel a constant stir of excitement every time there would be a spontaneous text from him. The days where he would always let her know that he was thinking of her. She put it down to the honeymoon stage where it was a matter of time before it would all come to an end. It was probably that way for all couples.

It was normal.

Her thumbs drew back, not knowing if it was a good idea to send him a text, not wanting to wake him. She was frustrated for even wrestling with the thought of how he would react if she did, hated that she had become so reactive with him.

Her message was short, letting him know that she had arrived safely and would be spending the day in the theatre so reception might be patchy. She wished him a good day and let him know she loved him. She switched her phone on silent and sent it back into her bag by her feet. The lights began to dim and the old burgundy curtain slowly draped down. She shifted her weight sideways on her seat, trying to find a window of space between the woman and the tall man who had annoyingly blocked her view in front of her. She glanced down her row. All seats were taken. She would just have to stay put until the section was over.

He was really tall. The longer she sat there, the more agitated she became as the back of the man's head became the feature of the show. The first couple of solos had come and gone and she had pretty much missed all of them. It didn't help that the guy was constantly whispering to the old woman beside him throughout every performance. How did he not know that it was distracting? Maybe if she wasn't so short it wouldn't bother her so much. But still, she just wanted to be able to sit and enjoy a morning in the theatre in peace. Was that too much to ask?

Clearly it was.

She glanced at the program. Competitor number three was to be performed by Ruby Kahler.

Kahler.

It was although someone had pulled a plug and all of the blood drained from her body. It couldn't possibly be his niece, could it? She quickly did the math in her head.

Yes, it was possible.

The last time she had seen Ruby the girl had been a toddler, running around in a diaper. It must have been at least six years ago. Seven maybe, or even eight. Which meant her family was somewhere in the auditorium cheering her on.

'The poor girl is petrified.'

Again, her attention was drawn to the tall man in the row in front of her. For the first time this morning, she recognised the voice. It belonged to the man who, after all of these years, still left a mark on her heart.

Ethan Kahler.

Her body stiffened as she found herself staring attentively at the back of his head. She was unable to move, let alone breathe properly. Even in the darkness she could confirm the silhouette belonged to him. His broad shoulders and long neck gave away that much. He still had the same mop of thick brown hair, the only difference being that his once distinctive curls had managed to unravel over the years.

She barely paid any attention to the solos that graced the stage, she was far more intrigued by the man before her. She wanted to get his attention somehow, but every time she decided against it. She wouldn't have a clue what to say to him if she did. It has been *years*. She knew better than anyone, how time could change a person. He was probably completely different. He could be married, or even have a family by now. Anyway, he wouldn't be interested in small talk with her. His silence after all this time told her that much. But it wasn't just him. She hadn't kept in contact with anyone in Aringdale in almost a decade. Of course, she had ways of checking in; Facebook, Instagram, WhatsApp. It was the twenty first century after all, where technology was constantly evolving. She had searched for his name several times over the years, unable to find him which she didn't understand. Everyone was on social media. She did have his mobile number though. She should have been able to memorize it after it had been basically engraved in her contact list for half her life. Maybe it had even been the first number to make it into her pink Nokia mobile phone back in seventh grade. But any chance of remembering it had disintegrated with her decision to delete his number when …

The lights of the auditorium were back on and the audience stood to their feet. The section was over. Who had won? Had Ruby placed? She couldn't believe she had completely missed the award presentation. Her focus had been that far gone.

Everyone began moving around her, yet she found herself cemented to her chair. Ethan was already on his feet shuffling towards the end of his row. If she wanted to say anything to him, now would be the time before another nine years passed. Part of her wanted to run out after him and see how he had been doing after all this time. But instead, she took out her phone just in time as she saw it ringing. It was Patrick. The conversation was quick. He told her about his plans to play golf with the guys before heading out for dinner. No questions were asked about how she was doing, her time with her parents, or how long she had decided to stay in her home town. She assumed he was fine with the idea that he would see her when he saw her.

It was fine.

'I could've picked that voice from a mile away.'

Her blood ran cold at the very sound of his voice. She lifted her head and instantly their eyes locked. She felt her heart quicken as the side of his mouth curled into the same crooked smile as the one etched in her memory. His dark eyes were gentle, echoing a warmth that had the rare ability of tickling her soul. Other than looking a little rugged, a little manlier and all grown up, he was exactly as she remembered.

'Hi stranger.' Her words came out like a yelp more than anything. She cleared her throat hoping to smooth it. 'How are you?' She couldn't help but feel a string of nerves tangle themselves into a neat little web inside her as she stood there. She was basically floating his presence.

He was looking at her with the dancing eyes he always had whenever he was around her. It was although he could sense her uneasiness, yet just by being Ethan, he found a way to comfort her restless soul.

'I'm great!' The crooked smile was larger than life itself. 'Can I give you a big hug?'

It was such an Ethan thing to say. It was hardly a question as he bent down and wrapped his arms around her and closing them over the small of her back. He warmed her instantly. With his neck inches from hers, she could smell the familiar scent of his cologne as it sent a trickle of calmness through her.

'How are you beautiful?' His voice soft as he held her in an embrace reserved for a long-lost friend. It was although no time has passed, and it was the year 2010 again.

She felt a tightness take hold in her throat. What was that about? and where had it come from?

'It's so good to see you.' She couldn't answer the question. She wasn't sure why.

He released his arms and took a moment to study her face. It was good to see him.

It was really good.

The inquisitiveness in his eyes withdrew any feeling of uneasiness inside. Instead of repeating the question, he took the seat next to her and searched her eyes. He had always been incredibly observant like that.

In fact, his intuition scared the hell out of her.

'What are you doing here? Tell me, what's news with you?' He scratched the nape of his neck. 'It's been a long time.'

She was seriously struggling for air. She couldn't help but catch herself staring at him. He was even better looking than she remembered. There were no pimples or scars, his complexion radiating an even, olive glow. Even through his woolen jumper, tight around his solid arms she could see he was still fit. His broad, strong shoulders was evidence of that. Did he still play football? Or had he finally freed himself from the sport that had once completely consumed him? Had he decided to settle down and …

'About five years, right?'

'Huh?' Oh no, she was all distracted again.

He brought his lips together and shook his head, smiling. 'I'm trying to work out the last time I saw you,' he laughed.

She uncrossed her legs, forcing herself to relax but all she was left with were shallow breaths leaving her gasping for air. 'Nine.'

He tilted his head at that and nodded slowly. 'Someone's counting,' he joked.

'Someone has to,' she giggled. 'I must say, you don't look any different.' She could feel her smile swallowing her face. She probably looked like a complete idiot right about now.

'I have to admit, you do.' He gave her a deliberate once over with his eyes.

She opened her mouth in a shocked, playful expression. 'Aged?'

'More beautiful than ever,' his response came quick.

Just like that they broke eye contact and she lowered her head, smoothing her hair behind her ears the way she always did when she felt uneasy. 'I'm sorry.'

She looked up and waved off his apology. 'It's fine,' she smiled, filling with a breath of sadness. 'Ruby did amazing!' She wasn't quite sure why the comment escaped her mouth when she had clearly missed her performance.

Ethan sat up straighter, his eyes lighting up at mention of her name. 'I'm so proud of her. She kind of had two left feet just like her uncle so we were skeptical when she started taking lessons,' he laughed.

Her smile only grew as she watched his eyes glisten with the obvious love he had for his niece.

'But she took us all by surprise! Dance has taken a hold of her. I have a feeling it will be that way for some time.' His eyes searched hers again. 'But I'm sure you know all about that.'

She nodded, careful in her expression. 'Dance does have a way of staying with you.' She breathed in and scanned her eyes around the theatre before landing them back on him.

His eyes were down at the program, supported by her left hand. She followed his glance, noticing her engagement ring glistening bright as ever under the dim theatre lights. She found his eyes, noticing his smile hadn't wavered.

'And it looks like these ballet people sure remember the talent you brought to the community here.'

He was referring to her face on the front of the dance program of course. Had he noticed her ring? It wasn't the right time to bring it up, not that she needed to rely the details anyway. He knew. His parents would definitely have told him. Either way, it still hurt that he had never bothered to congratulate her all those years ago.

His smile told her that he hadn't noticed, or maybe he had, and didn't care.

'I didn't really make it much further than that.'

The expression in his eyes changed. He tilted his head in a way he knew her heart had more to say than she let on.

'I mean, I tried. You know that.'

'You were well on your way when I saw you last,' he responded gently. He looked at her, and waited.

A flood of emotion swept through her. This was silly. Why was she feeling like this? She wasn't about to unload her sorrows and life failures onto him. Those days were gone.

So far gone.

She wasn't the same person as she was nine years ago. She was young and naive then, with the world at her feet, driven by the dreams and desires inside her undamaged heart.

'I got injured,' she said, shrugging. 'And that was the end of that.' She knew her response was abrupt and the curiosity behind Ethan's eyes confirmed it. He wasn't stupid. He knew better than anyone it was her life. But even then, she could tell that he knew she didn't want to talk about it and wasn't going to push it.

'So now we move onto plan B and I build you that dance school, right?' he asked, grinning.

Ah yes, the dance school idea.

It was something that they had talked about as kids. He always promised her he would build her a dance studio one day. It was going to be split into two studios, separated by a portable wall with the option to open up to serve as a function room. The memories of their conversations and banter over this single dream carried on for more than a decade. He had even drafted her up a plan once to prove that he was dead serious.

Somehow in this moment, it was more than her heart could take. A witty comment would usually slide off her tongue, thrown back and forth for as long as they allowed it to. But there was something inside of her stopping her from engaging that playfulness today. She needed to end the conversation, grab another crappy coffee and focus on what she had come here to do—to watch the dancing.

But she wasn't quite ready to leave yet.

'Life does seem to have a lot of plan B's,' she laughed, deceivingly.

His eyes searched hers again, as though he could sense a story behind the words she chose. She wished he wasn't so intuitive. She hated that he could read her like an open book. Especially when she was trying to keep it firmly shut.

'How long are you here for?'

She knew what he was doing and it made her panic. 'I don't know.' It was honest. To be fair, it was somewhere between two days and two weeks, but she didn't know that for sure. It wasn't a lie.

He stood to his feet and stretched out his long legs. She couldn't help but give him a quick examination all over. She still couldn't believe after all of this time, here he was, right here beside her. Her heart quickened all over again.

'I feel like you and I have a lot of catching up to do, Sienna. I want to know what happened to you.' The lightness was back in his voice. Thank god. She wasn't ready to be interrogated.

'You want to know what happened to me,' she repeated, slouching against her seat.

He nodded with a big toothy grin. 'You haven't given me much. But I'll work with what I have.'

'Persistence has always been your thing.'

'Some things never change.' He was still grinning.

She bit down on her bottom lip. He was wrong. Everything had changed.

'I can see that,' she said, instead.

'Mr Sogo?'

She clasped her hands together. 'That place still exists? Let's do it.'

He laughed, taking in the excitement that lit her face. And there was that crooked smile again. 'Are you free tonight?

She hesitated. What was she doing? Was it really a good idea having dinner alone with Ethan after all these years?

She glanced down at her ring sparkling away under the theatre lights. She tucked her arm behind her.

The last thing she needed was the questions.

She looked back at him, his eyes hopeful. Was she treading on dangerous grounds if she said yes? It would be a simple dinner, a couple of hours shared between two old friends. That was all. It was all that they had ever been.

She lowered her head as she thought about it. She would tell him everything, well the highlights anyway. She would be honest in telling him about her engagement and everything in-between. He would share his story too. They would acknowledge the two very different people they had become and how the years had changed them.

Especially nine years.

Then they would wish each other well and continue on with their lives. It was just dinner. One dinner. She wouldn't be doing anything wrong.

She pushed away any feelings of guilt before it had a chance to land there. She loved Patrick. A dinner wasn't going to change that, nor would it compromise anything they had.

She lifted her head and positioned her eyes on his. 'Tonight works.'

Eight

S HE COULDN'T REMEMBER the last time she felt as nervous as she
did now.

As she pushed open the doors of the restaurant, she felt herself
step back in time. Everything about the place was just the way she
remembered it. The buffet in the middle was laid out in the same way,
with the same brown tiled floor and laminated menus.

The blended aromas sent her stomach in a series of growls. She
was starving again, her stomach not having been exposed to such food
in a long time. To think she used to visit regularly with her friends
from school, made her long for the days where she could eat anything
without the psychological battle that came with every calorie she
consumed. Patrick would be completely against her eating out at a
place like this. It was a cuisine their nights out stood clear from. She
could almost hear his voice telling her not to be tempted. To be strong
and go for garden salad. If there was anything she was going to take
away from tonight, it would be the satisfaction of eating anything she
pleased, without feeling the need to apologise for a single second of it.

She spotted him in the far-left corner of the restaurant, sitting at
the same red booth as the one they had once reserved more times than
she could count. He hadn't seen her yet, allowing her a moment to

compose herself. The more she studied the man paved in her memory, the more she felt the years close over before her. It wasn't just that he looked the same, or that he carried himself the same way. There was something about his manner with her that afternoon that hadn't wavered. Even after all these years, he could still read and understand her completely, perhaps better than anyone. He had a way of unlocking a side of her she wasn't aware existed anymore. She didn't know how open she was willing to be with him tonight. If their connection was as strong as she imagined it would be, then it would only be a matter of time before he would have her heart exposed like open heart surgery.

With her heart beating quicker than normal, she slid into the seat opposite him. His eyes quickly found hers and a fluid of calmness trickled through her.

What was it about him that had such a power of ease over her?

'You're here'—and there was that crooked smile again.

'Surely you didn't think I'd stand you up?'

He directed his hand towards the buffet behind them. 'Not a chance. Anywhere else, maybe.'

She grinned. 'This place used to be pretty amazing.'

'This place *is* still amazing,' he corrected her.

'I guess not much has changed in little old Aringdale.'

'You're not wrong. But that's hardly a negative here,' he laughed.

'Well, that all depends if they still make my lemon chicken risotto.'

He chuckled. 'You mean the one where you used to drench your food in that horrible cheese crap?'

Her eyes lit up. 'That cheese sauce is called Haloumi. And it wasn't horrible.'

'It really was.'

'Well?'

'Yes, it hasn't gone anywhere.'

His eyes were doing that thing again where they tickled her insides, sending her heart into irregular rhythms.

'It better be as good as I remember it.' She stood to her feet and smirked. 'My stomach is about to eat itself. I can't wait another second. Let's go, like right now.'

'Still as excited by food I see,' he laughed, joining her to collect a plate.

She shook her head, smirking. 'You still think you have me all figured out.'

'Like I said, I'm working on it.'

After piling her plate high with risotto, garlic cheesy bread, gnocchi, meatballs and whatever else she managed to fit on there, they went back to their seats. There wasn't an inch of white left on her plate.

He was right about one thing; She had never been so excited to see so much food. And to think she didn't need permission to eat it, well, that just added a whole another level of excitement. She felt like a kid outside her parents' watch.

There was a lot of surface level talk at first, bits and pieces she had heard through the grapevine over the years. Other parts, news to her ears. The last time she had seen him he had completed his building apprenticeship. But now years later, he owned his own business. Football was still very much part of his life, but his desire to become a professional was long gone. It was more of a social thing for him now and found coaching to be just as fulfilling. Even though his dream of playing AFL had left him, he was still in a prestigious league, playing at a high enough level to be paid for it.

As she listened to him share the details of his life, she realised all over again, how much had shifted.

It only felt like yesterday where he was still a big kid dripped in talent, standing at a cross road with more opportunities than he knew what to do with.

But now in front of her, stood a man.

A man who was no longer driven by the things of the world. A man who held a value for travel, relationships, family. A man who had found his place in this world, ready to find someone special to share it with.

She could see this all within minutes of talking with him, sensing that he was waiting for her to share her story. But whenever there was the smallest gap in conversation, she would fill it with another question. Luckily for her, he seemed happy to talk. But after about an hour the formalities fell off, and he dove straight in.

'Congratulations on that by the way.' His eyes were down at her left hand that was caressing the empty glass in front of her.

'Huh?'

'Your engagement … a bit late of me, I know.'

She felt herself squirm. She expected her heart to behave differently. Instead of feeling a joy at the mention of the topic, she felt a darkness cloud over her.

'Thank you.'

He brought his lips together and gave a subtle nod. 'He must be pretty extraordinary.' His voice sounded different this time.

Their eyes met again. She didn't know how to respond.

Extraordinary.

It was a word that defined everything Patrick meant to her. Maybe it didn't reflect who they were as a couple at this particular point in time, but it didn't mean he wasn't worthy of the title.

'We were young and he won me over.' The words came from nowhere. Did she really just say that? Did she really just try to justify her relationship with the man she was about to marry?

He let out a forced laugh. 'Are you saying he isn't extraordinary?'

Come on Sienna, what are you doing?

'No, not at all. He's wonderful.' She shifted her weight side to side. Her stomach started to feel uncomfortably tight.

'So, when are you getting married? Didn't this happen ages ago?' She didn't mean to sigh. But to be asked that question one more time …

She shrugged helplessly. This time she didn't have a story in her. He lifted an eyebrow.

'You are still marrying the bloke, right?'

'Of course, I am.'

There was his crooked smile again, in teasing form. She knew this particular smile too well and started to feel skeptical where he would take it.

'Does your family love him?'

She nodded and sipped away at the ice in her cocktail, biting into the half-melted ones.

'As much as my family loved you?'

She swallowed hard, sending the shards of ice to the back of her throat. 'What are you doing?' she questioned him.

'What do you mean?'

His sarcasm always annoyed her. And still annoyed her.

'Why are you bringing us into this?' She was suddenly agitated and for the first time, felt the heat of the room like a furnace.

'I'm just trying to figure you out.'

He was still smiling. Was he serious? How was this him trying to figure her out? She lowered her body further down into the booth.

'It's been nine years Ethan and you want to figure me out now? After all of this time?' Her smile was gone, hating the uneasiness she was feeling. 'Ok.' She cleared her throat. If he wanted to figure her out, she would save him the time and put it all out on the table.

'I'm not the eighteen-year-old girl anymore who believes she can be the next prima ballerina if she sets her mind to it. I'm not the girl who believes you get out of this world what you put in, or when one door closes, another one opens.' She crossed her arms over her stomach. She felt sick. She had eaten way too much. 'I'm the girl who has come to realise that life is very rarely fair. It will chew you up and spit you out if you don't hold on tight enough and more often than not, can be completely ruthless.'

She took a breath. She hadn't meant to be this dramatic. But she wasn't here to play games, even though a small part of her enjoyed him persisting in cracking into the hard shell formed over her.

'Nothing can withstand time, because time doesn't have the ability to stand still. Therefore, no good thing can last forever, no matter how badly your heart may want it to,' she mumbled the last part.

She really shouldn't have had that extra cocktail.

Bad move.

For the first time that night there was a silence between them. She slowly built the courage to lift her eyes to find his down at his hands. After what seemed like forever, he finally looked up at her. His eyes were filled with a sorrow she hadn't seen before.

'What happened, Sienna?'

'What do you mean what happened?' She let out an exasperated laugh. 'Life happened, Ethan.'

He nodded. 'I'm sorry I haven't been part of it.'

'I assumed you didn't want to be.' She regretted the words as soon as she said them.

His eyes narrowed. 'Don't be like that.'

She exhaled a little laugh, one that was perhaps, a little too sarcastic. 'The last time I saw you I basically laid out my heart to you, and you ran.'

He was shaking his head, looking down again. She wanted to say more while she was on a roll. She could totally do this, let it all out once and for all. But tonight, wasn't the time. There simply was no point digging up the past.

Not now. Maybe not ever.

Besides, she didn't want him to see how much hurt he had inflicted upon her. The past was the past. She had to keep it that way. She inhaled a shaky breath. Never mind her emotions that had swallowed her whole, she wouldn't let him see that. She had to keep this light if it was even possible to backtrack at this stage.

'We were kids,' she started, feeling her heart shattering into a thousand pieces all over again. 'I guess I was just always smitten by you.' She sighed and forced herself taller in her seat. 'Anyway, I think you would like Patrick.' She changed the subject. 'I think he's exactly the type of guy you would have imagined me ending up with.'

He nodded and managed a smile. 'Not just handsome, intelligent and quirky'—he paused—'a man who would without fail, be by your side through all seasons of life.'

His head was lifted, but his eyes avoided hers. She felt her heart land in her stomach like a ton of bricks. How was it possible that he remembered this? After all of these years, he had remembered such detail from a single conversation that happened a lifetime ago.

Word for word.

What that meant, she didn't know. But it was enough to make her want to cry. Not that she would allow that to happen.

She nodded, forcing a convincing smile through her quivering lips. 'Yeah, that's him.' It was all she could manage. Did she believe it?

She wasn't sure.

'Then I couldn't be happier for you.'

For the first time that night, his crooked smile was gone. She stared at him, wondering if it was just her, or if in this moment he was further away than any of the years that had separated them.

She had learned a lot about Ethan over the years and the way he ticked. But one thing she never seemed to have fully worked out, was his feelings for her. He was slow to express himself but was always quick to notice whenever there was a guy in her life. He would either jump into protective mode, or disconnect from her entirely. When she thought about it, it had always been that way.

And it started as far back as the year 2005, when she was an eighth grader at Mason Grammar.

THEY HAD BASICALLY known each other since their bums were wrapped in diapers. Their sisters had been close friends which saw their families spending a lot of time together at play dates, parties and school events. It wasn't that they were pushed into their friendship, that wasn't the case at all. They had always connected on an uncanny level, their time together often spent in constant fits of laughter whether it was at his grandparents' pool, the park, the movies, or dining with their closest friends at Mr Sogo stuffing their mouths with their hyperactive metabolisms.

He was a year above her at school, but this hadn't stopped them from spending almost every recess and lunch together. While their friends obsessed over who would be the next king or queen in the game 'Foursquare' which seemed to be the thing back then, they would find themselves walking countless laps around the school, deep in discussion about anything her little heart desired. She never saw herself as an open or vulnerable person, but Ethan had a way of changing all of that. He was the first person she felt safe enough to confide in, finding the ability to completely unload all her fears in his company, refreshing. Perhaps it was the way he always took on the role of a big brother that made her feel this way.

Writing became an outlet where she could express herself freely. She would often find herself taking out a piece of paper from her binder book in class, writing him a letter whenever she got the chance. She was always on top of her school work, so finding a spare five or ten minutes was easy. There were times her teachers would be suspicious when she sheltered her letter with her hand while the rest of the class had their books out, working away. But being the star student that she was, they never once pulled her up for it.

What did she write about? Whether it was a fight with her parents, a boy she liked, her dreams—she wrote about it all. She wrote with a freedom and trust she only now realised, was admirable.

And rare.

A trust that if she was really honest with herself, was one she was yet to come across again. But if she really thought about it, she was just a kid back then. Naive and unharmed by a world she was yet to experience, without the layer of bubble wrap securely fastened.

Of course it was easier for her to trust back then.

She would fold the letters into quarters and keep them in her dress pocket until the bus ride home at the end of the day. As Ethan lived in the same neighborhood, they would catch the same bus together. It was that way for most of their childhood. She remembered how it was always her favourite part of the day, being able to spend time with him, just him and her. Although she never voiced it, she secretly enjoyed being able to sit beside him so closely, feeling the way her pulse accelerated whenever his arm brushed beside hers.

She wasn't sure why her body behaved the way it did. Perhaps it was the way he deeply cared for her in a way no one else did, and during the best of times, knew her better than she knew herself. Or maybe it was the way he made her laugh more than anyone. Not just a giggle here or there, but seizures of laughter that left her stomach muscles in agony.

The letters.

There had been many of them passed back and forth over the years. His responses even back then, had been full of wisdom, kindness and encouragement. So much so, she had kept every single one of them in her 'special box,' hidden away in the back of her cupboard in Aringdale. They hadn't been romantic letters but held a depth to them that made her heart glow like a ray of sunshine on an overcast day.

A man who would without fail, be by your side through all seasons of life.

As soon as the words surfaced in her thoughts, she dismissed them. Why they presented themselves there, she didn't know. They were irrelevant, and well and truly expired.

Especially in reference to him.

He hadn't been around for half her life. Well, not for the significant part anyway. He hadn't been there when she moved to Melbourne, where she struggled months on end with home sickness. He hadn't been there when her dream of becoming a dancer came crashing down.

He hadn't been there for the myriad of setbacks she encountered before she eventually found her feet again.

He hadn't been there for well, everything in between that too.

So, no, he hadn't been there for every season of life. As kids he had been, but not during the most pivotal events of her life, and that was the reality.

She wasn't bitter, at least she didn't think she was.

She was disappointed. But equally disappointed in herself. Seeing Ethan again and the way it felt like home in his company like no time has passed at all, validated that.

He had always felt like home to her. So much so, she never had the courage to cross that line with him while she was growing up, in fear she would lose that exact feeling of what home meant to her.

And it meant everything.

Even though her feelings for him had developed into something deeper that year, she knew it hadn't been worth the risk to express them. How many couples that got together in their teens actually stayed together forever?

Next to none.

She knew the statistics and it was enough to make her keep quiet. He was her best friend that and in itself was something she definitely hadn't wanted to stuff up. Especially during a time where puberty was striking hard. She didn't want to make any impulsive decisions when her flying hormones were doing exactly that.

When her best friend, Sadie, took an interest in him, she was flooded with waves of jealousy and an anxiety so intense—she felt as though her world was coming to an end. A world she had created, consisting of him and her living happily ever after in. As a best friend, she felt as if it was her duty to set them up in some way, especially when Sadie was constantly gushing about how wonderful he was, asking every question under the sun about him. How it all came about, she didn't know, but she remembered how difficult it had been to see her best friend so smitten over someone she had secretly claimed as her own. But she was careful not to give away how much this bothered her.

Come to think of it, she had been a master at putting on a front—even back then. She would smile through the many tedious conversations, feeling her heart break a little more after every one. She didn't know if Ethan liked her back at that point in time, but either way it hadn't eased the pain. But he had never spoken about her in that light before. She remembered confronting him about it one afternoon on one of their many bus rides home.

'What do you think of Sadie?'

He had looked at her with that cheeky crooked smile of his. 'She seems like a cool girl. She's quite the head turner, real pretty. Why do you ask?'

It was like taking a bullet.

'Well, she likes you.' Her smile so forced she swore he would have picked up on it. He must have known every one of her expressions. He knew her that well. But this time he hadn't, or simply had overlooked it.

Instead, his eyes had lit up. 'Really?' His arm brushed beside hers, taking notice of the butterflies that usually danced inside become violently squashed.

'Yeah. She kinda can't stop talking about you.' She found a laugh. 'Can you please just ask her out already so I can get her to shut up?'

He grinned. 'She can't stop talking about me?'

She wanted to slap it from his face.

'Well, yeah.'

'Hmmm …' His smile turned to a smirk, making Sienna feel sick.

'What?'

'Nothing.'

'So … are you going to ask her out?' She knew she sounded desperate, but she hadn't cared. She needed to know the answer.

'Calm your farm,' he laughed, 'I barely know the girl.' He jabbed her sides playfully, sending her body abruptly back against her seat. 'But I'd definitely like to start. Maybe we can all hang out tomorrow.'

She didn't have a single doubt that he would like her, that he would fall for her. She was a beautiful brunette, not to mention athletic, intelligent and witty like himself. It was then she realised from that day forward, their recess and lunch times would never be the same.

'Why do you do that?'

His face gave away nothing. 'Do what?'

'Tickle me like that all the time?'

He scrunched his face up. She wasn't sure where the question had come from, but at that point of time she felt it was her last chance for some indication of his feelings for her—If there were any at all.

But the vague look on his face told her it was all in her head. It told her everything she was feeling, that home feeling, was simply not shared. She would shut up. The vibe was definitely tense for the rest of the bus ride home as she stared glumly out the window. She had nothing left to say.

Just as she anticipated, everything did change.

The days where they would walk laps around the school soon became nothing but a distant memory. Instead, she fell straight into being the third wheel. It wasn't long before he was laughing with Sadie in the way he once had laughed with her, making her feel as though everything she believed they had, was solely in her imagination.

When the two of them weren't all over each other, they were talking about each other constantly. The bus rides she once looked forward to, soon became something she dreaded. She would stare out the window as Ethan rattled on about how amazing her best friend was and how crazy it was that he could see a future with her already. To say they were smitten was an understatement.

Eventually she stopped writing letters to him, not that he seemed to notice anyway. Not once did he ask after them, even though their letters had become a daily occurrence by this point. As soon as she stopped writing, her desire to be open with him left her. She could feel their friendship slip away somewhere into the background as Sadie soared to the foreground.

And just like that, her walls went up and she closed her heart off to him.

It wasn't until a couple of months into their relationship where she took an interest in one of Ethan's close friends. Tommy was cute, a little scrawny, but a sweetheart. Best of all, he seemed to like her just as much. It wasn't long before the four of them were hanging out, doing all the things and going to all the places she and Ethan had once found tradition in. Whenever Tommy held her hand or grabbed her waist as he swung her around, in the corner of her eye she would catch Ethan flinch. Even though it was subtle, she saw it. He would stop whatever he would be doing at the time and just stare, even if it lasted for a moment. She would pretend not to notice as she spiritedly flung her arms around Tommy's neck, planting kisses on his cheek. She felt a bit guilty using him in this way, when all along she had the intention of making Ethan jealous. But at the same time, it had strangely filled her with a sense of confidence and made her feel desired.

Empowered.

Not only that, it ignited a thought. It made her wonder if it wasn't all in her head after all, that there was actually a possibility that Ethan liked her. Even though Tommy was one of his closest friends, he was still protective over her as although his mate was a complete stranger. It was a side she hadn't expected to see after she had convinced herself he had forgotten about her.

'Do you think you love him?' he asked her one afternoon, on one of their usual bus rides home.

'I don't know,' she answered, 'but I know I'm falling for him.'

'Yeah, ok.' He sounded defeated, jealous even. That made her smile. Pretty big actually.

'Why do you ask?'

'Just checking in.' His eyes met hers and he shrugged. 'Just take it slow. You know … don't rush things.'

This didn't make sense to her.

'You love Sadie and, well, I love Tommy. It has nothing to do with rushing. It's a feeling I have little control over.'

'Sienna, love's not just a feeling,' he stated dryly.

'What?' Irritation inflamed inside of her.

'It's a verb, an active choice that you—'

'Are you seriously correcting me?' she interrupted. 'You don't think I have that with Tommy?'

'So, you *do* love him then?'

'Maybe I do,' she snapped.

'Maybe?'

'Yes. No! I mean …' She sighed heavily and pushed her hair erratically behind her ears, avoiding his eyes. 'Yes, I love him!'

With her head hanging low she slumped down in her seat and fiddled with the Pandora bracelet around her wrist.

'Ok.' his voice small, beaten.

She couldn't work out why she was so frustrated at the time. Why his questions bothered her so much. But now, looking back on the memory from eighth grade, it had all been so clear. It wasn't Tommy she had been in love with.

It was Ethan.

Nine

S HE DIDN'T ASK him if there was anyone in his life.

She wasn't sure why. Maybe she didn't want to relive the scene of listening to him rave about how wonderful his girlfriend was all over again. No, she didn't want her heart dragged back to that memory. Maybe she wanted to avoid a situation where her relationship could be compared against his. That could well have been it.

Or maybe she just didn't want to hear it.

No further questions were asked about Patrick after that. It was a topic that held a tension far too strong to revisit. Besides, it was meant to be a simple dinner between two old friends. Or whatever they were.

And she was determined to keep it that way.

A part of her wanted to pour out every emotion held captive inside of her, screaming to be freed. Yet the other part simply didn't have the faintest idea on how to go about it, her heart having been closed off to him longer than it had ever been open.

But truthfully, she was afraid. Terrified actually.

Terrified of what could be brought to surface if she looked deep enough.

THE REMAINDER OF the night could have easily taken a turn after her little breakdown, but awkward silences rarely entered their repertoire. It hadn't been back then and strangely, wasn't now. It didn't make sense that two people who no longer had a thing in common could still share a connection so strong.

She glanced at her watch to find that it was already nine thirty. Where all that time went, she didn't know.

As they went to pay the bill she realised she wasn't in any state to get behind the wheel. She had only had two drinks, but it was two more than she would normally have, and her head was left in a spin. Ethan, being as observant as always, noticed this straight away. They agreed to extend the night and get a coffee at the café a few blocks down until she was sober enough to make the drive home.

But as soon as they stepped outside, rain began to bucket down out of nowhere and they found themselves sprinting to her car for shelter. As they scrabbled inside and slammed the doors shut behind them, she found herself starting to laugh. She was drenched. Her blonde locks had quickly turned to a wet, matted mess. The rain on the roof was pelting down so violently, she could barely hear the sound of her erratic breathing that transpired. She turned to face him, her laugh growing louder at the sight of his hair that had been perfectly placed, now collapsed over his eyes like a sheep dog. As soon as he saw her laughing hysterically, he started to join in. The more he laughed, the harder she did. Just like old times, she found herself in seizures of laughter, leaving her stomach muscles in agony.

It felt good to laugh that hard.

That well.

They found themselves that way for a good five minutes before finally managing to pull themselves together. She inhaled, allowing the crisp air to fill her lungs. 'Let me drive us there.' She inserted her keys into the ignition.

'Not yet.' He sent her hand back into her lap. 'Let's just stay here for a minute.'

The combination of the smoothing tone of his voice and the therapeutic patter of rain allowed her to exhale, freeing any uneasiness as she fell back against the seat.

'Ok.' She was happy to be still. Still from her thoughts. Still from the anxiety wrapped around the walls of her heart.

'Is it nice to be back here?' His question took her off guard.

'Here?' As in, right here next to him the same way as a decade ago? She wasn't sure she was ready to dive into …

'Home.' He shifted his body to face her. 'Is it nice to be back home?'

She tilted her head back and took a moment to think. After being bombarded with a flood of conflicting emotions over the past ten hours, she hadn't had the chance to make sense of any of them. Being back in Aringdale had never been so exposing.

A town that once had her fastened securely in a safety net, had somehow left her vulnerable. So vulnerable it forced her to confront every suppressed memory as her guard loosened, leaving her completely exposed.

She never expected being back in her family home after years would make her feel although she had never left. She never expected that every cell in her body would come alive again at the sound of Tchaikovsky; the famous classical music that filled the theatre that day. And she certainly didn't expect to feel an inconsolable loss every time Ethan looked into her eyes with that damn crooked smile of his. It was her honest answer. If it was the year 2010 she might have voiced it.

But it was 2019, and everything had changed.

'It has been like a breath of fresh air.' It was close enough to the truth, just without the weight of emotions behind it.

He searched her eyes in the way where he knew her heart had more to say. She didn't give him a chance to investigate.

'Do you ever see yourself leaving here?'

'I don't think so. Everything is here that I need. My family, my business, my …'

Girlfriend. She waited in anticipation. Any time now.

'My mates,' he finished. 'Aringdale is home to me. I don't see myself leaving any time soon anyway.'

She nodded, not quite understanding the relief that had washed over her.

'Do you think you will ever come back?' He reclined the seat all the way back, allowing his legs to fill the space between. 'To raise a family with Patrick?'

To raise a family.

Naturally, it was the next step they were heading towards. But out loud the idea sounded a million steps away. A step she hadn't had the chance to process until now.

His face changed at the silence of her hesitation. 'You haven't discussed it?'

He was prying now. She hated it when he took things further than his business to know. So, what if they hadn't talked about the exact location they were going to raise a family? Not every detail of her life had to be mapped out. It wasn't even an issue.

She shrugged.

'Ok then,' he said, frowning.

It turned out that he was the one who clearly had more to say.

'What?' she asked, curious to learn his thoughts.

'The Sienna I know had her whole future worked out since she was, what? Thirteen? Fourteen? And as far as I remember, kids were definitely part of that plan. That's all.'

She let out an abrupt snort. 'The girl you knew,' she corrected him. 'Anyway, your question wasn't whether we want kids, it was where we would raise them.'

'So, you still do want kids then?' he tested her.

'Of course I do.'

'Does Patrick?'

She sighed. Did he? She mentally sifted through their conversations over the years. Travel, yes. Marriage, yes. A German shepherd, yes. A house with a theatre room, yes. An annual holiday to Europe? Yes. But kids? No memory of such conversation came to mind. How has she not brought up having a family with him? Especially when family was everything to her.

Had been everything to her.

'... I,' the walls of her throat began to cave in. 'I don't know.'

Now it was his turn to sigh.

They sat quietly for a long moment, only the sound of the rain outside wedging their silence.

'Ok ... wow.'

He was looking out the window now, his eyes narrowed to slits with his lips pressed together as though the whole thing was a lost case. She could quite literally feel his judgement. She could only imagine what he was thinking. Something along the lines of how could she go into a marriage without having such discussion. He probably thought she was foolish for choosing to sign her life away to a guy who wasn't on the same page as her. That didn't want the same things as her. But how was it of any concern to him anyway? How could he just assume her plans were identical to the ones she expressed as her thirteen-year-old self?

'You don't know my relationship with Patrick, not a single detail. So, come on, please don't speculate.' There was a hostility behind her composed tone.

To her surprise, his lips curled.

'There she is.'

She folded her knees to her chest and hugged them. 'What do you mean?' she laughed at his sudden liveliness.

'This is more like the girl I know. The Sienna who isn't afraid of telling me off. You're still a firecracker. I like it,' he smirked.

She shrugged, annoyed at herself for being unable to hold back from smiling.

He really was contagious.

'A firecracker? Really? I'm not so sure about that one. But me telling you off, that's something I can't see changing because you always have to know everything about everything,' she giggled. 'Someone has to put you back in your place. It feels quite satisfying to finally tell you so.'

He laughed. 'It's been way too long since we have cut through all the crap and had a completely honest conversation.'

'Are you saying that our conversations today haven't been honest?' she questioned him playfully.

He pretended to look offended. Surely, he knew she hadn't shared her heart? She hadn't shared a fraction of it. It has been securely shut like a vault in safe keeping. He shook his head.

'No?'

He shook his head faster this time. 'No,' he agreed.

'No?' she asked again, laughing with him.

'No, because you are holding something back, I know you are,' he added.

Instead of answering, she hugged her knees even tighter towards her body.

'Even though you seem so convinced I don't know you anymore, I know you well enough to have a pretty clear idea that there is a lot more going on in there.'

He extended a finger towards the direction of her heart. She slapped it away before it had a chance to reach her.

'Are you questioning my honestly, Kahler?'

He nodded confidently. 'Maybe I am, Henderson.'

'And what am I not telling you?' she tested him.

'That I don't know. But what I do know is that you haven't brought up your fiancé once today and that doesn't sit right with me,' he pulled a face. 'Especially since this guy is meant to be *extraordinary*.'

'And that he is,' she shot back.

'Hmmm' he murmured and looked away.

'You're so infuriating.'

'Not as infuriating as you.' He was staring at her again, his smirk indicating that he wasn't going to back down on the banter.

'How so?' she challenged him.

'You've just become hard to read.'

'Guess you can't figure me out after all,' she joked.

'Not yet anyway.'

Not yet? What did he mean by that? She wasn't planning on staying in Aringdale long. Even if she was, it wouldn't be a wise idea to spend any more time with him. She held the thought long enough for the momentum to be broken.

He cleared his throat. 'What I mean is, let's not let another eight years go by without seeing each other again.'

'Nine,' she corrected him.

'Nine,' he repeated, smiling—but it stopped short of his eyes.

'I never wanted that in the first place. You do realise that, right?'

She knew better than to go there, but she couldn't help herself. The truth of the matter was, it had never been her intention to distance herself from him for any of those years. It had been out of her control and in no way had been her decision.

She could see that he was somehow affected by the way his focus was down in his hands. He knew she was right. He had to. The regret in his eyes told her that much.

'I never wanted that,' his voice came weak, almost a whisper.

She bit down on her bottom lip, feeling her chest fill all over again with that horrible ache. She looked at him, unable to speak in fear that tears would leave her eyes. She inhaled a shaky breath, confused at the tide of emotion that had overcome her. 'What did you want?' It sounded more like a desperate plea. It must have come across this way too as his eyes met hers.

'More for you.' He didn't blink. 'More than I could give you at the time.'

To have him look at her this way was more than she could handle. She refused to let herself break. She squeezed her eyes shut in hope that the tears would subside. But when she opened them, they willingly spilt down her face.

Instead of hiding them she let them fall.

'What couldn't you give me Ethan?' She hated herself for loosening her grip on that damn guard of hers. What was she doing exposing her heart like this? She was stronger than that.

She had to be stronger.

'You left. You spread your wings' he started, his eyes firm on hers. 'You grew up Sienna. You became independent. Your dance career became everything to you, your sole focus. You didn't need me anymore.'

'You were everything to me,' she responded, abruptly.

She unfolded her legs as a combination of resentment, fury and hurt washed over her. His face was down again, his features holding that same, sorrowful expression from earlier. She didn't wait for his response. She didn't want to hear it. It was irrelevant now, it didn't matter what he said. It wouldn't change things. Not now.

Maybe she just needed this moment to release all the suppressed feelings time had failed to loosen. Now she had voiced as much as she prepared to, she could get back to her life.

And she would.

Aringdale had made her sentimental for long enough. It was time to shake off whatever this was that has overcome her and get a hold on herself.

On reality.

'I'm sorry,' she sighed. She brushed away the few tears that remained. 'This is the last place I expected tonight's conversation would go. I didn't mean …'

He gently took her knee and gave it a gentle squeeze. 'I don't think either of us did,' he started. 'I'm so sorry. The last thing I want is to make you all upset.'

Now she felt embarrassed, silly.

She would never drink again. Another reason not to go near that stuff.

The rain outside had stopped, yet the silence between them was thunderous. What now? They had parted ways before and would do so again. It's time to say goodnight.

And goodbye.

'I should probably get back,' she smiled forcing the door closed on her unsettled feelings. 'Thank you for today, for this evening. It was lovely to see you again.'

He nodded, accepting the distance she placed back between them. 'Sienna …we never got the chance to talk about what—'

She held up her hand and shook her head. Never got the chance? He had almost a decade of opportunity. 'It's really ok, we don't have to go there. It was so long-ago Ethan, please.' She swallowed, hoping to soften the lump that expanded in her throat. 'Let's just leave it at that.' Her guard was back up. This time she would be stronger. She didn't need to be reminded that she had been friend zoned the entire time she had been in love with him. She didn't want to hear it.

And there was no reason to justify it.

She couldn't understand why he seemed to be so affected by this. Not when he had had years to make it right. Clearly their friendship didn't mean as much to him to have given up on it, to have given up on her. She had every right to be angry. Every reason to feel hurt and rejected. But strangely, being back in his company made her feel everything but that. She was disappointed, yes. But somehow amidst the unsettling ache, he gave her an unexplained sense of comfort.

'When do you leave?'

'I haven't decided. I won't be here longer than a week, probably.'

He looked at her intently and nodded. 'Can I see you before you head back? For old times' sake?'

For old times' sake.

Really? She didn't want him doing her any favours.

'I'll probably be at the theatre for the rest of the week,' she ignored his question. 'Maybe I'll see you there.'

'You'll be seeing me,' he responded, sure of himself.

She wasn't sure if he meant it, or if planning to see her again was his way of dealing with the guilt of time they had lost. Either way, she would be at the theatre without any expectation of restoring their friendship. Things would never be the same between them again. Too much time had passed, too much had happened. If their bond had been strong enough, it would have survived the years, maybe even thrived.

But it hadn't, and that spoke in itself.

ALL THE LIGHTS were out by the time she returned home. She stood in the middle of her old room, confronted by the whirlwind of emotions weighing upon her. She wasn't used to having time to just, stop. To be still, to reflect. She wasn't used to her mind racing a million miles an hour like this.

She threw her handbag down on her white embroidered doona and took out her phone for the first time that night.

Three missed calls and a text message. All from Patrick.

With weary eyes, she scanned the text over.

> **Hey. Been trying to reach you. Why won't you answer your phone? Thought the theatre didn't have reception.**

Not only was it controlling, it questioned her motives. Where was the trust between them? She threw her phone down, missing the mattress completely. It landed on the floorboards with a thud and it would stay there. She didn't have the energy to respond. Not in a way that would be safe, words carefully structured in a way where a fight could be avoided.

She collapsed onto the bed feeling the load of the day weighing on top of her. After her parents' confusion of her surprise arrival the night before along with day she had, she hadn't had a moment to digest exactly what she felt being back home. Back in her old room staring at the same ceiling where she had once pondered all her dreams.

The box of letters.

It must have been six years since she last added to it. Back when her Nanna passed away. She had kept hold of the memorial booklet along with half attempted poetry and cards her friends made over the years. Then there were the letters her and Ethan had exchanged over their countless bus rides home.

She rolled open her cupboard door and knelt down to take out the black cardboard box containing the depths of her soul. It was full to the brim with layers of paper spewing from beneath the lid. She carried the box to her bed, crossing her legs as she settled down with it. She removed the lid, feeling overwhelmed at the quantity of letters inside.

She suddenly grew nervous at what she would uncover. It would take hours to sort through what appeared to be a hundred letters, all identical in nature, all folded into quarters. How many had they exchanged over the years anyway? She quickly did the math. They had begun in 2005, daily, weekly, then monthly before the odd letter was written by the time 2010 came around. There would have been at least seventy or eighty letters exchanged over the space of those five years. Thousands of written words that once held so much worth. A worth that slowly lost its value as the years rolled over, as their friendship washed-out to nothingness. Even now she struggled to shake the bitterness wrapped firmly around her heart.

Nothing lasts forever, she reassured herself.

Tonight was going to be a lucky dip, she didn't have the energy to sort through them in any sort of order. Her already weary eyes were growing heavier by the minute.

Her attention was drawn to a letter half in size of the others, folded four or five times into a little square. Whatever words were hidden beneath appeared to hold some sort of secrecy. With her heart beating quicker than normal, she opened the letter and smoothed out the creases.

11th June 2008

So, the other day I heard that you were going to the movies with Brody. I thought 'Oh no!' My little sister is going off with a boy that I have no idea what he wants from her. It scared me. But after hearing the way you feel about him made me realise that this guy means the world to you.

Please Sienna, as one of your closest and caring friends I'm asking that you get to know this guy better before you rush into a relationship. Get to know him out of school, get to know his friends, his values, his attitudes. Once you know him well it will be so much easier to go out with him. You two can even hang out with Sadie and I, we would love to get to know him.

Love you Sienna. I'm always here, thank you for opening up and sharing your heart.

She folded the letter exactly the way she found it. Folding it four times over, then five.

Then wept.

Ten

S HE WASN'T SURE what drew her to Brody Manis.
She did remember it was a season where all her friends seemed to be in relationships and hadn't wanted to be the odd one out. It was the second term of eleventh grade. The year she made the transition from a private to public school. A school literally eight times the size of her previous one as it hadn't offered VCE at the time.

Aringdale Senior College was a maze.

A large school meant there were a lot more guys. A pool so much bigger, she could hardly wait to start fishing. She didn't have her rod out for long with how quick Brody took her attention. Every morning she would walk past his group of friends that hung out at the main stairwell of the locker rooms. Every time she would feel his big blue eyes on her each time she passed. But even then, not a single word had been exchanged between them. This continued on for at least three or four weeks before he actually had the courage to approach her. Like her, Brody was shy, although on the outside anyone would assume he had all the confidence in the world. He was intimidating to say the least; tall, broad with sandy blonde hair and a perfect olive complexion that only made his eyes glow brighter. His friends weren't half bad to look at either, footballers, known as the school 'jocks'. In other words;

the popular boys. A group of guys every girl wanted to be seen with if they ever wanted to be anyone. Just like high school there were distinct groups, a classification system, a hierarchy.

And Sienna was determined to be at the top.

She didn't want to be a nobody, especially during her final years of school. So, when Brody took an interest in her, it was a big deal.

From the moment he asked her out, her whole world changed. She went from wearing clothes she never thought twice about in the past, to shopping at the high-end stores in town, purchasing the latest trends she couldn't really afford. Until then, she never really wore makeup other than a light foundation and a touch of mascara. With her natural beauty and even skin tone, she never had to try very hard to look beautiful. But as a young adolescent she hadn't learned that less was more. Especially with her desperate attempts to be noticed.

It wasn't long before she found herself in the bathroom for an hour each morning before school, curling her hair and applying heavier makeup around her eyes. As soon as she realised her physical beauty she became more conscious of the attention she received and had soaked it up like a sponge. It wasn't just Brody. Whether she was passing by in the corridor or lining up at the canteen, all looked at her with lustful eyes.

Her friends were quick to notice the change in her, the air of confidence she acquired almost overnight and the way she started holding herself. She brushed off any questions whenever she was asked if there was a boy in the picture. She hadn't wanted to share the news. Not straight away anyway. The whole Brody idea seemed too good to be true. Besides, there was always the fear that he would get bored and trade her in. So, she kept her mouth shut.

But soon enough she reached a point where she had to tell someone. And unfortunately, her parents had to be the first. Planning her way to and from the movie theatre was a too difficult to plot without a license.

There was no other way around it.

She had no idea how to approach them, what to say, or how to say it. Confrontation had never been her thing, she knew she would come across defensive as soon as she opened her mouth. Brody was her first official boyfriend which meant her dad would definitely be over the top about the whole thing. She needed advice on how to approach the situation. There was one person's advice she respected more than anyone's—Ethan's.

So, she wrote him a letter. She was a little apprehensive at first as they weren't exactly close having slowly grown apart at the same time as his relationship with Sadie had progressed. In the same space of time, her friendship with Sadie had fallen by the wayside. It wasn't intentional, but she hadn't tried very hard either. How could she? She was tired of putting on a front every time they hung out together in a group, looking in on their endless displays of affection. An emotional affection she believed he once had for her, a physical affection they had the potential of sharing.

Yes, even after three years it still left a persistent sting.

Ballet had begun to chew up every minute of her spare time. When she wasn't at school, she was in the studio training hard for one of the many performances she was involved in that year. Luckily for her, it was her passion, offering a distraction from dwelling over their relationship despite having years to adapt to this change.

It may have been the year 2010, but the condition of her heart was as raw as it was in 2005. Time hadn't changed that, whether she was able to admit it to herself or not.

As soon as she placed her pen to the paper the words had flowed freely. There was no hesitation, no fabrication in the language she used. Just an authenticity she always wrote with. Though her heart had been guarded, her letters hadn't been. There was a beauty behind every written word. Although life had changed the course of their friendship, their letters never reflected that.

It had been weeks since she had seen Ethan. She barely saw him around school anymore with their separate friendship groups hanging out at opposite ends of the campus. Being a senior and a year above her, his locker was in a different building to hers too. In a school consisting of over two thousand students with personalised class schedules, it wasn't unusual for them to not have crossed paths.

The next morning, she arrived a little earlier in hope to catch him before her biology class. She had felt a bit weird lurking by his locker as she turned the letter over and over in her hands as she reconsidered the whole idea. But after a couple of minutes she decided she had nothing to lose and had slipped it under his locker door. She sent him a quick message to let him know so she didn't look like a complete psycho.

He never replied to her text, but she did find a letter inside her locker first thing the next morning. Without opening it she knew it was from him. It had been folded the same way as they always had; in quarters on the same white lined paper he always used.

11th June 2008

So, the other day I heard that you were going to the movies with Brody. I thought 'Oh no!' My little sister is going off with a boy that I have no idea what he wants from her. It scared me. But after hearing the way you feel about him made me realise that this guy means the world to you.

Please Sienna, as one of your closest and caring friends I'm pleading that you get to know this guy better before you rush into a relationship. Get to know him out of school, get to know his friends, his values, his attitudes. Once you know him well it will be so much easier to go out with him. You two can even hang out with Sadie and I, we would love to get to know him.

Love you Sienna. I'm always here, thank you for opening up and sharing your heart.

She smiled as she read over it. Smiled at his protectiveness, his wisdom and the way he seemed to still care about her. She had needed that reminder, that reassurance.

She suddenly couldn't wait to have Brody in her life, to go on double dates with and have someone to care for, to love.

And to be loved in return.

Ethan knew of Brody. They had competed against each other in football a handful of times. It was comforting to have his approval, making breaking the news to her parents a whole lot easier. Like she had expected, her dad was hesitant at first, insisting that he came over for dinner first before being open to the idea of her being alone in a cinema with him. Meeting the parents wasn't something she had wanted to jump into before their first date, but she hadn't had the choice. Thankfully, Brody had been open to the idea and ended up acing the whole thing.

Her parents loved him.

He was a true gentleman and knew how to turn this on around them. But it wasn't just her parents, he could hold a conversation with anyone. He was one of those guys that you could throw into a cell of criminals and would still find a way to connect with them on some sort of level. He was funny too, often leaving her mother in stitches of laughter with his humorous jokes and interpretative dance moves. Not only did he have a sense of humour, he was intelligent too. He was in his senior year, and like her father, aspired to be an accountant. That alone gave them common ground as they spent countless hours over the next few months in her father's office discussing all things financial.

He was pretty much perfect, quite the catch; intelligent, athletic, funny, good-looking, charming—the list went on really. The more she got to know him, the harder she began to fall. It was like a chain had been broken, a freedom every time she would go away from a double date without feeling a twinge in her heart for Ethan. She was grateful for Brody. Not only for making her feel like she was special, but for finally allowing herself to let Ethan go.

It had been the best year yet. She was excelling in all her subjects at school, received a high distinction for her advanced ballet exam. Her friendship with Sadie was stronger than ever and she had a boyfriend who seemed to adore her. Everyone loved him and openly expressed so. Well, everyone other than Ethan had expressed their opinions.

She had confronted him one day about it. They happened to have the same free period one week and were both in the library studying for exams.

'You've never really told me what you think of Brody.'

He had looked up from the text he was reading and scrunched his face. 'He is a nice enough guy. He seems to tick all the right boxes.'

'Nice enough?' His response had bugged her. 'Nice enough for me, you mean?'

He laughed. 'Oh, come on S, don't put words in my mouth. No one will ever be good enough for you.'

Her heart did a flip flop in that moment. She studied his face, but for the first time, was unable to read it.

'So, in other words, you don't think he's good enough for me. You think I can do better, is what you're getting at?' She laughed, but his comment had stung her.

He closed his text book and settled himself deeper into the beanbag. 'Why do I feel like you are still looking for validation?' He looked at her inquisitively.

'I'm not,' she snapped. 'He's amazing. I am so happy. Everyone thinks he is great, but you've never commented about us together. I guess I just want your support.' She hadn't meant to come across as bluntly as she did, but his remark had hurt her.

He is a nice enough guy.

'You have my support.'

'Good,' she responded stubbornly, 'thank you.'

He still hadn't answered her question, but she knew the conversation would stall there.

'I guess I have my concerns,' he admitted.

Of course he did.

'And what are you concerned about?' She couldn't think of a single reason why he would be.

'The dude is attractive, a flirt. He can have any girl he wants—'

'And he chose me.'

'Yes. He did. I mean, yes, he has. But not long before you there were at least three others. I don't think he has ever been with anyone for more than a couple of months. I just worry that you'll get hurt. He'll be off to Uni next year and will meet so many new girls. You—'

'I can't believe this.' She let out a frustrated laugh. 'You don't think I'm different from all the others?' her voice was weak. Somewhere stuffed in the back of her head it had been her biggest fear. For Ethan to have voiced it, made her feel sick.

'God Sienna, yes I think you are different. But it takes a special person to be able to see that.'

'So, you really don't think Brody is that special person for me,' she snapped.

It hadn't been a question, but he shrugged and shook his head.

'I thought I made that clear already.' His cheeky smirk made her want to slap it right off his face.

'Why can't you just be happy for me?' She started to pack away her text books.

She was well and truly done.

'I want you to be happy more than anything. I just don't see that with this guy. Not long term anyway. You asked me what I thought of him and I was honest. Isn't that what you wanted? Or did you want me to be like everyone else and tell you what you want to hear?'

She hated his blunt honesty. Hated the way he made her question the good thing she and Brody shared. But most of all, she hated that there was a possibility he was right. She had been so desperate for a boyfriend she had failed to do a background ground check. Maybe Ethan was right, maybe his past didn't check out. Or perhaps her frustration stemmed from the truth of his words.

'Of course, I want you to be honest with me.' She had never packed her books away as fast as she had that afternoon. 'But I would have also appreciated for you to put your personal, judgmental feelings aside and be supportive of the guy I deeply care about.' She knew she loved Brody, but she wasn't about to throw that word out there. He had grilled her about that word in the past. It wasn't worth a fight.

'You keep saying I'm not supportive,' he was clearly frustrated too. 'Yet I've done everything I can to welcome him in, to help him feel part of the group. I don't even remember the last time Sadie and I have had a weekend alone together with all these group hangs we keep on having.'

He made a valid point. Why was she being so ignorant? Part of her wanted to apologise but the other part of her hadn't wanted to swallow her pride.

He is a nice enough guy. The comment still burnt her.

'Well, we will be away for his auntie's fifteenth on Saturday, so you get a free pass this weekend.'

He raised his eyebrows at this. 'Wow, Ok Sienna.'

She knew he hadn't deserved her last remark but she was upset and hadn't wanted to back down. Without another word, she swung her book bag over her shoulder and marched out of the library with prickling tears clouding her vision.

Ethan's lack of approval had bothered her at first, yet its effect dissolved as the weeks and months went on. They soon became one of those couples that did everything together. When her weekends weren't swallowed by a dance class or rehearsal, they would be on a road trip exploring cute little cafes or riding their bikes along the famous track that stretched almost fifty kilometres behind their house.

The debutante had come and gone and everyone had gushed over the picture-perfect couple they had made. She had secretly envisioned it as their wedding day as her dress made from lace and silk swept gracefully as their bodies moved in harmony with each other across the dance floor. Sadie and Ethan hadn't done theirs together. It wasn't Sadie's thing to get all dressed up like that. In fact, she didn't think she had ever seen her in a dress at all in her life. She had always been a bit of a tom boy like that. Sadie had wanted to be there for her, but for whatever reason had something on that night.

But Ethan had been there.

He hadn't even registered his attendance but rocked up anyway, an hour after the presentations had begun. She had no idea how he found his way in without a ticket but had somehow managed to pull up a seat at her family's table. He had been pretty proud of his efforts, but Sienna had been annoyed at the whole stunt, wondering why he had showed up at all. It had all been quite odd really, and rude the way he casually waltzed in. He didn't say more than a handful of words over the course of the night. Not to her, or to anyone for that matter. He was just there, hovering around aimlessly. He left before the night had concluded, rushing a goodbye with a forced smile that had left an unsettling pit inside of her. She knew him well enough to know that something rested behind the animated smile that influenced his peculiar actions that night. She thought that maybe he and Sadie were having problems, but when Monday came around the two of them were hand in hand, like always. Nothing had changed. Nothing was said, nothing was wrong.

She had imagined it.

The following weeks were basically a write off, being the busiest season of the year for her dancing. November was drawing to an end with rehearsals and performances overriding every social event on her calendar that year. Other than the sporadic catch up for an hour or two when she was free, her weekends had been spent in her point shoes instead of Brody's arms.

The year twelve graduation was set the week before her first performance of 'Coppelia' where she had been lucky enough to land the main role of 'Swanhilda'. She had somehow managed to make an appearance at presentation night despite the clash of rehearsal time at the theatre. She had remembered standing tall, beaming with pride as she watched her boyfriend cross the stage dressed in his black, yellow and purple graduation gown before shaking the principal's hand and being handed his certificate. She had so badly wanted to make the after party that followed but had to get back to the theatre. After sending Brody off with a speedy kiss and cuddle, she hurried back just in time for a warm up before the final show run of the night.

Sunday brunch had been a tradition they shared from the beginning. Macy Lane Café. It was the place they had gone for their second date and had fallen in love with their eggs benedict ever since. She hadn't heard from Brody that morning but hadn't expected to after what would have been a big night celebrating the end of an era. But when he hadn't shown up at the café that morning and didn't respond to any of her text messages or calls, she had an inkling something wasn't right.

And it wasn't.

She did receive a text, but not from Brody. It was from an old school friend she had known since kindergarten. Ashley had been at the after party the night before and asked to meet for a quick chat. She remembered feeling faint as Ashley walked into the café that day with an apologetic look painted across her face.

Brody had cheated on her.

She had witnessed the whole scene play out on the dance floor with his tongue jammed down some girl's throat neither of them had seen before. Apparently, Brody had been dirty dancing with this girl until she approached him. As soon as he saw her, she said his eyes widened before he removed himself from the girl's provocative body and bolted. As soon as she heard the news she felt unsettled. She wasn't sure if she believed it. It didn't sound like something Brody would do.

Not her Brody.

He loved her too much to even contemplate doing such thing. He would never hurt her, surely not. The dreaded thought crossed her mind whether things had gone further as soon as he was free from Ashley's view, but she dismissed it immediately.

She had left the café that morning barely being able to breathe and with trembling hands, called Brody nine or ten times, getting his message bank after every failed attempt.

A couple of hours later he arrived at her house. She had never seen him so hungover, his eyes blood shot from the excessive drinking the night before. Luckily her parents weren't home that afternoon, she hadn't wanted them to see the way she looked as though she had been hit by a freight train. But mainly because she didn't want them to see the emotional wreck she was. Her heart was sitting somewhere inside her throat as she waited for him to explain himself. She had expected him to be defensive, all over her with a swarm of apologies, but he had been completely calm and composed. She studied him, unable to detect a trace of guilt as he convinced her that he wasn't at fault. According to his story, he had been dancing with mates when a group of girls threw themselves at them. He said a random girl approached him blind drunk, forcing her lips on his. He had pushed her away as soon as it had happened. That's what Ashley must have seen—him removing himself from the situation.

That was what happened.

Nothing more.

After Brody left that afternoon she had expected to feel a peace, but her heart felt everything but that. It didn't help that the seniors had finished school for the year, with only year eleven's filling the campus for the remaining few weeks of the term. The time they usually spend together at lunch gave her more time to stew over the feared possibility that Brody had lied to her. But, no one else had seen what Ashley had. No one else had confronted her about the incident. But then again, everyone had been intoxicated that night. Ashley was one of the few people she knew that didn't drink.

Sadie had noticed her distance and confronted her about it straight away. Sienna told her the story, Brody's version of the story, shrugging it off as though she was unaffected by the whole thing. Brody couldn't control if a girl threw herself at him, he could only control how he reacted to the situation. And he had put a stop to it.

Everything was fine.

It had been after nine the next night when there was a knock on the door. Her mum had answered, her ears quickly responding to the familiar voices that filled the kitchen. Ethan and Sadie had rocked up, insisting to take her out for a late-night dessert run. It was at that point where she knew that Sadie had told him about their conversation earlier that day. She hadn't expected anything less. She was well aware that they told each other everything and that it was only a matter of time until he would know about it.

She fiddled with her fork, hacking away at her slice of cheesecake as she waited in anticipation for one of them to bring it up, knowing it was the reason they were out. But somehow through their many obvious exchanged glances, they had communicated against it.

Ethan had driven that night, dropping Sadie off first on the way before dropping her home. There was an uncomfortable silence, both avoiding the obvious elephant in the car. As soon as he pulled into her driveway, he turned off the engine and had sighed heavily.

'Sienna ...'

She knew what was coming. As soon as he had said her name, her eyes welled with tears. She wanted to say goodnight there and then, climb into bed, wishing she had never said anything to Sadie in the first place. She should have known better. Instead she faced him, unable to form a single word as her mouth started to quiver. She had expected him to have given her the whole 'I told you so' speech, but his eyes held a concern that made her tears fall.

'What.' It was all she could manage, yet it didn't come out as a question. Deep down she knew the truth despite her internal battle against it. She hadn't wanted to accept it. She wasn't ready to. She knew she would lose Brody the moment she did. And that thought alone scared her more than anything. She couldn't lose him. Not after falling this hard for him. She had given too much. Invested too much.

It was all too much to bear.

'Please don't tell me you'll go back to him.' It was more of a commandment. An order he had no place in giving her.

She shook her head in denial. 'He didn't do anything wrong,' she responded, weakly.

He slammed his hands down firmly against the steering wheel. 'You aren't seriously just going to let this go?'

She bit down hard on her lip and stared out the window as another batch of tears broke the surface. She couldn't hold eye contact with him. She wouldn't. She didn't want to talk about it. He hadn't been there. How could he force her to make a decision only knowing half of the story?

'I ... gotta go.' Her tears were falling harder now. But instead of brushing them away she had fumbled out of the car and started powering her way down the porch to the front door.

He got out after her and took her in a firm, yet comforting embrace before she had a chance to turn the handle. She stubbornly pinned her arms against her body, knowing that if she embraced his hug she would fall apart.

'Please walk away from him.'

To her surprise he began to weep, his heart breaking for what broke hers. She had never seen him cry before. Not since they were six years old at a friend's birthday, fighting over a party bag that had the most sherbet bombs in it. Seeing him shed tears over her, for her, only made the ache in her heart intensify.

She felt herself slowly giving in as she wrapped her arms around her dearest friend, wishing more than anything for the pain to shallow.

'You're stronger than you know.'

His words should have been reassuring, but she brushed away the comment before they had the chance to encourage her. She dropped her arms, brushing off his words, even though deep down she knew he was right.

But it wasn't going to happen.

'I ca ... can't,' she stuttered through her flood of her tears.

With his arms still around her, he lowered his head and aligned it with hers. 'He cheated on you. Crawling back to him will only tell him what he did was ok.' He shook his head in dismay. 'It's not ok Sienna. You know that. How he treated you was disgusting, and he'll do it again.'

Part of her still held onto her resentment of his long-standing disapproval of Brody. He had always been judgmental of him, of their relationship. Trust him to expect the worst.

'You don't know what you're talking about.' Her words were nothing short of pathetic. She was being pathetic, she knew that. Yet her pride had formed a stronghold over her, one she wasn't willing to break free from.

He rubbed his forehead vigorously as his eyes glazed over with angry tears. He bowed slowly, processing her response. Then without another word he turned his back on her and walked back to the car, slamming the door behind him.

She wrapped her arms around herself, sheltering herself from the ache in the pit her of her stomach that had made its way to her extremities. She felt paralysed, motionless as she watched him speed out of the driveway, his wheels making a mess of the gravel as he left. She inhaled sharply and wiped away any evidence of tear stained cheeks before she opened the front door and let herself inside.

Eleven

DANCE HAD ALWAYS been an escapism for Sienna.

A physical expression that granted a freedom and vulnerability to find and lose herself, all at the same time. A place where music had the rare ability of capturing her soul, transporting her to a place where her heart was content. A place through the stillness of sitting inside the theatre, she felt invincible.

It was a feeling she had lost. One that had been an essence to her being, a fire to her spirit.

She spent countless hours in the same seat at the back of the theatre, watching the competitions unfold over the course of the week. She was content in her own company as her spirit slowly refilled with a fire that had once fizzled years ago. The competition had changed since her teenage years, and not in a way that encouraged her. There were less competitors now, less schools across the region participating. She noticed that there was now a lack of classical ballet sections compared to theatrical ones. In fact, not a single school competing had teachers with any professional background in ballet yet had entered their students into these sections. Solos that had fallen short of the standard. A standard much lower than what had graced the stage a decade ago. Although she enjoyed watching the dancing, this observation frustrated her. Aringdale needed more qualified ballet coaches, especially now hers had moved on. They needed someone fresh, with industry experience and the knowledge to raise the standard before it was too late.

So now we move onto plan B and I build you that dance school, right?

It had been four days since she had seen him. She wasn't surprised he hadn't made an appearance, even after reassuring her that he would. He probably went away that night realising that seeing each other again wouldn't be wise, the same way she did. Not when there had been tears involved the first time. It was all too much, far too heavy on her heart and perhaps, had been on his too.

In just three days she would go back to the life she had created. A life she would press forward with, without the memories of Aringdale haunting her. She had a relationship to restore, a wedding to plan, and an accountability to her grade three class. An accountability to one student in particular, whom she wouldn't let down.

At least once a day during intermission, she would find herself at the foyer at the cafeteria with a lukewarm cup of instant coffee in her hands as she conversed with past students and teachers. Many of the conversations consisted of them pleading for her to come back and teach for them. She had managed to lock down a couple of workshops, not having a clue when she would find the time to come back and teach them. Whether she would commit to teaching one or not, it felt nice to be wanted, for her talent to be recognised and appreciated after all this time. She would have been silly to have refused the opportunity.

The little gold bell rang indicating the session was about to begin. She tossed her half-drunk cup in the bin and made her way back up the red carpeted stairs and into the auditorium. She took her usual spot, centre back, standing clear of the competitors and their tribe of support that filled the rows in front. She maneuvered her way through the crowd of people to her seat, keeping her eyes down to avoid stepping on any belongings. There was a bigger crowd this afternoon which was expected with popular theatrical solos and championships scheduled.

She reached her seat just as the lights dimmed, took out the program and settled herself in for what would be at least another three hours of performances.

'What section are we watching today?'

She turned, startled to find Ethan in the seat next to her with his familiar cheeky grin. Without thinking, she wrapped her arms around him and squeezed as much of him as her little arms could manage. A flood of happiness took over her. He had come after all.

'Hi.'

'Hey,' he said, grinning.

'You're here.'

'I told you I would, didn't I?'

She couldn't help but grin, too. 'What about work?'

He patted her knee. 'Slow day. I thought I'd spend it here with you instead. Much better than building another deck, I reckon.'

She physically wasn't able to wipe the smile off her face as he said this. He looked good, dressed in beige chino pants and a blue knit top. His big brown eyes look at her with an admiration that warmed her heart.

'So, what are we watching?'

'Oh!' She sat up straighter and passed him the program and a pen. 'Hip hop. You can fill this in.'

'What am I filling in?'

She pointed to the awards section on the page. 'I'll teach you as we go.' She could see the outline of his crooked smile, even in the darkness of the theatre.

Her spirit felt light, full.

She could hardly concentrate as the sections carried out that afternoon. Every time a solo ended, she could feel his eyes on her as their hands came together in applause. She could have sat there for hours but hadn't wanted to put him through it. He had been too polite to suggest a bite to eat, not wanting to take her away from the dancing knowing how much it meant to her. After a section of over twenty competitors concluded, she motioned him outside.

As soon as they exited the double doors and exposed their bodies to the cold, she felt her joy disintegrate as swiftly as the breeze. It was as though stepping out from the theatre had transitioned her from a fictional place where her heart was light, to an instant heaviness as reality festered its way in.

What was she doing uniting a place that had once been her safe haven with a man whom she was meant to guard her heart from?

She was playing with fire. That was what she was doing. And it would destroy her a second time if she wasn't careful.

'Where are you taking me?' he asked, stretching his arms wide, open to adventure.

She didn't do adventure anymore, she knew that much. Even if she did, it wouldn't be with him. She suddenly felt guilty for being alone with him, especially with the emotional turmoil she was in. She wasn't thinking straight. Maybe if she sent a quick message to Patrick, forcing him to the front of her mind she would feel better about the situation. She needed to move, walk, get out.

Something.

'The park?' she suggested.

'Ok, sure. Let's go! Will you be ok? You won't get too cold?'

Stop being so damn beautiful.

'I'll be fine.' She didn't smile. It was as though he could detect the change inside of her the way his eyes positioned on hers longer than normal. What was wrong with her? Her emotions were all over the place. She hated her inability to be able to make sense of them.

They reached the park in silence. She breathed in the beauty of nature surrounding them as their footsteps synced together along the footpath. It was the same park they hung out at as kids, eating fish and chips and countless boxes of pizza under the tallest Oaktree at the top of the hill. It was a place where they would sit and observe anyone that passed by below, making predictions what their lives were like, and what type of people they were. Maybe Ethan had found the same memory as their footsteps led them along the path and towards the tree that played a role in their enduring bond.

She felt her phone vibrate on the inside of her handbag. She quickly opened it to find Patrick calling. Part of her wanted to hear his voice, especially since he hadn't responded to any of her messages the day before. But a part of her was afraid of how the conversation would play out, knowing she would be more hesitant than usual with Ethan next to her, listening in.

'You can take it,' he said, studying her.

She stared at her phone as Patrick's name persisted to flash at her. She hit decline and sent it back in her bag. She would call him later.

'He must be missing you.'

She shrugged. 'It hasn't been that long.'

'Still, it's never fun being apart.'

She shifted her focus to her feet that were still moving in sync with his. 'It has actually been nice having some time away,' her words came slowly.

His lips coiled. 'It must be nice catching up with your folks, I bet they're loving having you home. Do you get to see much of them?'

She shook her head. 'Before a couple of weeks ago, I hadn't seen them since … well, probably since October,' she said, remembering the trip she made after one of their many fights. This particular one had been bad.

'Wow really? His eyes widened. 'You haven't seen them in what, eight months? Why?'

'I know.' She felt her throat stiffen at that. Of course, he was shocked, he knew how close she had once been to her family.

He stopped walking and narrowed his eyes. 'Talk to me Sienna. What's going on with you?'

The gentleness in his voice unlocked a chain around her heart within seconds. Instead of responding, she pointed to the tree that had once been theirs. It still looked the same; layered in jagged bark—its strong branches stretched wide, covered with ripe, green leaves. Even the trees hadn't changed in ten years. They sat down under it, taking shelter from the brisk air.

'I don't know what happened,' she began, confused at the turmoil her relationship was in. 'I don't know how we got here.'

He waited patiently as she took a long moment to articulate her thoughts. She began to share the details of her relationship, from their perfect beginning, Charlie's accident, to Patrick's addiction to alcohol, her work issues and the wedding she had almost given up on. He leaned back against the tree as she talked softly rubbing her back every so often as she poured her heart out to him as though she was a teen again. She didn't mention the emotional manipulation and the way he constantly had her in tears. She wanted to avoid a judgement being made of him, the same way a judgement had been made over Brody all those years ago. She refused to acknowledge that perhaps it wasn't Patrick she wanted to protect, but herself. For she was yet to realise if Ethan had the complete story, he would confirm what she knew deep down to be true.

She shared all she felt was safe enough to disclose, feeling a burden lift as soon as they were spoken aloud. He still had a way of making her look at herself as though a mirror was held against her heart. He always had a way of uncovering the truth inside her, no matter how deeply buried. She felt the breeze wash over them as they sat through the stillness of silence.

'Sienna,' his voice came gentle, sending a peace through her. With his hand still loose on her back, he crossed his legs and turned his body to face her.

She inhaled, preparing herself for what was to come.

'This is the biggest decision of your life. You need to take the time to figure out if stepping into a marriage with this guy is one hundred percent, the right thing. It shouldn't be something that puts your heart at unease or leaves you with any doubts. From what you have told me, I assume you guys have lost the ability to communicate and at some point, stopped being a team. It's okay to reevaluate.'

He drew back and searched her eyes. She kept her eyes on his even though she had a sense of knowing that she was about to be challenged.

'Do you really believe Patrick is the man who's going to encourage you, support you and champion the desires of your heart? Is he a man who complements you, builds you, pursues you and prioritizes you? I'm going to throw an obvious one out there okay, annnnnnd, this might be really confronting. Sort of cliché, but still valid.' His eyes clouded with a sorrow similar to the one resonating inside her. 'Can you really say with confidence that Patrick is the one you can see yourself truly happy with, for the rest of your life?'

As soon as the words were spoken, she found herself catching her breath. She could have responded quickly, reassuring him that he was. But if she looked at herself the way Ethan was looking at her, they would both know she was being dishonest. She had her fears, yes.

But she wouldn't give up.

She would be happy again. They would both find happiness again. It was a hope she would cling onto, a hope that would carry her through whatever was thrown their way next. Because of that hope, she was unable to answer the question truthfully.

'So many questions,' she sighed, 'can I write them down?'

He held her glance but said nothing. She kept her eyes on him. 'But … I also have a good memory too,' she joked, trying to keep the mood light in hope to ease the pang in her heart.

'You already have.'

She was confused. 'What?'

His eyes explored hers before he takes out a folded piece of paper from his pocket. She stared at it, feeling her blood run cold. Instantly she recognised the blue paper. It was the same paper as the one from the writing kit she had used to write her letters to him, all those years ago. With trembling hands, she took the letter from him ever so cautiously, unfolded it, and began to read.

January 17th 2009,

Hey you,

Can I just say again how sorry I am for doubting you? For not trusting that you knew what was best for me. Even though my heart is broken, I am grateful that you helped me find the strength to walk way. I am even more grateful that we are talking again. I would be lost without you.

Now, this might sound weird, but I have created a list for my future boyfriend, or husband (I know, I'm getting way ahead of myself). It's sort of like a check list I guess, but I wanted you to have it because I know that no matter what, you will be in my life forever. You're probably still wondering what this has to do with you, so listen up. Whoever I consider ending up with I want you, as one of my best friends to help me make sure that the person who is lucky enough to marry me one day (poor sucker, lol) matches this criteria.

Before Brody, I admit I was so focused on superficial qualities wanting him to be intelligent, handsome, tall, good sense of fashion, quirky etc. But I have learned that these things are simply not enough. So, I have made a list! Don't laugh, but here it is. But please remember, I need you to help me with this, so I am holding you accountable for when that day comes! Please don't let me walk down the aisle to a man who falls short of these! No pressure! Hehe... love you.

1. He should be teachable

2. He should challenge me

3. He should cherish me

4. He should respect me

5. He thinks before he speaks, slow to anger

6. He should be trustworthy

7. A good communicator

8. A good listener

9. Family orientated

10. Faithful

11. Practices humility

12. Most importantly, a man who would without fail, be by my side through all seasons of life.

Love always, your friend

Sienna

With stinging tears, she folded it up and instead of giving it back, she stuffed it in her jacket pocket.

'Out of all the letters, you found this one. What made you bring it?' She couldn't look at him.

His body shifted closer to her. 'I had a feeling it was something you needed to read.' Very gently, he placed his hand on her knee and together they stared out at the trees swaying gently in the breeze.

'You knew we were having problems?'

'I sensed it as soon as I saw you.'

A tear slid down her face and she found his eyes with hers. 'You still have it?'

'I have all of them.' He stopped for a moment then nodded. 'Every single letter you have ever written me.'

She shook her head. How could he have kept every one of them and hadn't kept in contact with her? He hadn't even tried to reach out once.

'Why would you tell me that now?'

'What do you mean, now?'

The kindness in his voice bothered her. She circled her fingers through the strands of grass beside her. She made a fist around it and yanked out a chunk.

'I didn't know they meant anything to you. I mean,'—she breathed in, struggling to bring oxygen with her—'everything could have been different.' A million thoughts were whirling inside her head. Had he really loved her, after all?

She didn't dare ask.

He squeezed her hand. She looked down as he laced his fingers between hers. She suddenly felt hot all over, despite the wind slapping her face like ice.

'This is why I wanted to talk about what happened between us.'

She shot her eyes up at him. 'Ethan, if we hadn't met by coincidence at the theatre last weekend, we wouldn't be in this position to have such conversation. Are you saying if we hadn't had crossed paths, you would have found a way to hunt me down after all these years and share everything that you're sharing with me now?' Her face was pulsing with heat. Angry, hot tears burned down her cheeks. She couldn't control them. Not this time. How dare he say such things when it was too late?

He took away his hand and sighed heavily. 'You keep playing the victim here. Yes, I disappeared eight years, nine years ago or whenever it was when I was young and stupid to not fully comprehend what I was actually walking away from. It doesn't mean that I haven't thought about you every single day since then. Even though I lost you, you were always on my heart. Yes, I should have reached out. Yes, I should have tried harder. I know that.

'But have you forgotten that you pushed me away during a time I pushed for us to be something? It was back when Sadie and I had broken up, back when you were still broken up with Brody. Before you gave in and crawled back to him. Do you remember that? Do you have any idea how that made me feel?' Tears shone in his eyes. 'That you would choose someone who broke your heart over someone who had always protected it? Who would always protect it? Sienna, you wanted a man who would guard your heart through all seasons of life.

'I could have been that man, Sienna. By the time you moved away for dancing and poured out your heart to me in your tiny little shoe box apartment that night, I couldn't do it. I just couldn't do it. It hadn't felt right. It felt forced. And truth be told, I was still wounded by you.'

She met his eyes feeling her heart break all over again at the stinging truth of his words. How had she spent this whole time blaming him when she was equally responsible for the damage of their friendship?

'You know what had scared me the most?'

She wanted to ask him, but the lump in her throat was about the size of Mount Everest.

'I didn't want to lose you. I knew there would be no way we would be able to salvage our friendship if we hadn't have worked out as a couple. It was something I hadn't wanted to gamble with … or maybe deep down I knew that you could have been it for me. Either way, it was all too much to think about as a twenty-year-old. I just wasn't ready for that.'

They lapsed back into silence. The loss between them too strong for either of them to continue. She wanted to look somewhere else, anywhere else. But she couldn't. Not when he was looking at her this way. A fresh batch of tears formed at the crushing sight of his.

'I'm so sorry,' she inhaled, feeling the weight of her heart slam against her chest. 'I wish more than anything that I hadn't screwed things up for us.'

He shook his head reassuringly and smiled the warmest kind of smile. 'You didn't screw anything up. It was all about timing. And let's face it, timing was never our thing.'

'No, it wasn't.'

She reflected back on the years that followed that particular night. They had both been in and out of relationships, never being out of them at the same time. There had never been the opportunity for them to explore the fullness of all that was lost between them.

As the seasons changed and the years rolled on, so had they. And now here they stood in a position no different from the previous nine years. Although there was one difference.

She was getting married.

The wind picked up. They eventually stood to their feet and walked in silence once more down the path that led to the gazebo at the base of the park. Without a word, they stepped inside and their eyes locked again. He wrapped his arms around her, shielding her from the gust of wind that carried a strength similar to the one of her broken heart. She buried her nose against his chest feeling the loss, a second time. He bowed his head and ever so gently planted a kiss on her forehead, sending her skin ablaze as it trickled through her like a ripple effect. She held his embrace, taking in every detail of what it felt to be in his arms.

A moment that would be their last.

Twelve

IT WAS THE last time they saw each other before she left Aringdale. As liberating as it had been reuniting after so long, they both knew it would be ephemeral. A collection of ephemeral moments where feelings were rekindled, all over again.

She never expected it would be so difficult leaving her childhood and everything it represented after just seven days. Saying goodbye to her parents had heightened emotions in the same way they had when she left home the first time all those years ago. After seasons of absence, a single week of connectedness had narrowed the gap inside her heart.

The drive back home was a complete blur—an out of body experience, her mind and body refusing to adjoin as one. With conflicting emotions strangling her, she felt numb as she stared out at the road ahead, the whirlwind of emotions inside her depleting with every passing kilometre.

By the time she pulled up she hadn't wanted to get out. She glanced at the dash board. 8:47 p.m. With a heavy sigh, she turned off the engine and took her bag. Instead of getting out, she sunk down into the seat and dug her nails into the synthetic. She had sent Patrick a text that morning letting him know she would be back by evening. She hadn't given a time, but he hadn't asked for one either.

Eventually she emerged from the car, collected her belongings and made her way up the flight of stairs, catching herself braking as she neared the door. From the outside, she could hear the TV accompanied by loud voices, sending an echo down the stairwell.

Boys' night.

The last thing she wanted to deal with. She turned the key, let herself in and shut the door behind her. Instantly, she came more alert at the sheer state of the place. Furniture had been shifted around, clothes sprawled everywhere, dishes piled up to the ceiling with a years' worth of empty cans of beer stacked against the kitchen wall.

It looked as though a bomb had hit it.

She could already see herself spending the next morning cleaning up after his mess. She rested her head against the wall of the lounge room, peering in at his friends circled around the coffee table, submerged in a board game of some sort. The football was on in the background, the T.V framed by more empty cans of beer.

'Hey babe,' her voice came weak, lacking the enthusiasm she normally had whenever she would greet him. Especially after days apart.

'What the hell man! I didn't see that coming!' He reacted to a move on the board. His head was down, immersed in the game. A couple of his friends noticed her standing there and nudged him.

'Hey man, your girlfriend's back.'

Girlfriend.

She felt her eyebrow lift at the comment. He rolled the dice and hovered his hand over the board like a magician.

'Hey babe. How was it?' He still hadn't looked up at her.

She shifted her feet and stared at what might as well be a stranger before her. 'It was great.'

He reached for his beer and swallowed hard. He leaned over to view something his mate was showing him on his phone. She stood there in silence with her back against the wall watching as they all carried on with the game, throwing their heads back as they dissolved into fits of laughter.

It was like she wasn't even there. He was yet to acknowledge her, his laughter mocking her already trampled heart. She turned on her heel, collected her bags and went to their bedroom. The noise from the living area only made her feel even more alone as she lowered herself onto the edge of the bed. She just sat there, motionless.

Scattering her eyes around the room, everything once familiar suddenly felt like it belonged to someone else. Whose life was she living anyway? Since when did she love all things mahogany? Crystal lamps, and a thousand grass photo frames? Was she serious? Simplistic was her style, or at least had once been. Yet, everything in their room was marked with over the top, fancy finishes. She shook her head, shaking off the thought. Of course, she was going to start questioning everything when the past week had confronted her with an avalanche of emotions. Especially after being confronted by her past the way she had. After a good night sleep, she would wake up feeling better, in Patrick's arms, or not.

She would be just fine.

She slipped her hands in her jacket pocket and inhaled sharply as her fingers found the folded paper. She took out the blue square shaped letter feeling herself exhale as a sadness whispered over her. She unfolded it and read over her own words, two times, then three.

I would be lost without you.

Her eyes were drawn to the six words that breathed a truth as she reflected on a life she created without Ethan in it. She didn't need to be told that a partner should complement you, and not complete you. Was it wrong to think that you could lose your way without them? Clearly, she was trying to seek happiness in all the wrong places if she was relying on a man to fill the gaping hole in her heart.

Her eyes jumped down to the bottom of the letter.

*Please don't let me walk down the aisle to a man
who falls short of these!*

Her heart slammed against her chest. She once was convinced that Patrick ticked every quality, but now?

She wasn't sure.

She was under no illusion that the best of relationships were a fairytale. She was aware life had a way of throwing every couple with seasons of trials and challenges to overcome. But had these qualities been upheld during the drawn-out season they found themselves in? Did they even exist at all? Were they really facing the storm together with a love strong enough to see them through?

She stared at the list of twelve, paying specific attention to the last one.

*… You wanted a man who would guard your
heart through all seasons of life. I was that man
Sienna.*

She couldn't get him out of her head even if she wanted to. His face was etched in her mind, tattooed to her heart. He wasn't only the man who had guarded her heart, he challenged her, cherished and respected her. He always listened to her heart before he shared his. He was someone she could always depend on, someone she found freeing to share her heart with. A man who prioritised those around him, a man who was faithful with a heart that always protected her. He ticked every single quality on her list.

He always had.

'There you are.'

Her thoughts were stunted as Patrick steadied himself against the door with another can of beer in his hands.

She discreetly tucked the letter back into her pocket. 'Here I am.' She managed a smile, refusing to let his drunkenness to infuriate her.

'Have you had dinner?' he slurred.

'Yeah, I ate before the drive back.'

'Didn't drive through anywhere through, yeah?' His eyes finally met hers for the first time that night. She could only imagine that he was seeing duplicates of her.

'No, I didn't get any fast food, I ate at home.'

'Good,' he mumbled and sat down next to her.

'You have another week off until you go back, don't you?' He patted her knee as though she was a mate from his football team. She placed her hand on his, hoping the heaviness would lift as soon as her fingers weaved between his.

But it didn't.

'Yeah, one more week.'

'You should have stayed longer babe.'

His words sent another shard of pain through her. 'I know.' She squeezed his hand in hope to feel something. 'But I wanted to get back to you.' She honestly felt nothing.

'I can't promise we'll see each other much this week. I've a lot on with work,' he said platonically.

She inhaled a shaky breath and nodded. What happened to the days where he would come bounding in after time apart, telling her how he missed her?

'We will just have to do the best with the time we've got,' she responded half-heartedly.

'Yeah.' He paused, listening in to the voices coming from where all the action was. 'Well, it's probably my go again. I better get back to it.'

'I won't keep you.'

He patted her knee again, stretched his back and tripped on a pile of clothes on the way out. She stared out after him, the pain in her heart expanding wide across her chest. The voices from the other room grow louder as their bodies filled with alcohol. She collapsed onto the bed and stared at the ceiling, feeling every essence of hope slowly dwindle as she sank deep into the mattress.

She took out her phone and scrolled through her contact list. She searched under E then K, for probably the hundredth time. His number definitely wasn't there. She refreshed her Facebook page, then Instagram. He was nowhere to be found, even after trying every possible combination. Who didn't have social media these days?

The thought baffled her.

Her mobile started buzzing, with Jacqui's name demanding her attention. Only then did she realise how much she had missed her best friend. Jacqui had spent the past few weeks in Thailand with her boyfriend at some fancy resort on some tropical island drinking cocktails, getting massages, loving life as she loathed hers. She longed for their chats more than she longed her next breath.

As soon as she heard her voice, her spirits lifted. 'Oh, my, gawwwd, I have missed you so much, we have so much to catch up on.'

She couldn't help but smile as her friend filled her in on their perfect little getaway.

'And yes, to catching up. Let's make it happen soon please. Talk to me, how was it back home? Are you still with your folks?'

And just like that she felt the darkness close in on her again.

'I'm back. I got home about an hour ago,' she paused. 'Jac … I have so much to tell you. I don't know where to begin.' She felt her throat thicken with emotion. There was a hesitation on the other end of the line.

'You sound different. Something happened, didn't it? I'm coming over.'

Something inside of her panicked at that.

'No! No. Probably best that you don't. Patrick has the guys over. I'll come to you.' Already she had picked up her keys and slid her feet back in her boots.

'Is everything ok between you two?'

Jacqui knew of Patrick's drinking problem but that was the extent of it. She had never really shared her heart, having spent too many years behind the mask she had carefully crafted. One that made them appear as the happy couple everyone assumed they were. But that was all about to change.

She couldn't hide anymore.

'Not really. But it's so much more than that, I'll explain it all soon. Give me twenty. I'm leaving now.'

A surge of anxiety built inside her at the thought of leaving the apartment at this hour with a drunk fiancé who would barricade her like a guard dog, determined to keep her caged. She sent her phone into her handbag and walked down the hallway. She peered over at the guys who were now engrossed in a show of some sort. There was lot of hysterical laughter as their beers splashed around with every chuckle.

They had better clean up after them.

Patrick looked up with a confused expression as he watched her lingering there. He eventually stood to his feet and stumbled over to her. 'You're heading out?'

She turned the keys in her hand. 'Jac's back from Thailand. I thought I would pop over to hers for a bit,' her response came quick.

He narrowed his eyes and looked at her as though she had committed a crime. 'You've been gone for a week, I see you for like five minutes and you're already running off?'

His words shot a flute of adrenaline through her body. And not a good kind. Was he serious? The look on his face told her that he was.

'This is clearly a boys' night.' She motioned her hand to his friends whose eyes were still glued on the TV. 'I'm not going to crash that.' She didn't have the nerve to tell him he hadn't given her five minutes of his time, or love or care for that matter. But she knew better, especially in his drunken state where his emotions were always unpredictable.

'You can always join us. You're more than capable of making that decision without waiting to be asked.'

'I'll remember that for next time,' she said, her defense weakening far too obediently. She leaned over and sent him a quick kiss on the cheek even though her insides were fuming. He stood there immobile, completely unresponsive to her affection.

'Well, off you go then.'

'I'll only be an hour or two,' she said submissively. He had already joined the others.

He shrugged with his back turned from her. 'Whatever. Stay as long as you like.'

A few of the boys exchanged a look, aware of the tension between them.

'See you soon.'

Jacqui had been her closest friend for years. If it wasn't for her, she wasn't sure how she would have survived the grueling ballet years at the National Premier Ballet. They had been each other's source of encouragement and sanity as their fragile bodies and minds tolerated the daily physical and mental abuse of their Nazi director. Similar to herself, Jacqui had chosen a different path after deciding enough was enough and hung up her point shoes in their third year of full-time training. She now worked as a nurse at the Royal Children's Hospital and hadn't looked back. If only Sienna felt a peace about the path she chose for her own life. After spending a week in her past, she wasn't quite sure how to pick herself back up and find momentum again.

Sienna collapsed into her friends' arms as soon as the door opened. They stayed that way for a while, allowing the moment of their reuniting to linger.

'You're so brown!' Sienna pulled back and studied her once pale skin that was now bronzed from the summer sun.

'I know, right? This never happens to me!' She rolled up her sleeves showing off her tanned skin. 'But let's be honest it will all probably peel off in a matter of days and I'll be back looking like Casper again!' Her humour instantly made Sienna feel better.

'Well, you look amazing, Casper or not.' She stepped inside and squeezed her again. 'Gosh I missed you. Don't ever do that to me again.' They broke apart. Jacqui's deep brown eyes locked with hers and her expression deepened.

'How have you been?' her words came slow, careful.

Sienna sighed. 'Is it possible for someone from a lifetime ago make you question everything you have ever known?'

Jacqui raised an eyebrow. 'Patrick?'

Sienna shook her head, her spirits sinking back into the deep, black hole. 'No,' she answered, her breathing suddenly strained. 'Ethan Kahler.'

'Who?' Jacqui's eyes filled with a million questions.

They settled into the living room, curled their legs up on the couch and lifted a blanket over them.

'I reconnected with someone from my childhood while I was in Aringdale.'

'An old high school boyfriend?'

Sienna waved the question off. 'No, we were never …' she exhaled, 'we never dated, but easily could have.'

Jacqui nodded with understanding, waiting for her to go on.

'I know. I've known Ethan forever, yet I haven't mentioned him once to you the entire time we've known each other. Some friend I am. You're probably thinking, how can a guy so far back in my past possibly affect me in the way he has so strongly now? And out of nowhere.' She wrinkled her nose, feeling the prickling of fresh tears emerge from the corners of her eyes.

What was with her emotions lately? She couldn't seem to keep them under control. Jacqui reached for her hands. She took them.

'It sounds like whoever this Ethan guy is, he's obviously opened up wounds you didn't realise you had,' her words came slow, 'or maybe haven't worked through yet.'

This must have been a rare sight to her, Sienna wasn't a crier.

'He's done more than that Jac, he's made me feel alive again.' She brushed away an escaped tear. 'I used to be so different. I used to be brave, daring. I was this little ball of energy and nothing ever stood in my way. I used to embrace life with curiosity, a wonder, and I approached it to its fullness. I was always inspired, motivated, always working towards something. I had clear goals, ambitions … I knew exactly where I wanted to be and when.' She inhaled sharply, unable to unravel the knot that has become of her thoughts.

'And you know what? Family was everything to me. I used to be so close to mine. You wouldn't have guessed that, right? I know, I never talk about them. You haven't even ever met them. I'm lucky to make the effort to see them once or twice a year! Don't know what happened there, how I could ever have considered spending time with them to be a burden.' The suffocating lump failed to soften in her airway no matter how many times she swallowed.

'I guess what I'm trying to say, through all of this word vomit is that in the short time I spent with Ethan, he somehow managed to delve in and rip out everything that had made me, me. Every single detail, and it's confronting as hell. He somehow gave me the courage to want to find that person again, the girl I once was. The girl I recognise more than the one staring back at me in the mirror each day as I hide behind this bloody mask I've been wearing for god knows how long.' She started to cry.

Oh god, she was actually *crying*.

'And now I feel like I'm existing, floating, surviving. I don't know what my future looks like. What our future looks like. I've been wanting to believe that I do, that there's this whole plan, but I've got no idea. I can't even begin to imagine it. Sad, I know, right? It is sad, and to honest, I don't even know if I'm happy.' She huddled her knees in closer to her and wedged them under her chin.

'Patrick doesn't look at me the way he used to. He's only ever affectionate when he knows he's being an ass, or when he's drunk.' She hung her head and shook it. 'The way he speaks to me Jac … the way he belittles me. The way we can't hold a single conversation before all hell breaks loose. I was aware of it, but not in the way that it all shouts at me now.' Hot tears were rolling down her cheeks, yet somehow, she felt a freedom in her openness. 'It only took a dinner, a box of old letters and a walk in a park to realise all of that.'

She probably had no idea what she was rambling on about, but it didn't stop Jacqui from wrapping her hands around her and holding her tight. She didn't say anything for a long moment.

'Do you think that maybe you've been trying so hard to be the woman Patrick wants you to be and it took reuniting with this other guy to realise that while you were trying so hard to please him and be that perfect partner, you lost yourself along the way?'

She released her arms and looked into her eyes in a way that gave her the courage to confront her feelings, head on. 'I think it's more than that,' she said slowly. Even under the warm blanket she somehow broke into a cold sweat.

'It's normal for a first love to stay with you. To make you take a step back and question how you have evolved and changed since they held your heart.' Her smile somehow calmed her. 'First loves are pretty powerful like that, no matter what people say.'

'What if he has always stayed with me.' It was hardly a question, rather a sense of knowing, knocking her down like a cannonball.

'What do you mean?'

Sienna drew a shaky breath. 'I don't know if I've ever stopped loving him.'

Thirteen

B Y THE TIME she set foot inside the classroom, the old Sienna was back.

The submissive who kept her focus on the task at hand, protecting the pressings of her heart from overriding any sense of reason.

Perhaps it was a coping mechanism, a façade that allowed her to carry on without breaking. It was a version of herself that was familiar, safe and numbed her from the emotional shackles Aringdale chained her with.

Now she was back, her identity wouldn't dare be tested again.

Her conversation with Jacqui had provoked feelings, old and new, feelings she didn't even know existed. Even though they had been brought to shore, they were washed away in the same wave of time.

Patrick was right in saying they wouldn't see much of each other over the next week. Meetings for company projects and business proposals saw him focusing more on his relationship with work, than the strained one at home. She had used these lonely evenings fine tuning details of the curriculum plan for the school term ahead before making some last-minute classroom arrangements.

By the time the weekend came around, he had spent their last potential day together playing golf with friends, returning home in the early hours of the morning after a pub crawl. He had tried to gain her affection as he cuddled in behind her, wrapping his arms around her waist as his beer stained breath tickled her ears. She had been half asleep as he planted a series of kisses along her neck, whispering her name, along with a string of other words she hadn't understood through his intoxication. Part of her wanted to embrace the sporadic moment of his hands over her neglected body, but another part of her didn't know how to respond naturally to his touch in a way that had once been so instinctive. She was afraid her attempts of pleasing him would fall short of his expectation.

Expectations she no longer knew how to fill.

Instead, she had gently squeezed his fingers as they curled between hers. So gentle, she hadn't been convinced he had felt the acknowledgement of her presence. By the time she considered rolling around to bring her face to his, soft snores had bristled her ears.

There had been a small window to rekindle a connection lost, but within moments, the opportunity had passed. Maybe there would be another window.

But even then, only a miracle could change things.

SHE LEFT HOME a good hour before she usually would when Monday came around. Patrick was sound asleep by the time she walked out the door and made the drive to school in the dark. She had been one of the first staff members to arrive, even beating Damian who basically lived at the campus.

She switched her classroom lights on and drew her attention towards the Indigenous humanities display she had set up in the corner of the room. Boomerangs, dotted art fabric, clay and print outs of famous traditional paintings covered the table. She had even sourced out a digeridoo and various puzzles representing the Dreamtime stories, all thanks to her father and his well-preserved childhood collection.

Presentation and attention to detail was something she always put a lot of energy into, especially when introducing a new topic to the kids. She was all about getting her students to explore as many senses as possible with their learning. Her detailed little set up made her feel confident that they would be inspired by this particular unit.

'Good morning Miss Henderson.'

Her attention was directed down to the smiling, freckled face standing behind his desk in a well-trained manner.

'Good morning Nolan. My goodness, you are here early.' She peered at the clock on the wall. 7:47 a.m.

The bell wouldn't go for another hour.

'I hope that's ok? I won't disrupt you. I have my book to read. Actually, I think I have a couple. Aunt Lindsey had to get to work early, that's why.' He began unpacking his bag.

'Oh, your aunt dropped you off today?' She was glad he hadn't travelled alone on the bus so early in the morning when it was still dark.

'Yeah, she lives in the city so we had to leave super early. But I didn't mind, it meant that I got to have McDonalds for breakfast. I'm never allowed that stuff!'

She smiled, nodding as she tried to piece it all together in her head. 'That's nice you got to spend some time with your aunty. I'm sure she enjoyed having you with her.'

Nolan shrugged a little too casually as he took a seat at his desk. 'She doesn't seem sick of me yet. So, I suppose we are having a good time.'

She took a seat next to him. 'Don't be silly! There is no way that she would be sick of you! A bright, kind, polite boy like you Nolan, she must be so proud! Tell me, how were your holidays? What was your most favourite thing you did?'

He wrinkled his nose and turned the colourful pages of his book.

'Probably staying with Lindsey.' His red matted hair flopped over the rim of his glasses. He whisked it back. 'We did things I never get to do. We went to the movies and I was actually allowed popcorn. I even got to go to the aquarium and asked the tour guides a lot of tricky questions.' He giggled at the memory. 'He couldn't tell me how many species of fish there are, or if it's true that female seahorses release up to fifty eggs into the pouch of the male's abdomen during mating. I think I may have embarrassed him actually. I didn't mean to put him on the spot, I just wanted all the answers.'

He looked up with dancing eyes. 'Anyway, we went home, well, back to Lindsey's house and looked up some facts on the internet. There are over thirty-three thousand species of fish Miss Henderson, isn't that incredible?' He pointed to a great white shark on the page open in front of him. 'Did you know that they have three hundred teeth, arranged in many rows? Maybe you can read this book to the class, if you want, and maybe we could have a quiz or something on it. I probably shouldn't participate in the quiz part though. That wouldn't be fair, because I'd know all the answers.' He took a breath through his racing excitement. 'I guess my most favourite part of the holidays was getting this book. Lindsey is so kind and she loves books just as much as I do. Finding that out was probably my second favourite thing. I think that was pretty cool.'

A smile filled her face. 'Well, we can certainly share this book to the class, that's a great idea.' She watched Nolan beam as he flicked through the pages. 'Maybe you can read a page or two to everyone during show and share this afternoon, would that be something you'd like to do?' If there was an opportunity for him to interact with his peers and get him reading, she would jump on it.

A smile tugged at the corner of his lips. 'Even though it's not my day?' He hesitated ever so slightly. 'Sure, I guess I can do that. What pages should I read?'

His willing attitude surprised her. 'Any page you like. You can choose. Maybe the one that talks about the great white shark, you seem to have a brilliant knowledge about that.'

He nodded with a confidence she hadn't seen before. 'Ok, I think I can do that.'

Sienna passed him the white board marker. He stood to his feet and began writing the days' date in cursive before arranging the days' timetable in order with the subject magnets. It was his special job, an unspoken routine since he was always the first student to arrive.

He enjoyed the responsibility of helping her out each morning. It was a simple task like this where she had seen Nolan slowly break away from his shell in a way he had become more vulnerable with her. A side of him she so badly wanted to come to light every morning as the bell went, and the classroom filled.

'So, when do you go back to mum and dad? They must be missing you.' She was over at her laptop now, sending resources to the printer she would later laminate.

'I don't think so,' he said carefully. 'They are always working heaps. They're doing more overseas trips these days. But that's ok, I don't want to go home. I'm having fun with Lindsey.' His eyes still firmly focused on the board.

She looked up at him, his robotic response rested uncomfortably upon her. 'It is a very busy career, that one,' she commented, knowing that Stuart was a pilot and Miranda an air hostess for Qantas. 'But also, a very exciting one. Have you flown much Nolan?'

He shook his head. 'I've never been on a plane before.' The joy in his voice from earlier was gone. He sat back down at his desk, adjusted his glasses and turned to a new page in his sea animal book.

She pursed her lips together, trying her best to hold her tongue from firing the many questions bound around it.

Something didn't add up. She could feel it in her bones.

'SHOW AND SHARE' ran every afternoon during the last period of the day. It was a time where students had the opportunity to stand up in front of the class for two minutes and share something that was important to them. Being the first day of the week, there was always news to be shared, especially after a weekend. Some weeks were themed but being the first week of term with holidays behind them, she had left the topic open.

As students took their turn before him, Nolan fidgeted with his book, turning it over and over in his hands. It wasn't unusual for him not to participate in the 'questions and comments time' at the end of each presentation. He rarely ever put his hand up, but he always listened intently. She couldn't help but watch him as he sat at his desk, clearly distracted. It pained her that she had no idea what. She wondered then if it had been unfair of her to put him on the spot, to get him to present today when it wasn't his day to do so. But he had been so enthusiastic in telling her about the holidays and his book she had wanted to give him the opportunity while his spirits were high and his knowledge was fresh.

It was Nolan's turn to present.

He stood from his desk and made his way to the front of the classroom. She flashed him a warm smile, but his eyes avoided hers. They were focused down at his feet as he swayed back and forth. A student set the timer on the interactive whiteboard.

'Good morning everyone,' he mumbled.

'Good morning Nolan. What are you presenting today?' the class responded in unison.

His book dangled down loosely in hands in front of him, his eyes still lowered. 'Today I've brought this book.' He lifted it slightly, his hands covered the words.

She could see the children twisting their heads about as they tried to take a glimpse of the title. She felt her heart sink. Where was the confident, articulate Nolan she had seen earlier?

The seconds on the timer were escaping as he stood there frozen as though it was the first time he has ever presented to the class.

'How about that page you were showing me earlier Nolan? What was that one about?' Her eyes exuded with warmth as she did her best to encourage him.

He looked up and nodded tentatively. 'Um …' He awkwardly positioned the book over the length of his arms and flicked through the pages.

Thirty seconds gone. Ninety remaining.

'I like this page the most because it has some interesting facts about the great white shark.' He waved it slowly in the air side to side for everyone to see before his hands lost grip and it sailed to the floor.

A few giggles escaped around the room.

He quickly bent down to pick it up, losing his glasses in the process. Sienna sent a stern scowl to the class and the giggling stopped in an instant.

'They are amazing creatures, that's for sure!' she commended him a little too heartily. 'What are some facts you can tell us about them?' Usually questions and comments were reserved until the end, but she had to help him through this.

Fifty-two seconds remaining. He could do this.

He was wiping his glasses now, studying them a little too hard before he put them back on while the other hand awkwardly juggled the book.

He looked blankly at her, his eyes unnaturally wide.

'How many teeth do they have, Nolan? Does it mention it somewhere in there?' She was trying hard, praying he would regurgitate the information he had shared with her earlier.

He shrugged, fear and uncertainty clouded his eyes.

A few more snickers.

She sighed. What had she done?

'Why won't you tell us something from your book? We're all waiting!' Jacob called out, smirking as his eyes darted around the room for validation.

She felt her blood boil in record time. 'Jacob! That's very

disrespectful. You can stay back with me when the bell goes,' her words came sharp. She rarely raised her voice. There were other means to managing behaviour.

Jacob shrugged, pretending not to care, but his body language as he sunk in his chair told her otherwise.

Nolan started rocking forward and back, panic spreading over his features. 'There are three hundred of them,' his voice sounded breathless, 'three hundred or more sharp … really sharp … first two rows that grab … and cut like. I mean, the others in the last rows replace the front when they are broken and um, worn down …'

It was a jumbled, incoherent mess.

The giggles grew even louder.

Just as she stood to her feet to address the class, the timer went off. The confronting buzz unleashed an inner panic as Nolan plunged towards the door. It was the first time she had seen him freak out like that. Bolting had never been in his repertoire. It took her by surprise. The silence that invaded the room confirmed that she wasn't the only one.

AFTER BEING NOTIFIED of his where about, she dismissed the class swiftly as the bell went minutes later. She found him in the library sitting on the floor in the nonfiction aisle with his chin in his hands, unresponsive to the librarian whom she was grateful had been in the room. As soon as he saw her, he lifted his chin, his expression filling with the same panic as the one flickered earlier.

'I'm sorry I ran away.' The sincerity in his voice made her long to reach out and comfort him.

'It's ok Nolan.'

His face softened. 'I'll try again next time. I just can't … I don't know why that happens. I got all dizzy up there and,'—he gulped, struggling to inhale—'I got all embarrassed and everyone was laughing at me. I couldn't stand there and keep stuffing up like that. I couldn't think. Everything got all foggy.'

Her heart ached as his distress multiplied with each word. 'What happened this afternoon won't happen again Nolan. No one will be laughing next time. Only twenty-one pairs of respectful, listening ears and eyes.' She hoped it wasn't an empty promise. Especially after the stern words she had fed the class after he ran out.

He nodded and slowly got to his feet, collecting the books beside him. 'Mrs Jennings said I can take them home with me.'

She smiled as he tucked three or four books under his arm.

At least he hadn't lost his desire to read.

'How are you getting home today?' They began walking back to the classroom together.

'Lindsey. She's probably here now.' His pace quickened, realising that she might already be waiting for him.

'Oh, lovely. I would love to meet her.'

His eyes quickly met hers. 'Please don't tell her about before.'

'Nolan, you know grown-ups need to know when things like this happen at school. I can't hide that information from her.'

He groaned, his pace having now halved in speed. 'As long as Miranda and Stuart don't find out.' There was a fear in his voice. 'Especially Miranda.'

Miranda and Stuart?

'You mean, your parents?' she corrected him.

He shook his head assuredly. 'They aren't my parents,' he answered dryly.

She felt the blood thump in her ears. What was she missing here? She was suddenly desperate to speak with Lindsey.

She needed answers.

Surely enough, as soon as they reached the classroom his aunt was standing in the corridor with Nolan's bag around her shoulder. She was a pretty woman. Short, with cropped dark brown hair and an hour glass figure. Unlike Miranda—she dressed modestly—in a pencil skirt that fell just below her knees—complimented with a clean-cut silk blouse. The way she held herself and her warm smile, made her appear as though whatever line of work she was in, she was a successful, confident woman with her head on her shoulders.

Sienna shook her hand and extended a smile.

While Nolan went inside to tidy his desk, she filled her in on the afternoon's incident. She told her about Nolan's anxiety of his parents finding out and all the factors she believed had led to his breakdown. Lindsey listened intently, showing a care and genuine concern for Nolan that Miranda was yet to show. Without saying too much, Sienna informed her that she hadn't had any luck getting in contact with his parents. Lindsey didn't seem surprised but hadn't heard anything about it either.

'All I know is that things are a bit strained at home at the moment since Nolan found out about everything.' Lindsey peered over at him, making sure he wasn't listening in. He was over at the white board, wiping it down ready for the next day. 'He hasn't been connecting very well with them. They haven't been able to get a single word out of him, he's been completely unresponsive. I said I'd take him for the holidays. A bit sooner than we'd planned, but I'm glad I did. It seems to have all worked out well.' She let out a deflated sigh. 'I haven't wanted to bring any of it up with him, I haven't wanted to risk it with how well we've been getting on, you know?'

There was an honesty Sienna was drawn to, even though she didn't have a clue what she was talking about. But still, she could feel the woman was holding back. That there was more behind those eyes than she was letting on.

'Haven't wanted to bring what up?' she politely asked, even though her insides were screaming for clarity.

'His adoption.' Lindsey's eyes didn't flicker, as though she assumed Sienna knew all about it.

'Right, of course.' She released a breath she didn't realise she was holding.

'Being as inquisitive as he is, he has been questioning everything that's taking place. Which is understandable, the poor kid is getting roundabout answers, it's confusing for him. But the more he prods, the more things have flared up. It's been a bit of disaster to be honest.' She wiped her brow. 'They probably haven't been sensitive of his emotions either, mind you, the way they—'

'I'm ready.' Nolan's eyes rested on Lindsey suspiciously, as though he knew they were talking about him.

She smiled freely, giving away nothing and passed him his bag. 'Fantastic! Let's get you home. I was thinking of making blueberry muffins.'

His eyes dilated. 'Home?'

'Back to mine honey.'

He nodded, his lips curling ever so slightly. He looked at Sienna. 'Bye Miss Henderson.'

Her mind was racing trying to assemble all the information, yet her smile remained solid. 'Have a lovely evening Nolan, enjoy those muffins. Feel free to bring any left overs in tomorrow for me,' she joked. His smile broadened. 'I can't make any promises.'

They all shared a laugh.

'Thank you,' Lindsey whispered under her breath as Nolan took off ahead of her. 'The work you do with him, he is always talking about you. He adores you, you are really making a difference, so thank you.'

It was possibly the nicest thing anyone had in a long time. Her throat tightened. She swallowed to loosen it. 'I appreciate that. Nolan is an absolute pleasure to teach.' She had more to say, more questions to ask. There was so much more to learn. But part of her was still holding out for a conversation with his parents. Or adopted parents.

Whatever they were.

They were the ones she knew she had to talk to if she wanted the answers.

She wondered if Damian knew any more about the situation. If he knew of Nolan's adoption, when it took place and its implications. Yet, his surname *Livingston* was the same as Miranda and Stuart's. It didn't all make sense. Having the answers might explain why Miranda was so hesitant to speak with them, why he was alone most of the time and why he had a relationship with his aunty, and not with his parents.

With every burning question she found herself taking another step towards his office. She couldn't shake it this time. She couldn't just let all these questions slide.

She knocked on the door and waited a few seconds before opening it just enough to see in.

The room was empty.

She went to his desk and took a note from his sticky pad. She began scribbling a message, then decided against it. She would email him or drop by tomorrow. It could wait a day. She took the half-written note in her hand, almost smacking into Allie on her way out.

Perfect.

The note sailed to the floor. Slowly, Allie darted her eyes from the note on the ground with Damian's name on it, to his office behind her, before positioning them back on Sienna. She lifted a brow and let out a soft snort as though she had made a connection between the three— that her theory of their love affair was correct all along. Without saying a word, she picked up the note and slapped it into Sienna's hand like a self-righteous teen. Then, with a devious smile she shook her head scornfully, and paraded off.

What a fabulous first day back.

Fourteen

T HE FIRST WEEK had come and gone in a flash.

It was always that way at the start of every term. New units being introduced along with the challenge of settling the children back into a rhythm after the holidays. She was grateful for the distraction and the way it kept her mind from wondering.

The mystery case concerning Nolan still stood exactly as that. Damian knew no more than she did. He hadn't had any luck getting in contact with his parents either, but hadn't pressed the matter which only bugged her more.

Nolan was scheduled to have his first appointment on Monday with Anita Moore; the school counselor. She hadn't received his parents' consent but with Damian's approval, had taken the risk and decided to go ahead with it.

She must have left about a hundred messages by now but was holding onto hope it was something significant enough they would respond to. Nolan was under the impression that he was meeting with the literacy support coordinator to work on self-confidence skills following his little breakdown. She hadn't directly lied about it but hadn't been a hundred percent honest, either. She was worried if he knew her position, he wouldn't cooperate.

To her knowledge, he was still staying with his aunt Lindsey. She hadn't seen her again since that Monday afternoon but felt better knowing that he was in her care, even if it was short term.

In fact, the situation was better for everyone.

He had a spring in his step that hadn't sprung prior to that. Sure, he kept to himself most of the time, his head down more often than not when it wasn't preoccupied in a book. This hadn't changed and she hadn't expected it would overnight.

But what she had noticed was a quiet confidence take root inside of him, in a way that instilled resilience when he would usually give up.

And that was a transformation in itself, even if it was a small one.

It was Friday night and as usual, Patrick wasn't home. 'Bowls with the boys' he had told her, promising he would be home in time for a movie together later.

She wasn't holding her breath. But strangely, wasn't as affected by his absence as she once had.

She had become accustomed to it now.

Sinking down into the couch, she placed her bowl of chicken curry on the coffee table as her phone vibrated in her pocket. Her eyes were drawn to the unfamiliar number on the screen. She opened the message, her mind blank before realisation sent her heart to lurch.

> **You're right, the lemon chicken is amazing.**
> **Wasn't brave enough to try the white sauce**
> **with that fancy cheese you like with it though.**

She was suddenly filled with enough energy to run a marathon.

Ethan.

Just when she didn't think she would hear from him again …

Halloumi. That fancy cheese is called Halloumi.

Her fingers danced over the keypad, pressing send before she has a chance to reread her response. Seconds later there was another ping.

Are you sure? What's this then?

Attached to the text was a picture of what appeared to be a chunky blue vain cheese scattered over the dish. Something she wasn't even brave enough to eat. She burst out laughing and cozied her legs up under her on the couch.

That is blue vein cheese. I would never be that brave.

With a smile as wide as a Cheshire cat, she googled a photo of halloumi cheese and attached it with her message. Again, his text was almost instantaneous.

Haha … wow. Well, now I'm feeling a bit stupid. :P

Their messages went back and forth for a bit before she asked the burning question. He had retrieved her number from a mutual friend after learning her old number belonged to some old lady living thousands of kilometers north.

It hadn't felt that long ago where she had lost her phone during the days she was at the Academy dancing full time. She had reached in her bag during a stage rehearsal one afternoon to discover it gone. Although no one admitted it at the time, she was convinced it had been stolen. She had had her suspicions, as spiteful girls like the ones from *Centre Stage* and *Black Swan* didn't only exist in fiction. Especially in the ballet world where girls would attempt anything as they competed for the very few contracts that existed.

Her mind drifted back to 2010; the year her heart was left brittle after her falling out with Ethan. It was the September holidays and she had been dying to get out of the city over the break, away from the toxic ballet environment. It had been almost a term since she had been home last. Being a first year, she missed the comfort and dependability of being around her family. And after losing contact with her oldest and dearest friend, she was fragile. Her parents were finishing up their final week of their trip around Canada and had mentioned that Ethan's parents Tamara and Rod, had offered for her to stay in their little cottage situated behind their house until they returned. It was a kind invitation, and not an unusual one as both their families had established a strong friendship over her childhood years. She was tentative at first, worried she would run into Ethan while she was there. She had been told that he had moved out just months prior and was now living with two friends from his footy league. It was only two nights, she figured she wouldn't run into him.

So she accepted the offer.

Like the rare connection she shared with Ethan, the one she shared with his parents was no different. She loved them as if they were her own.

And they embraced her as a daughter.

She never made it to the cottage. Tamara insisted that she stayed in the main house with them. Funnily enough, they had set her up in Ethan's old room, even if the situation hadn't been humorous at the time. She was tempted to decline, but rude wasn't in her. She wouldn't be petty. As far as she could tell, they were oblivious to the fact that the two weren't friends anymore and she had wanted to keep it that way.

It wasn't until that night when she was getting ready for bed, where she stepped into his old room. A collage of old photos spewed over his walls, slashing open scars as the memories peered back at her. Many of them were selfies of himself and Sadie over the years. Her eyes had been drawn to the ones of them in a group, and more so, the odd photo of him and her. The way his eyes shone in each picture as her arm hung loosely around his shoulder with their cheeks smooshed together said a thousand words.

Until that night, she hadn't quite realised the strength of their relationship, the pure joy and happiness that oozed from every photo. A friendship that had been left behind as the photos remained on the walls of his abandoned room.

She remembered waking up the next morning to the blended smell of bacon, eggs and tomato wafting down the hallway, landing right underneath her nose. The kitchen table had been set up in decorative china—all fancy in its layout. There had been fresh bread, scones with jam and cream, five assortments of tea and fresh fruit accompanying what would have been a satisfying breakfast with just the bacon and eggs alone. She had been looked after, that was for sure, and had wondered if Ethan had always been spoilt the same way she had.

The day only got better from there on. After offering to help with the clean-up and being told she would do no such thing, she had spent the morning in the sun curled up with a book on the patio surrounded by wild flowers, chirping magpies and the playfulness of their gorgeous Border Collie. It had lasted a full five minutes before Tamara appeared with a tray of iced tea and a fresh batch of chocolate chip cookies, straight from the oven. They spent hours in conversation as her white, starved skin had hungrily soaked up the sun rays.

That afternoon Rod had taken her out to the flying range where she took the passenger seat in his Tecam II plane, adrenaline exceeding every level performing had ever given her. She had never felt so scared, yet exhilarated all at the same time as they glided through the air, feeling every bump as the wind picked up. She had never experienced Aringdale in the way she had that day, taking in all of its beauty as she viewed the town in its entirety from a thrilling dimension.

He had asked her whether she had been in touch with his son. She told him she hadn't, without devouring into the details of how their friendship had taken a turn south and because of her, would never be the same again. He had looked at her in the way Ethan used to; with attentive, gentle eyes. Even his smile was crooked, sending her heart in a frenzy as their uncanny resemblance made her miss him all over again. He mentioned that he could tell Ethan missed her. When she asked how, he said his son didn't laugh the same way he did when he was in her company. That he was 'searching,' filling his time with 'empty things'. Even his friendship circles had changed. He didn't elaborate what he meant by 'empty things,' but she hadn't pressed it either.

The world around her stopped in that moment, or at least it felt that way through the distraction of her million thoughts as the engine rattled away. His hearty laugh was quick to fill the air.

'Well, I'm going to say this Sienna.' His smile was infectious, sending her lips to coil. 'If you two aren't married by the time you're thirty, then you'll marry each other. It's already decided.'

She wasn't sure why he had made such comment when their history had only been one of friendship. Maybe Rod had sensed something deeper between them. Which only hurt her heart more as she had seen the potential too.

But Ethan hadn't.

She was at a loss but had thrown her head back and laughed at the comment anyway.

She had collected her thoughts once, spilling them over a series of journals. There had been several of them over the years. Beginning from ninth grade right up until she met Patrick at the age of twenty-one. From then on, she stopped writing.

The way many things came to a stop once they got together.

She pushed the thought aside. She didn't have to put an end to anything, only she was accountable for her choices. She placed her phone down, neglecting her cold chicken curry and took out the steady ladder from the closet. Positioning it in front of the cupboard in the bedroom, she reached to the top shelf and took down the plastic tub containing what she assumed were her old journals. She placed it on the bed, the weight of the contents causing the mattress to sink a little. Images of rings, hearts and flowers invaded her sight as soon as she lifted the lid.

Their engagement cards.

As her eyes ran over the poetry of messages written by their loved ones, a peculiar sense of guilt filled her. Out of all emotions, she hadn't been able to make sense of. It was the one that stumped her the most. It has almost been five years since their engagement—just shy of four years since their celebration. Most engaged couples would have pieced together the details of their wedding, gone forward with their wedding, perhaps travelled the word and had a kid or two by now.

They had been spoilt that day, showered with gifts of money, homeware, wine, vouchers—the list went on. Presents that remained packaged and hidden in the far top cupboard somewhere.

Maybe that was where the guilt came from. That there were hundreds of dollars' worth of abandoned presents stashed away when they could be of good use. She cringed at the thought of all the vouchers that would have expired by now.

What a waste.

Reading over the heartfelt words as they were wished a life time of happiness, felt as though the words were meant for someone else. Why was it that she felt completely emotionally removed from the joy everyone else seemed to have for them?

Wish you all the love and happiness as you embark on your life together.

They had all read. Three key words stood out to her.

Love, happiness, life.

Words that laughed at her squarely in the face. She opened the cards one by one, each one having read similar to the last. Yet the one from the Kahler's had laughed the loudest:

> *We are so sad that we are unable to be there today to celebrate your engagement. Our hearts are bursting with happiness and we so look forward to your special day. We love you very much and thrilled that you have found each other. May you continue to cherish each other for years to come.*
>
> *Our love always,*
>
> *Tamara and Rod xoxo*
>
> *… You have found each other.*

Why did she feel as though she was still searching?

It was probably something to do with what Jacqui had mentioned about her having lost her identity over the years. But that hadn't been Patrick's fault.

… May you continue to cherish each other forever.

Ok, so maybe she couldn't justify that one. But when things were good, they did cherish one another. Didn't they? They would find their way back.

Enough.

She couldn't keep doing this, picking apart their relationship like a wood pecker. Yes, right now they were standing on shaky grounds, but that didn't mean that a solid groundwork hadn't been built.

Did it?

For whatever reason, Rod and Tamara hadn't been able to make their engagement that day. She remembered feeling over the top disappointed without really knowing why. It had been years since she had seen them, that night in September probably having been the last time she had. The Kahler family left an imprint so profoundly on her heart making the years fall away, no matter how many had elapsed.

The thought crossed her mind that Rod may not have wanted to see her with anyone other than his son. But that would have been taking his comment in the plane that day about them marrying each other a little too literally. He loved her like a daughter, and sure, he had been protective of her the same way a father would. It made sense for him to have concerns over a man he had never met. But even if it had been the reason, it would have never stood in the way of them being there that day.

After her trip home she wasn't sure how well she would handle seeing Rod again, with Ethan's features reflecting back at her. Their characteristics and mannerisms were practically identical, even if Ethan had never congratulated her on her engagement. Out of all the moments to reach out—that would have been a perfect opportunity.

She lowered her head onto the pillow. Curling her body into a ball she turned to her side and stared at the cards around her. It was a position they once spent hours entangled in each other's bodies, connected in a way that now felt like a life time ago.

She wanted to blame living together for what they had become. That the four walls enclosed over them barracked their relationship before it had a chance to grow. They had moved in too soon, trying too hard to establish foundations, all in the wrong order.

But they were head over heels in love, the excitement of their prolonged honeymoon phase, fast tracking them to a place their relationship wasn't ready for. They had jumped the gun. They had wanted the victory without putting in the hard work. Had they really approached the finishing line without having run the race? Now it was almost impossible to retrace their steps and go back to the start. And if they did, would they find anything worth running for?

Think.

She searched her brain. What did they share in common? What brought them together in the first place? Sure, they were physically attracted to each other. They were both adventurous, or at least had been. They loved the outdoors and enjoyed going out for a nice meal. They both had secure jobs and shared a desire to be financially secure. That was great and all, but placing these things aside, what values did they share if these things fell through? What happened to championing the passions inside of them, the ones that set their souls on fire? What about the unconditional love of a family? Children of their own?

Oh god, what if he didn't even want children? How had they not talked about that? Out of all the things, it was something she wanted the most.

They needed counselling.

She couldn't sit back and watch their issues fester a moment longer. Getting through each day without breaking down wasn't an achievement anymore. Something had to shift. Things had to change. Otherwise they would wake up one morning without a single thing binding them together.

Counselling.

The idea terrified her. Counselling meant they had hit rock bottom and just maybe, would anchor there. Counselling sounded like a destination, not a pit stop.

It was a place where all their issues would be brought to light—thrown into the hands of a stranger. Issues they hadn't been able to speak about for years, let alone acknowledge. What if they were just too far gone? She made a mental note to at least suggest it. He will probably laugh in her face, but at this point, she had nothing to lose. She already felt as though she had somewhat lost him.

Her eyes grew heavier as her head span with a storm of questions. The whole thing was exhausting.

WITH A SLAM of a door, she woke. Battering her eyelids, she peered at the clock and caught herself gasp. She had been out for almost two and a half hours. Before she had a chance to process a thing, Patrick appeared at the door. He stood there for a moment, taking in what must have looked strangely odd with a pile of cards sprawled around her as she laid there.

'Are you okay?' He almost looked concerned—*almost*.

She propped herself up onto her elbows. 'Yeah.' She rubbed her eyes. 'I didn't realise how tired I was.'

He nodded slowly, his eyes stopped cold at the tub sitting on the bed. 'What's all this about?' He walked over and began flicking through the cards.

'I was looking for something and came across these ... It's nice to look through them again.'

He nodded again. 'Everyone was very generous, that's for sure. Did we ever send out thank you cards?' He didn't look at her.

'Yeah.' She sat up properly this time and folded her legs under her. 'They went out.'

He smiled. It had to be the most he had given her in weeks. She sent him a little smile back. She wanted to ask him how his night was, but while she had him, she knew it was now or never.

'Looking at these and reflecting back on the happiness that day...' She had no idea if she was going about this the right way or not, but he seemed to be listening. 'And looking at where we are now, I feel as though we've lost our way a bit and think it could be a good idea for us to be open in exploring anything that might help us find that joy again.' She felt breathless as the thump of her heart interfered with every word.

He crossed his arms over his chest and sighed. She leaned in ever so slightly, expecting to take in a beer stained breath. But instead it smelt minty, almost fruity. It was a pleasant surprise and held potential for their conversation to actually lead somewhere this time.

'What are you suggesting?'

'Counselling.'

'Jesus, S.' Hard lines formed on his forehead. 'You've got to be joking.'

It wasn't the reaction she had hoped for, but she had anticipated it. 'I'm really not.' She squeezed her fingers, hyping herself to be brave and continue. 'I think it could be good for us. I know it might sound scary but I know that we'll be able to put everything on the table and work through it all together. We just need a starting point, a bit of guidance. Advice has never hurt anyone. We don't have all the answers, maybe there's strategies we can—'

'No.' He shook his head firmly.

'Patrick—'

'No S. If we have reached the point where we have to rely on some professional who doesn't know a single thing about us to fix our problems then that speaks volumes.' His eyes became fierce, sending a flute of adrenaline through her. 'Their knowledge derives from text books. They'll just give us text book suggestions and text book solutions based on how they perceive and categorise the information we feed them. The only two people who ever know what's going on in a relationship are the two people in the relationship. You and I.

No one else. Not some stupid counsellor who probably chose their career because they couldn't solve their own problems, delusional in thinking that they can solve the problems of others.' He was standing now, clearly done with the discussion.

'Well that's my suggestion.' She threw her hands up, too irritated to let the tears fall. 'What's yours? Or are we going to keep going on like this until we break?'

'We're already broken.' His eyes persisted firmly on hers, holding no emotion. He sighed heavily. 'You know, I was hoping for us to spend some quality time together and work on us before you decided to get up and leave to go to Aringdale for two weeks.'

'One week!' she snapped.

'Well, whatever. You still left when we weren't in a good place.' She couldn't believe what she was hearing. How dare he put that on her like that? How manipulative he was being!

'I have been wanting to fix us but you're up early sneaking into work before I have a chance to open my eyes.'

He was actually *blaming* her.

'And you're always home late! I feel like you're avoiding me completely,' she whimpered. 'And then there's your drinking problem, what are we going to do about that?' She could barely see him through her tears, just enough to catch a glimpse of the outline of his features.

'We don't have to do anything. Maybe I've already been talking to someone about it. If you cared to check in with me once in a while you would already know that. I haven't had a drink all week. Not a single drop. Not since you got back home and ran off to Jacqui's house.' He was shouting now. 'If that's even where you went.'

'Oh ok, so we have trust issues now, do we?' Her fingers were turning blue the way she was squeezing onto them.

He threw his hands up, landing in a loud slap to his sides as they fell melodramatically from the air. 'Fuck off,' he roared, rolling his eyes. 'Well, let's just add that to the list too shall we!' His eyes were fierce on hers, ignoring the tears streaming down her flushed face. He paused for a moment. 'I'm going out,' he muttered and stomped out the bedroom.

'Will you be home later?' she squeaked.

'Don't know.'

With that, the front door slammed behind him. She scrambled off the bed, scooped the cards together and stuffed them back into the box without care. With quivering hands, she climbed the step ladder and pushed them deep back into the cupboard until she couldn't physically see it anymore.

She wandered back to the lounge room and took her cold bowl of dinner and transferred it into a plastic container, and into the fridge. She wasn't hungry.

Her phone was still open to her conversation with Ethan. It was amazing how only a few hours earlier she was laughing, and now, submerged in tears. Not that crying was unusual for her these days, but still. Through the torment of her emotions at an all-time high, she found herself calling Ethan's number. After two rings, he picked up.

'Sienna?'

'You said you wanted to figure me out but it's me that needs to figure myself out,' she gasped, shaking. 'But here you go, you might as well know everything about the girl you once knew. He isn't fighting for us. He hasn't been fighting for years. I don't think I've heard those three words from his mouth for just as long. Maybe he doesn't know how to love me anymore. I don't know what to do, I sure as hell can't talk to him. And when I do, he doesn't listen or respect a single word I have to say. I don't know if he even respects me anymore. He's too busy telling me to fuck off or playing victim for every problem we have. And that's when he's apparently sober. When he's drunk his behaviour is even more erratic. I lied to you Ethan. Extraordinary doesn't even cut it. The only thing that's extraordinary is the mess I'm in.'

'Sienna—' he started again.

'And you should know this too. I've completely changed. I'm not the girl you remember, Ethan. It's best you stay away from me. After a few more conversations you would see that there is so much more going on than I let on. You saw it that night we were in the car and I know you saw it the day you gave me that old letter. You wouldn't have brought it unless you knew something was off. You knew something wasn't right. That's just it, you know what I need before I do. God, maybe I'm the one who needs counselling, not Patrick—'

'Sienna …?' His voice was calm on the other end of the line. Always so calm, always so gentle.

'Yeah?'

'Come home.'

Fifteen

SHE DIDN'T GO home.

Instead, she spent an hour on the phone that night releasing every suppressed feeling while she was so wound up. Although her heart was bleeding, it was somewhat healing to be able to unload the weight of what she felt with Ethan in a way she had so long ago. As always, he listened without judgement and hadn't preached at her. He was disgusted at the words Patrick spoke over her, the way he disrespected her and the control he kept taking advantage of. He wanted to punch the guy when she told him he would often return home drunk and aggressive. He demanded for her to be honest in telling him whether he ever had hurt her in any way. She told him that he hadn't, which was the truth. Not physically anyway. Only emotionally, which in ways she believed was more painful.

He had asked to see her again, to talk through things. But as their phone conversation went on, her emotions learned to settle. They had settled enough to know that she couldn't allow such catch up to happen. Especially after Patrick had accused her that their recent problems stemmed from her little visit home. Her setting off again would only add fuel to the fire, especially when there were trust issues she hadn't realised were there, until now. The call had ended with him letting her know that he was there for her. That she could come to him whenever she needed. The support was comforting, nursing the ache inside of her. They had been words that her soul craved and had carried her through the week.

By the third week of the term, Nolan had completed three sessions with the school counsellor. To her delight, they had actually gone really well. She had asked Nolan if his parents knew about his meetings with Anita after having spent weeks with his aunt Lindsey. He told her when he mentioned it to them they were mad, scorning him for not trying hard enough at school. He even feared that he would be kept down which only made her wonder what the hell his parents were filling his brain with. It was then it occurred to her that they might not have known that Anita was a counsellor, and not a literacy coordinator she had initially told him. When she thought about it, she hadn't been very clear with the details in her futile communication with them as her anticipation of hearing from them became less and less.

In just weeks she had noticed a difference in him—Anita's work proving to be a success. She had implemented the 'Mood Meter' into their sessions. A visual platform that helped kids better manage their emotions, with studies proving an improved mental health and emotional intelligence. At the start of each day, Nolan was encouraged to identify where he sat on the mood meter graph, deciphered by a low to high axis with a corresponding colour. He was prompted to make decisions throughout the day on how he could improve where he was positioned on it, empowering him to take control of his emotions. He had responded well to the program, his confidence and self-awareness noticeably improving. Even his body language began to change. His slumped shoulders became more rounded, his once hanging head, now noticeably lifted. Now that he had become a little more confident, he had become less of a target. Even if he did continue to keep to himself with his head in a book.

But that one, would take time.

It was Thursday afternoon when Miranda showed up at the classroom. It was bucketing down with rain; the bus route Nolan usually took home disrupted with delays due to an accident on the highway. It had made sense for him to be picked up but seeing her lurking by the door had still taken her by surprise.

'Miranda.' She stood from her desk as soon as the woman entered with a distinctive stride to her step.

'Miss Henderson.' Her lips tightened to form a hard line.

'You can call me Sienna.' She made the effort to smile despite her heart being thrown into a flip flop.

'Right.' She darted her eyes around the room before positioning them squarely on hers.

She was dressed no differently from the last time Sienna saw her. Her style the same, distasteful, and in ways inappropriate as her soaked white satin top revealed her black bra underneath. Her face tired, droopy, yet her eyes lacked any hint of submission.

'I'm wanting to talk to you about these sessions Nolan's been having, without our permission too, mind you.' She wasn't wasting any time. She hitched up her tight black leather pants and plonked herself down on a chair.

Sienna took a seat too. 'I have tried everything I can to bring the matter to your attention Mrs. Livingston.' For some reason, using her full name seemed more suitable, formal. Seeing as the matter was precisely that. 'As I briefly mentioned to you earlier in the year, Nolan has been struggling. There have been some issues—'

'There's nothing wrong with my kid.' She lifted her perfectly manicured fingers, cutting her off. 'In today's world, we are creating a generation of psychologically fragile children, protecting them from opportunities to take risks, learn from their mistakes, preventing them from developing a thick skin to face challenges and failures.' She glanced at her nails, frowning as she studied them. 'We are wrapping them in cotton wool, what's happening here is no different,' her tone sure, so certain. She raised her flawless sculpted eyebrows. They were actually quite impressive.

Sienna tried her best to stop staring at them.

'I apologise that my husband and I haven't been around to sit down with you, nodding our heads like robots over this triviality. Ok, so Nolan had a little melt down and ran out of the room as soon as his head went blank. I'm sure it's not an unusual reaction for kids to start giggling if he was standing up there like a stuffed mullet. But running out of class is just a little bit dramatic. I have told you this before that he is over sensitive and needs to grow up. He doesn't need special attention over it. Having someone standing over him, patting his hand, will only feed his insecurity that he is different when other kids in the classroom aren't receiving the same treatment,' she went on, barely taking a breath. 'And I know there are other matters such as your concerns that Nolan is being bullied and that his work is falling short of the standard.'

She finally stopped lecturing, her expression softening ever so slightly. 'I don't mean to sound harsh, and I'm aware that this may be coming off that way. But if you saw how Nolan behaves at home you would understand where I'm coming from. He sits in his room and does nothing but read. We have guests over and he doesn't acknowledge them. He isn't interested in mixing with other kids either. He sits and reads and shakes his head whenever we ask him if he has any homework to do.

'For a long time, we let it go. But then things had to change. He was aware of this, and we were firm about the consequences if he didn't pull his finger out. He needed a kick up the butt and as soon as that happened, he started becoming less sorry for himself.' She tilted her head and sent Sienna a condescending smile. 'Maybe you're seeing that in Nolan now. That he is finally being accountable for his choices and realising he needs to take ownership of his actions. Some responsibility. I'm a big believer that change comes from within. If Nolan is having others make decisions for him, then how will he grow? It will only hinder him. Wouldn't you agree Miss Henderson?'

How this woman could speak such words over her son was beyond mind blowing to Sienna. It took all of her might to contain the rage swirling inside of her. Miranda couldn't be further off the mark.

She gritted her teeth together, forcing her tongue behind them. 'I can assure you that no one is wrapping your son up in cotton wool Mrs Livingston. As a teacher, it is our duty—my duty—to be aware of those students who are facing challenges, whatever they are. It is my responsibility to help identify them and address them the best way I can. Anita has been equipting Nolan with skills to reengage him in learning through self and emotional awareness techniques. "The Mood Meter" that derives from an evidence based approach called "Ruler" has been very beneficial for him.

'This has been transferred into the classroom where Nolan has been able to make better meaning of his learning whilst building emotional intelligence such as understanding, expressing and regulating his emotions. It's more than quick-fix strategies or a bag of tricks. It is a purposeful, philosophical, and ethical code of conduct and that's what we are trying to do with Nolan. We want to support him with skills that will benefit him beyond the classroom.' She sat up straighter and tried to stay composed. 'This positive learning framework provides a basis for us to develop a management plan that assist students, like Nolan, to develop a quality learning environment that is nurturing and accommodating to the needs of the student. No student is the same, therefore our approach can differ depending on the child.'

She took a breath, relieved to see that Miranda was beginning to tune in even if she did have a blank expression on her face. 'The change we're seeing in Nolan is a reflection of the work that has been invested in him. I don't believe for a moment that neglecting the issue by telling him to "harden up" will help him in any way, or provide him with the skills he needs.

'I can assure you that we are not signaling him out or making him feel as though he is any different from the other children. Nolan does not receive any special treatment nor is treated any differently than the other children. I'm not sure whether there is something going on at home that could be potentially contributing to—'

'Excuse me?' Miranda's eyes narrowed, her tone switching to one of defense.

Sienna knew then that she had crossed thin ice.

'To my understanding, your work commitments are quite demanding and I am aware Nolan spends a fair bit of time on his own and more recently, with his aunt. He has expressed to me that he feels as though you are often disappointed in him when I know he is so desperate to please you—'

'This is just absurd.' She threw her head back towards the ceiling. She took a dramatic breath and brought her head forward again. 'I hope you aren't questioning our fondness for our son.'

Fondness?

Even her choice of word made her stomach clench. She wondered in that moment if they even loved him.

She couldn't see it.

'That's not what I'm saying at all. I wanted to check in to see if there were any outside factors that I need to be aware of in order to gain a better understanding of Nolan,' answered Sienna, warily. She considered bringing up the information she did know. But she quickly decided against it. Miranda didn't need to know about her conversation with Lindsey. The last thing she wanted was to give her another reason to be upset with her.

With Miranda so focused on her eyes she hoped that this was the moment where she finally got some answers.

'We've both recently been in Los Angeles for work which I'm sure you know about because Nolan stayed with his aunt, my ... sister. I can't see how that could possibly be a deterrent to Nolan's self-confidence, staying with a family member for a couple of weeks. He had a ball,' she responded sarcastically. A reaction far too animated to be genuine. It was although she was trying hard to hide something. It killed Sienna that she didn't know what. All she knew was the woman sitting opposite her wasn't fit to be a mother.

She was a monster.

She needed to be more assertive, firmer.

'Mrs. Livingston, I'm sorry if anything I'm saying is being misinterpreted as an attack on you, or your parenting, as that is not my intention. I'm just wanting to have an open conversation with you about your son's progress at school. In all honesty, I'm concerned at what appears to be a lack of acknowledgement on your behalf of what's going on when Nolan needs a support—'

'There's nothing I don't accept here Miss Henderson. I'm not by any means disregarding Nolan's difficulties, I'm just merrily stating the fact that the whole counselling thing is not necessary. Anyway, I'm not sure what good it will all do when we are moving soon.'

The knot in Sienna's stomach tightened. 'You're moving?'

A pleasant smile tugged at the corner of her full, red lips. Miranda nooded. 'Yes. Stuart has landed a once in a lifetime offer with American airlines so we'll be moving to Los Angeles late September, early October at the latest. Still working out all the logistics,' she said with a matter of fact tone.

'How does Nolan feel about this?'

The frown from earlier spread wide across her face. 'I don't know yet, it's not really his decision to make. It's not a nine-year old's call to be honest, to approve or disapprove a decision made best for the family.'

Her sarcasm made her want to punch the woman square in the face. How could pulling Nolan out in the middle of the school term and throwing him into an entirely different school system half way across the world be what was best for him? It would be completely disruptive and would unravel all the progress he had made. She wanted to scream it to her, but she knew it wasn't her place to voice it. As badly as she wanted to, as much as Miranda needed to hear it.

Her silence only encouraged her to rattle on further.

'We're planning to sit down with him on Saturday. Nolan loves the U.S, he always wished he was born there. You know, he loves the snow, pretzels, curly fries, candy, squirrels, the whole thing. It will be like a giant playground for him. We have no concerns how he'll settle. Nolan has learned to adapt. He has moved so many times already with fost …' Her face changed as though she had already said too much.

But in a flash, it was gone.

Sienna wanted to focus on whatever it was that stopped her from finishing her sentence but all she could think about was Nolan's comment about him never having flown before. Why did she feel like something seriously wasn't adding up?

'Anyway … I don't need to justify any of this to you. I just thought as his teacher you should have an idea of our movements. It's all very fresh and new, but it has been decided.' Her eyes thinned again. 'Just like I had the right to know that Nolan was seeing a bloody counselor behind our backs. Still not impressed with that.'

Sienna was certain this impossible woman just wanted to pick a fight.

'We did everything we could to inform you about that,' her words came slow. Her mind was still on the comment before that had been cut short. Had Nolan moved around a lot, handled back and forth between foster homes? How old was he when this happened and why hadn't he mentioned it to her when he had been open about everything else? Was there a chance that Miranda and Stuart didn't treat him with the love and care he deserved because there was a possibility they weren't his parents? It was Nolan's first year at the school so it made sense if he had moved around.

A wave of nausea formed inside of her.

Then there was the thought that terrified her the most. What if the Livingstons weren't really moving to Los Angeles but were palming Nolan off to another family? What if the conversation that sent Nolan to stay with his aunt was entirely made up, that he never was adopted in the first place? What if Lindsey wasn't in fact his aunt at all, but a potential adoption prospect? Surely Nolan wouldn't have played along with all of that? Come to think of it, he looked nothing like the woman. But they did share the same surname. And what was all that crap about Nolan loving America? His favourite country was Poland. That was what he had told her.

Miranda abruptly dismissed herself shortly after. It all had been a blur as Sienna walked her out, her mind spinning with a million scenarios playing over in her head.

She knew something wasn't right. She knew it, and the uneasiness inside of her confirmed it. Her intuition was too strong to ignore, yet she seemed to have done just that—ignored the situation as it snowballed into a million of possibilities before her. The whole thing didn't make sense, and she was itching to get to the bottom of it. But she knew that there was little she could do, little she could say. The hypotheticals would just have to stew in her mind for now.

Even if there were far too many unanswered questions.

SHE WAS HOME at a decent time. A good forty-five minutes before Patrick, given he wasn't out late drinking again, or at a 'work meeting'. This gave her enough time to prepare dinner and have it served, warm and ready to go as soon as he stepped through the door.

Just the way he expected it.

Tonight's meal was easy to prepare. Minestrone soup with baked potatoes. Although she wouldn't eat the potatoes.

Far too many calories.

As the soup boiled away, she turned on her laptop and jumped onto *Pinterest*, An app she often used to inspire her with creative classroom ideas. She logged on, her eyes drawn to the beautiful ivory gowns she had pinned under a board titled 'Wedding'. She hadn't updated it in almost two years. She scrolled through the dresses she once admired, surprising herself at how quickly her taste has changed. It was amazing what could happen in the space of two years.

Or even a week, if she was really honest.

The thought disheartened her. It proved to her over again that nothing stayed the same and how quickly things could change—how quickly life could change. How certain you can be about something, then not.

She clicked the X on the screen to shut down the window. She wasn't going to torture herself with pictures of dresses that in the five years they had been engaged, hadn't been any closer to trying on. Instead she opened her photos folder. The last album she uploaded had been over twelve months ago. She used to take photos all the time, documenting every moment, no matter how big or small. Looking at the blonde, wide eyed girl smiling back at her as she scrolled through felt as though she was prying into the life of someone else.

She stumbled across a folder labelled 'old stuff'. Hundreds of unordered images loaded all at once, all ungrouped. Her attention was drawn to a picture of a seventeen-year-old version of herself, standing in front of a red Ute. Next to her was Ethan as an eighteen-year-old, his mop of brown hair positioned in loose curls on his head, his crooked smile young and alive. She clicked into it, allowing the picture to fill the screen. He was dressed in a red and black footy jersey with tiny shorts exposing his long muscular legs. Like in all their photos together, her arm hung around his shoulder as his arm wrapped around her waist, holding her in close.

She remembered the day their picture was taken. It was about seven months before she made the move to the city. Footy season had just started up and she had just come back from her audition for the National State Ballet School. She had been broken up with Brody for a few months, Ethan and Sadie by a month or two.

Even the timing of that had been weird.

He had wanted to drive her to her audition as he had a new Ute and wanted to give it a decent go on the road and all, but had a game scheduled for the same day. They had arranged to catch up when she got back that night. It had been sunset when he took her out on the dirt plains out the back of his parents' two-acre property, back before the cottage had been built. She remembered the feeling of freedom as they zoomed up and over the dunes, the windows down, the cold wind slapping her face like ice. Their laughter had drowned out the roar of the engine as they took off as though they were racing in a dune buggy through the Las Vegas desert. She hadn't recalled a time where she had felt as audacious as she did when she took the wheel and with the guidance of Ethan's hand on hers, drove in erratic patterns until the sun set in brilliant shades of orange, red, yellow and violet around them.

She should have known then. The way his hand stayed on hers the entire time they shared that moment together.

She should have known when he invited her to stay for dinner, then for supper.

She should have known when he took her to the Ed Sheeran concert a few weeks after that. Free tickets he had told her.

Were they really?

It was a short time after that when she had crawled back to Brody. Stupid move that had been. It was only a month after that where he had cheated again. And they broke up, again. The cheating hadn't surprised her, well not really. She hadn't balled her eyes out or locked herself up in her room with a tub of ice-cream like all the movies say to. But by the second time she had completely emotionally removed herself from him. The whole getting back together had been a thing of comfort, security, even if she was emotionally removed. Yet her stupidity had cost her the one fleeting opportunity she had with Ethan.

The man who could have possibly, been it.

Ting.

She took her phone and unlocked it. Talk about timing. It was from Ethan. Her heart accelerated as she opened the message.

> **Hey you!**
> **Looks like work is calling me out of Aringdale**
> **and into your hood for a 6-week project.**
> **Would love to see you if you have the time.**
> **Think of you often, hoping you're alright.**

Just like that, the weight of the world lifted from her and she was back in his Ute again. With windows down, the wind in her hair, wild and free as they drove over the dirt dunes and into the sunset.

Sixteen

I T WAS THE weekend again.

What a shame it was that she dreaded them so much. It was the two days a week where neither of them had work to distract them. Time they were forced to spend time together. Well, that's how it felt anyway.

Forced.

At least lunch at Nancy's would suck up a good hour or two of the day. He would order the steak burger and she would order the warm chicken salad, the way they usually did.

If it had been Ethan opposite her, she would have ordered the carbonara with a side of haloumi, even if the two didn't go together.

Enough.

She stepped in the shower and let the warm water rinse away the negative thoughts. In order to have a chance of a functional day together, she had to first change her mindset. She dried herself off and took a glimpse of herself in the mirror as she stepped out. Her bony collarbones were protruding like drum sticks from the base of her neck, her twiggy arms closely resembling chicken legs. She inched her face closer to the mirror and rubbed the steam from the glass. Even her face looked gaunt, lifeless. Her jawline was as prominent as ever. She looked like a lollipop. An alien even. No wonder Patrick never touched her anymore.

She was ugly.

She dragged the scales out from under the basin and positioned her two feet onto them. Forty-six and a half kilos. It was the smallest she had been in years. Probably since her mid-teens. She stepped off them and pushed it back where she found them. She was clearly underweight. So why did Patrick feel the need to monitor her so persistently? He always had to have control over everything she did. Probably as for years now, he had lost control over himself.

She dried herself off and slipped into a pair of skinny jeans and a knitted turtle neck sweater. Even her jeans were too big for her as they hung off her tiny waist, her stomach almost concave when she looked down at it. How had she not noticed this before? She wrapped her towel around her and with damp feet pattering the floorboards, she walked back to their room.

Patrick was out for a morning jog, which wasn't unusual. He was either running off his hangover, in his study smashing down beers in preparation for the next hangover, or out with the boys drinking some more again.

But the past week had been different.

He had been out late but hadn't come home drunk. Sure, he was still cooped up in his study on the rare occasion he was home, but without the beer cans stacked up. Even the fridge was free from them. It was weird to see the bottom shelve so empty. She should have felt relieved, pleased, optimistic. After all, it had been a skeleton hanging over their relationship. A burden that they hadn't been able to free from.

So why did she feel as though nothing had lifted?

She should be happy. This was progress. Maybe today would be different.

She spent a little more time than usual on her makeup, attempting to hide the shadowed rings under her eyes. She didn't apply blush— she didn't need to make her cheekbones stick out any more than they already did. She dried her hair, allowing her soft blonde waves to frame her face, falling just below her shoulders.

There. Much better. Now she didn't look like a deadbeat.

Patrick was quick to notice the extra effort she had put into her appearance.

'You look nice,' he complimented her, walking in with his earphones still intact, music blasting away.

There was hope after all.

She smiled and for the first time in a long time, it genuinely filled her face.

SHE WAS SITTING on their bed crossed legged, flicking through a magazine when he returned from the shower, the smell of his after shave filled the room.

'How was your run?'

He took a pair of socks from the draw and slipped them on his feet. 'Yeah, felt good. Definitely ready to eat something though.'

Things had been strained between them, even more so after the way the counselling conversation had gone down the weekend before. But as usual, they had swept it under the carpet along with the rest of their aborted conversations and carried on existing.

He sat on the edge of the bed and leaned in towards her, squeezing her sides where her skin buckled at the waist line of her jeans. There was nothing on her, just skin and bone. Yet the caved position she was in still managed to form the smallest muffin top. He grabbed hold of them and sent them a series of quick, deliberate squeezes.

Squeezes of condemnation.

She looked at him, her smile slowly fading from one smeared wide on her face just minutes ago. He raised his eyebrows at her and without saying anything, stood to his feet.

'I'm ready when you are.' He continued to get ready as she flipped through the magazine, unable to focus on a single word as the soppy love stories—no matter how fake—stirred her misery.

Any optimism she had for a good day were dwindling fast.

As usual, Nancy Green's was spewing with people, with little chance of reserving their usual table. Not that a seat changed anything. If anything, it had only brought them bad luck so far.

Jeremy wasn't working which had to be a first. He had apparently flown to Cairns for his niece's wedding. Everyone was getting married these days.

Everyone but them.

They were seated by the door accompanied by the draft shooting an uncomfortably shot of wind every time the bell tingled, and the door opened. As predicted, he ordered the steak burger and she ordered the warm chicken salad. Which was fine. It still tasted amazing even though Jeremy hadn't prepared it. If anything, it was a slightly bigger serving which was a good thing as a handful of lettuce and the strip or two of chicken rarely filled her.

They discussed work as though they were two colleagues sitting in on a business meeting. She updated him on the Nolan saga and he talked about recruiting a new team for some upcoming six-month project. What the contract entailed, she had no idea as she kept zoning in and out on the conversation on the table opposite them.

A couple were talking about a wedding expedition that was taking place this weekend. An expo she was very familiar with, one that took place three times every year in Melbourne, Sydney and Brisbane.

And she hadn't been to a single one of them.

Fifteen Melbourne expos she had missed over the years. Her sister had bought a ticket for her once, but she had somehow double booked herself on that day and the ticket had been wasted.

The woman was going on about how she had been sent an extra set of tickets and didn't know what to do with them. She kept turning the envelope in her hands as her and the man she was with brainstormed potential recipients.

She was a deserving candidate, surely? Shame she didn't have a clue who the girl was otherwise she might have put her hand up.

Before she had a chance to pretend she was listening and come up with a convincing response to Patrick's ramble, she excused herself to the bathroom, breaking the momentum of the one-sided conversation.

She closed the door to her toilet cubicle and rested her back against the cold cement wall. She took out her phone for the first time that morning and scrolled through the thread of messages between her and Ethan. She hadn't brought up anything to do with her dysfunctional relationship since that Thursday night—he hadn't mentioned it either. Their messages had been light, filled with an overload of emojis and playful banter. It was innocent enough, being careful that what she sent couldn't be interpreted as anything more than friendship. She could understand if their words were read aloud, people would question the connection they shared. She found herself holding back at times, hitting the backspace key on words her heart desperately wanted to free. But she wouldn't enter such dangerous territory. Her heart would remain somewhat hidden and it would stay that way. But even her holding back it still didn't take away the fuzzy feeling she got with every message that came through from him. It was although after all this time, they were best friends again.

A friendship that picked up right where it left off, nine years ago.

He was due to arrive in Lilydale the next day and would stay at his cousin's house over the six-week period while he completed renovating in the area. They had arranged to have dinner on the Wednesday night. The one night where she didn't have a late finish at school. She hadn't told Patrick about it yet. There was a good chance she would be back before he got home anyway, considering he was always out doing whatever it was that he did after hours.

She no longer wanted to ask.

Maybe he wouldn't even question how she filled her night. Not that she would have to lie about anything, there was nothing really to hide. She would tell him. Wouldn't she?

She flushed the toilet and made her way to the basin. The woman with the tickets was by the hand dryer, smiling at Sienna's reflection through the mirror.

'You look familiar.'

'I think you might be sitting next to me,' Sienna replied with a smile, taking a paper towel from the dispenser.

'Possibly! But it's not that, I think I've seen you before. Your face rings a bell.'

Sienna searched her memory. Was the woman a parent from school? A friend of Patrick's?

Nothing came to mind.

'Devoted, loyal regular?'

'Used to be! Although making more of an effort now,' she joked. The woman lifted her finger knowingly. 'Sadie!'

The blood drained from her face. Was she a friend of Sadie's? She hadn't heard or spoken to her old friend in years.

'You know Sadie?'

The woman shook her head and took her handbag from the bench. 'No, I was trying to remember what your name was. I've been away with work, but I remember there being a celebration or something here years ago. Everyone was congratulating you. An engagement or something?'

'Yeah. Good memory.' She felt as though the story wasn't even hers to tell, as though it was never hers to begin with. 'The owner of this cafe put together something for my partner and I.' She sighed feeling a familiar waft of sadness over her.

Jeremy had hung a big silver banner along the back wall of the café, behind their usual table, filling the room with helium balloons that covered the ceiling. The staff had brought out a ginormous chocolate ripple cake, big enough to feed a small army. It had easily fed everyone in the cafe that afternoon, with leftovers stored in their freezer for weeks after.

'I'm Sienna,' she finally said.

The woman didn't seem to notice the smile drop from her face. 'Sienna, that's it! How was your wedding? Was it everything you imagined it to be?'

She wanted to run at the very reference of the word.

'Nice to meet you too. No wedding yet, but it's on its way.'

The woman didn't flinch, or ask any questions. Instead, she rummaged through her bag and took out the envelope from earlier. 'Here, have these.' She extended it towards her.

Sienna accepted sheepishly.

'There's a wedding expo at Exhibition this weekend. I don't know where you're at with your planning process, but just in case you're interested. I was sent an extra set.' Her kind smile made it impossible for Sienna to say no.

'That's really lovely of you, thanks.'

The woman nodded and sent her another smile before disappearing out the door.

Sienna didn't even catch her name.

After catching up on a few messages, she left the bathroom and made her way over to thank the woman again for her generosity. But by the time she neared the table she realised that they had left and their table had been cleared.

She hovered by the counter looking in as Patrick engaged in what looked like a flirty conversation with a passing customer. She was taken back by his sudden liveliness, the way his eyes lit up, laughing in a way he no longer did with her. The girl was pretty, with short, chopped, blonde hair dressed in the latest fashion. Her hip was cocked to one side, a hand on her hip, the other flouncing side to side as he chatted with her. She looked taken by him.

Of course, she was. Patrick was a head turner, and apparently, a womanizer too.

She should have felt jealous. Not because he was talking to another woman, but because of the way he was with her. It was then that she realised she had lost him. For his eyes glistened at the pretty blonde in the same way they had once glistened at her.

He casually picked up his phone to show her something. The woman leaned over to view it. Whatever was on there must have either been cute or funny by the way the woman's flouncing hand covered her mouth as she giggled some more.

Suddenly the tickets in her hand felt like a complete joke.

She walked over to her fiancé and stood behind the back of her chair, waiting for an introduction. He ignored her, keeping his smile steady as he conveniently waved the woman goodbye. The woman returned a playful wave, also ignoring Sienna as though she was invisible.

'What's this?' His eyes were fixed on the envelope she didn't realise she was now clenching.

'Who was that?'

'Louisa. Brad's partner,' he responded a little too quickly.

She had no idea who Brad was. She narrowed her eyes, watching him exchange another little wave as the woman walked out the door.

His eyes eventually focused back on her. 'What's this?' he repeated, taking the envelope from her hands, uncovering the tickets.

'Wedding expo,' she said, observing his muted expression. 'A woman in the bathroom just handed me them. She recognised me from a few years ago and asked if I was interested, noticing my ring.' It wasn't exactly the truth, but she wasn't about to explain how the conversation went down. She took a seat. It was probably a dumb idea to have accepted them. Not when they had issues to sort through first before attempting to fit with the hundreds of newly engaged couples in their little love bubble of happiness.

Especially when theirs had popped a long time ago.

His eyes inspected the square invitation. 'This weekend?'

'Yep. ' She fiddled anxiously with her hands in her lap. She was waiting for the quiet explosion, a hiss of aggression—one or the other.

'Did you want to go today?'

She almost fell backwards off her chair. Her heart pounded inside her ears, the world around her zooming in as lens narrowed and focused its position on the man before her.

'Yeah … sure, that would be nice … I have always wanted to go,' she stuttered.

Suddenly she forgot about the woman with the short cropped blonde hair and allowed his smile to smooth over the broken fragments of her heart.

Because this time, his ocean blue eyes were glistening at her.

SHE DIDN'T KNOW why he said yes, why he agreed to spend the next two and a half hours at an exhibition that represented everything he had resisted for the past five years. Yet, for the first time the very essence that had pushed them apart, seemed to have brought them together that afternoon.

To some extent anyhow.

It had been a long time since they had been out together like a normal couple. They didn't really talk, laugh or play, but he did take hold of her hand tight enough and long enough to make her palms all sweaty.

Upon arrival, they were asked to fill out a raffle for the chance to win a ten-thousand-dollar voucher towards their 'big day', along with fifteen hundred dollars' worth of flower catering. One of the questions asked for the date of their wedding. She had scribbled down a random date and stuffed into the box.

The exhibition had been set up in three rows comprising of countless stalls extending over a hundred metres in length. From venues, cars, flowers, dresses, cakes, photography, right down to the finest details—the event had it all.

It had been the first time she had seen everything in the flesh, under one roof. It made her feel as though they were newly engaged, looking at it all for the first time. Although there was some truth in that, it actually was her first time experiencing it all.

She couldn't help but notice the leap of excitement bound through her as she tasted samples of red velvet and the lemon meringue cake. Luckily the portions were so tiny, she didn't need to worry about Patrick slapping her hand away. Her excitement only intensified as they took a seat and watched the runway models strut down the catwalk in the most exquisite bridal gowns she had ever seen.

Passing the bridal stalls, she had spotted the dress that had caught her attention on Sydney Road, months ago. It was a stunning strapless, ivory gown with crystals and lace decorating the bodice, with a silk train delicately falling just below the hips. Women were lining up everywhere, conversing with the sale assistants as they set up their appointment times for dress fittings at the many neighboring stores. She had wanted to join the queue. She wanted to book in the appointment she had anticipated for years. But where their relationship stood at this particular point in time, it was an appointment that illogically, was still too premature to make.

They hadn't looked at suits, nor had they looked closely at photographers, wedding cakes, cars or a venue for that matter. She had spotted at least five or six of the venues from the top ten list she had made. She knew every detail about them all—the setup, the menu, the cost per head, the alcohol packages, the inclusions. She could have been mistaken as an employee there, her knowledge was that solid. She had had years of dissecting each one of them. She was basically an expert.

She had been discrete in throwing the flyers into their brown show bag as they strolled through. She wasn't sure if Patrick had noticed, his eyes scurrying left and right as they weaved through the crowd. If he had, he hadn't reacted.

Which she put down as a good thing.

It wasn't until they were walking back to the car later that afternoon where he continued to surprise her.

'I've thought about it and I think we could give counselling a go,' his tone sure, decided.

She squeezed his hand. 'Are you sure you're open to it? I mean after everything you said—'

'I know what I said.' He sounded annoyed to have been questioned. 'But surely it can't hurt us.'

She nodded. 'Did you want me to set an appointment up for us?' He shook his head, his face suddenly stern. 'I'll look into it this week. Let me do some research first.'

With that he took out his phone and for the first time that afternoon. For a moment she was impressed that he was on it already, researching counsellors. But as she caught his face dissolve into a devious grin as his fingers tapped away, she felt suspicion build inside her all over again. She parted her lips, wanting to ask him what was so humorous, wanting him to share whatever it was that lit his face. But closed her mouth before he had the chance to shut her down.

Maybe she imagined it, the way he intentionally angled his phone away from her eyes. But within seconds he had slipped his phone back into his pocket and took her hand again.

Why was she being so insecure? She could understand it any other day, but not today. Not when they had this amazing afternoon together. Well, at least a functional one. If anything, the success of the day stirred a motivation to fight for all she felt close to giving up on. They had a long way to go. She knew that. But she wasn't going to give up on the man who had looked at her today with glistening eyes.

Just when she thought they wouldn't look at her that way again. There was a hope in that single moment. It was the hope she needed for the long road ahead. He hadn't had a drink in a week, he had complimented her on her appearance, agreed to join her at the wedding expo. And miraculously, was open to counselling. These were huge steps forward.

And she wasn't going to do anything that would jeopardise any of it.

As they reached the car, it was her turn to angle her phone from him as she opened up a new message and cancelled her plans with Ethan.

Seventeen

S HE COULDN'T SHAKE him if she tried.

He was in Lilydale, closer to her than he had been in years. She couldn't help but wonder what he got up to when the sun went down each day in a suburb where he knew no one. Or why her phone stopped tinging with messages from him when they were just a short drive apart. Did he not think about her the same way her mind was sent in a constant frenzy every time he entered hers?

What was she doing? She was an engaged woman and Ethan was nothing but a friend. Something inside of her craved his presence, his attention, his company.

The whole thing was ridiculous.

And wrong.

Cancelling their plans to catch up was the right thing to do. But somehow nothing felt right about his silence from that day forward. She had grown fondly accustomed to his messages, enjoying the rush of adrenaline that came from being in contact with him. She could understand why he had backed off, why he had created distance between them a second time. Friendship was one thing but trying to salvage a friendship with an old flame, was another. Just as she suspected, it wouldn't work. It couldn't work. Not from her side anyway. Not when her feelings were electrified at the very thought of him, suppressing the throb in her heart all at the same time.

In a sense, Ethan was like a drug to her. Although now, the effects had worn off and the pain had set back in.

She thought things with Patrick would have changed. She had honestly believed they would. The way his eyes had found their way back to hers, the way he squeezed her hand tight, had all been convincing.

Or maybe it had all been an illusion.

But why? Why would he all of a sudden want to try and then not follow through? It had been over a week now—close to two in fact. From the way things looked, they were no closer to the counselling session they so desperately needed to book in. When she had gently asked about it, he had told her he was still reviewing potential places, making out he had made some sort of a short list. At this rate, their first appointment would take place within the same length as their engagement.

Or maybe it would never happen.

And truth be told, she wasn't too fussed. She had no desire to press the topic further. Deep down she hoped that as long as the whole scheduling of their sessions were in Patrick's hands, in his control, the better. It meant she finally had something over his head for their next argument. Something she could use against him, as malicious as that sounded.

But not only that, she was scared.

What if Patrick had been right about them being broken? What if the psychologist only confirmed it? What if they were too far gone? She wasn't ready to hear it.

Not even after five years of turmoil.

Besides, she doubted things would actually come to that. Couple therapy wasn't designed for relationships to come to an end, but designed to pick up the broken pieces and find a way to put them back together.

Their case would be no different because Patrick wouldn't give up on her. The same way she wouldn't give up on him.

It was really that simple when she put it like that.

THEY HAD A dinner reservation for six thirty. There was no special occasion, just an outing she hoped would rekindle the hope their relationship had sparked. Her choices were limited, with most cuisines not being an option with their excessive calories. She had booked a table at a Vietnamese restaurant a stone's throw away from Patrick's work. Apparently, his colleagues all raved about it and considering it was a week night, it made it convenient for him to get to. Patrick seemed more than happy about it, giving her a kiss on the cheek on her way out the door that morning assuring her he was looking forward to their evening together.

She had pottered around the house after work that afternoon, not quite sure what to do with herself. She wasn't used to having a spare moment to herself and felt guilty for it. In order to fill time, she had taken out the cleaning products for the third time that week and performed a spring clean of the apartment. Within an hour she had the place looking immaculate. Even more so than before. She then sorted through her wardrobe making a pile of clothes she hadn't worn, placing them into boxes to donate to Salvation Army, then threw out old shoe boxes that were taking up valuable space.

It was by the third box where she stumbled across her old journals. She had no idea why she had stored them there, of all places—perhaps she had run out of boxes when they moved last. There had been four or five different journals covering the years 2007 to 2010.

She opened the journal with the orange hardcover, remembering it being the most recent, and turned to the last page.

March 28th 2010

It's after midnight. Ethan turned up at my apartment tonight, out of nowhere. I hadn't seen him in months. Not since December last year where we awkwardly stared at each other from opposite rows at the Christmas eve carols service in Passel's park.

Anyway, he showed up with lemon chicken risotto, knowing quite well it's my all-time favorite dish. He kept hugging me, finding opportunities to hold my hand and stuff. Whenever I asked him what he was doing here he kept telling me that he missed our friendship and that it was his duty as my big brother, to make sure I was ok. That annoyed me. I don't want to be his 'little sis', I want him to love me the way I love him. I want it so badly that after a couple of pineapple vodka cruisers, I told him exactly that. I told him I loved him and it had been that way before I got him and Sadie together.

The next thing I know he kisses me and then I kiss him, empty bottles are going everywhere and I'm full of hope. Then he does a complete 180 and tells me he has to go and that 'he can't' and that he loves me as a friend and doesn't want to do anything that will wreck our friendship. He caught a taxi to his cousin's house about an hour ago and I'm left here in tears. Thank god Katie isn't home, I would die if I had to explain it to her.

I'm so mad at him. I feel so mislead, so deceived. He wouldn't have come here if he didn't think there was potential for us, if he didn't feel the same. Looks like I have stuffed things up between us, big time. I'm so humiliated, I deleted his number just now and everything. Immature and dramatic of me, I know. I'll probably regret it, but I feel like I can't face him ever again.

It all hurts like hell.

She squeezed her eyes shut, the memory so vivid as though it happened just yesterday. She remembered how distraught she had felt that night and the months following. Losing Ethan had felt as painful as a death. In a way, it had been just that. A death of a friendship, her identity dying shortly not long after.

Staying at his parents' house that September and sleeping in his old room had been the last straw. Every single detail about being home had reminded her of him, with every landmark and tradition, no matter how small, holding some sort of sentimental value. Even the fresh country air reminded her of the days where they would take his parents' canoes out on Lake Lingfield whenever there was a hint of sun. Her trips home became scarcer after that, once a month, then once a term. After meeting Patrick two years later, her visits became even less frequent. Once a semester, to once a year, gradually plummeting as she transformed into the person she was today.

Whoever *that* was.

She glanced at her watch. 6:22. She snapped the journal shut, stuffed it back into the box and buried it behind her mountain of shoes. The restaurant was a good twenty minutes away, she would be late. She was never late. The thought made her panic. She sent a quick message to Patrick, letting him know that she would be ten minutes late as she flew down the stairs.

Traffic had been kind, she had missed peak hour and managed to avoid every red light. Not quite understanding her frazzled state, she followed the waiter to their reservation. Patrick hadn't even arrived yet. She pulled out her phone, noticing he hadn't replied to her text either. She exhaled, allowing her body to relax as she took a menu and sat down. She allowed the tranquil melody from the talented pianist smooth over her edginess.

Why was she so on edge anyway?

She opened the leather-bound menu and ran her eyes over the fancy dishes; *Muc rang muoi, Banh gan, Cari ga*⊠—she had no idea what she was reading.

Where was the English translation?

She skimmed her eyes around the room. The place was fancy. She was underdressed, her white jeans and black turtleneck distasteful against the formal attire everyone around her were clothed in.

Anxiety began to circle inside her again.

She had all this time and hadn't bothered to do her research. Patrick would be arriving any minute in his navy business suit, making her look like more of an embarrassment. He would find a way to have a go at her for sure, amplifying how inadequate she already felt. She sighed, her eyes not having moved from the foreign words in front of her. Maybe if she googled the dishes to get some sort of understanding of what she would be eating, she would feel as though she somewhat belongs at a restaurant like this. She took her phone again and refreshed her web page. At the same time, a text came through.

Can you cancel? Been held back at work. Meet you at home in a couple of hours.

Sorry?

Hot tears prickled in her eyes. Was he serious?

'Madam, can I entice you with a beverage while you wait for your guest?'

She looked up at the waiter who had wheeled in a neatly presented array of wine and champagne.

She blinked back the tears and smiled. 'That would be lovely, thank you. What do you recommend?'

He selected a bottle from the silver trolley and began a rehearsed sales pitch. His voice quickly turned to white noise against her paralyzing thoughts. Her ears however, sharp enough to prick up at familiar words like *'Vintage', 'Moet'* and *'Chandon'*, so she agreed before he had the chance to finish. It wasn't until she opened the bill half an hour later where she had a mild heart attack at the damage.

$106.53.

That was one expensive glass of champagne.

Probably the most expensive glass she had ever had, and Patrick would lose his head over it. It was a shame she wasn't able to appreciate it as an anger intensified with every costly sip. Without a slither of remorse, she opened her purse and placed her card on the receipt. She hated that the waiter looked on with sympathetic eyes as she finished her drink alone, before waltzing away with her card to take care of the bill.

In a blink of an eye, every insecurity and worry weighing her down, lifted. She suddenly didn't care that she was dressed for the pub as she swung her handbag over her shoulder and marched out of the restaurant with a poise she could hardly own—given the elaborate setting. She was sick of being disappointed, sick of the never-ending supply of tears, sick of wanting to be wanted. What could be so important at work that couldn't wait? How had he not had the decency to let her know ahead of time? She read the text again as she slid into the car, her head spinning madly as she fastened her seatbelt.

He wasn't sorry at all, he didn't even care.

The next thing she knew, she made a turn right instead of left and pulled up out the front of Cortex Consulting. She turned off the engine and casted her eyes over the carpark in hope to locate his black BMW. It was now 7:26 p.m, and the only cars that remained were the ones that belong to the cleaners. She drove around the back, then along the streets bordering the building. His car was nowhere to be seen.

He wasn't there.

He lied.

She was tempted to call him then but didn't trust that she would be upfront with him. She didn't trust that she would actually say everything she wanted to. He would come home eventually and when he did, she would give him a piece of her mind. Well, that was the way she saw it in her head even if it wouldn't play out that way. She hovered her finger over his name in her call list. It took everything inside of her to resist hitting his name on the screen. Instead, she scrolled down a bit further and called the one person whose face refused to leave her mind. After seven rings she reached his voicemail.

'Hi, you have reached Ethan Kahler, sorry I'm unable to take your call right now. Please leave your name and number I will return your call as soon as I can.'

She took a breath. 'Hi Ethan, it's Sienna. Just want to let you know that I'm completely in love with you and we should run away together, get married and live happily ever after.'

Thankfully she hung up before the beep and didn't voice a word of it. Not that she meant it anyway. She was just upset, yearning for the comfort of her oldest friend whom she hadn't heard from in weeks.

And it felt like an eternity.

After stopping off at Macca's to slam down a large double cheeseburger meal and an apple pie, she decided to go home. She spotted the familiar BWM as she squeezed into the narrow parking lot beside it. She didn't know what caused her to feel more ill; the fact that he was home, or the burger that nested uneasily in the pit of her stomach. She felt herself almost running up the stairs, adrenaline driving her every step as she turned the key and swung open the front door. After a couple of very heavy strides she found him in the lounge room sprawled out on the couch, his feet resting casually on the coffee table, shirt untucked, laughing through a phone conversation. She leaned against the door frame watching him, her eyes raging. He seemed to have read her body language and ended the phone call swiftly.

'You look pissed.' He lowered his feet to the floor.

She didn't budge, not even a little bit. 'It would have been nice to have known you wouldn't be there so I wasn't sitting alone, dateless.'

'We were called into a meeting and I didn't have my phone on me. I let you know as soon as I could.'

Bullshit.

'But you're home now.'

'And?'

'We could have done a later dinner somewhere.'

'We still can if you want.'

'I've already eaten.' She threw her hand bag down on the coffee table with a little more force than she intended and turned for the kitchen.

He took her arm before she had a chance to brush past. 'What do you mean you've already eaten?' His grip held a possessiveness she no longer wanted to tolerate.

She shook him off. 'While I was there I thought I might as well go ahead and order the banquet. Your friends were right, the food there is incredible.'

He just stared at her.

She inhaled. She couldn't hold down this lie. 'Ok, so I just ordered a glass of wine and left as the waiter pitied me for being stood up. I went to Macca's.'

He looked disgusted. 'You went to *Macca's*?'

She nodded confidently. It felt good, actually. 'Where did you go?' She felt as though she had every right to ask.

'What?'

'I stopped by your work on the way home, you weren't there.' There, she said it.

His lips buckled together. She could almost see the stream emerge from his ears. 'You checked up on me?' He was on his feet now.

'Where were you Patrick?' she demanded, ignoring his question. He looked away, pausing as though he needed time to form an excuse. His eyes gave away nothing.

Silence.

'Patrick?'

'For fuck's sake.' He pushed past her and stormed into the study. She followed him in there. 'Where were you?'

He abruptly turned to face her and positioned his face inches from hers. She threw her neck back, startled.

'Remember how I told you that I was seeing someone about my drinking? For years you have nagged me about it and in the last few weeks I've had the courage to do something about it. I haven't wanted to talk to you about it because I didn't need you thanking me for it, praising, treating me like a five-year-old.'

She took a tentative step backwards, widening the distance between them. He only closed it back in.

'The last thing I need is for you to be constantly on my back. I've tried to be patient with you, I did the expo thing, I'm looking into bloody counselors to shut you up, but you don't know when to stop, do you?' He was barracking her against the wall now.

She felt herself being trapped in as he hovered over her possessively, like a lion claiming his prey.

'And now you are questioning me, questioning my faithfulness when I'm doing everything you have asked.'

She felt his breath heavy on hers as he secured his hands either side of her face and pinned her against the wall.

'I don't know what you want from me, I have a decent job, I work myself into the ground, I stop drinking. ' His eyes flickered an anger that suddenly frightened her. 'I come home to you every night, don't I? But nothing is ever enough for you, is it?'

Tears sprung into her eyes and she started to cry.

'DON'T PULL THAT CARD ON ME!' he shouted.

The sobs came harder now as she tried to break free from under him. But he had her trapped, closed in with nowhere to go.

He slammed his fists into the wall, missing her face by what must have been millimeters. 'Why are you crying?' he roared. The ricochet sent a vibration through the wall, rattling her head on impact.

She squeezed her eyes shut. 'You're scaring me, Patrick.'

With two hands, she pushed against his chest, maneuvered her body from under him and made a run to their room before he had a chance to pull her back in. She locked the door behind her and crumpled to the floor in a heap. She trembled all over, feeling the cheeseburger that hadn't had a chance to digest, sitting somewhere half way down her throat. She could feel the vile bubbling its way up her esophagus as she frantically scanned her eyes around the room. She reached for the nearest shoe box, throwing the journals that were inside across the room.

She vomited.

'Sienna…? Babe?'

She could hear his pleading voice from the other side of the door. She forced whatever was left inside to come up a second time and vomited again.

'Are you ok? Can you please let me in?'

With the vomit induced box in her lap, she rested her head against the wall and stared helplessly at the ceiling. Her eyes were clouded with salty tears and her throat burned like hell.

'I'm so sorry baby, can you please let me in and we can talk about it?'

She could picture him pressed up against the other side of the door, regret finally hitting him.

But it was too late now.

He kept calling out to her but all she could do was sit quietly and wait. She didn't know what she was waiting for, but she couldn't move, couldn't respond.

And she wouldn't.

AFTER ABOUT AN hour of silence, with wobbly legs, and very little energy, she stood to her feet. She felt as though her insides had been drained from head to toe.

It wouldn't be far from the mark.

Ever so quietly she unlocked the door, opening it just enough to peak through. The study door opposite was wide open, the computer screen turned off. She didn't hear any noise from the kitchen, or from the TV, so she tiptoed down the corridor into the lounge room.

It was empty. She entered the kitchen. It was also empty.

He was gone.

After disposing the vomit induced shoe box, she sourced a new hiding place for her journals. After washing the horror of the day off her, she dragged herself into the lounge room, reached for her handbag and took out her phone.

A single text.

She considered not opening it. She didn't want to hear a word he had to say. She went into it anyway, but It wasn't from him.

It was from Ethan.

She squeezed her eyes shut for a moment, took a shaky breath and read it.

I'm sorry I missed your call, hope you are well.

**I've done some thinking…and think it would
be best for everyone if I keep my distance.**

And just like that, she felt more alone than ever.

Eighteen

S HE STILL FELT shaky the next day at work.

The rest of the night was spent half slumped over the coffee table while the other half of her body hung on the hard, wooden floor. She must have spent a good hour staring vacantly at the message from the one person who had given her the slightest glimmer of hope.

Patrick never returned home. She had turned her phone off after that and hadn't looked at it since. She drifted through work with a fabricated energy, her mind shattered in pieces the same way her heart was. She didn't want to stop, think, or take a single moment to reflect on the hundred strands of thoughts knotted in her mind. She would get through today, then tomorrow, and press on every day after that.

Nolan was absent today. Somehow through her out of body experience, she had noticed that much. In a way she was relieved as she didn't have the brain capacity to dissect the parts belonging to his case. It could stay tangled inside with everything else, for now.

By the time the day drew to a close, she was wrecked. She had never felt so emotionally and physically drained, and she had barely scratched the surface of the new term. After conversing with a few parents with the usual; 'how is my child progressing at school?' conversations, she flopped onto her swivel chair and refreshed her emails. As always, there were about a dozen to go through ranging from parents, to upcoming seminars, lunch duty covers, fundraising campaigns, timetable changes, shout outs for extra volunteers for co-curricular activities, upcoming staff meetings—it just kept going.

She stared at the screen, massaging her temples with her two index fingers. She had no desire to respond to a single one of them. She pushed her laptop back and rested her head on the cool, tempered glass. Her heavy eyes flickered as she fought hard to keep them open. She hadn't slept a wink last night. She hadn't even made it past two feet of the coffee table. Instead, she had switched on the TV and let Netflix suppress her swelling pain. One movie rolled into two, then three. Before she knew it, she was in for the full marathon until the sun seeped through the blinds, signifying it was time to rise from the floor.

Bizzzzzzzzzzzzzz

Her head slammed against the desk. She was well and truly awake now. Probably bruised too. She took the classroom phone and held it to her ear.

'Sienna, are you able to meet me in my office?'

Everything about the question was so textbook, formal. Her stomach churned at the seriousness of his tone.

'Yes, of course. I'm on my way. Is everything—'

Damian hung up before she had a chance to finish. She pushed back her chair and felt her head spin from a blend of exhaustion, hunger and anxiety.

She didn't remember how she got down the stairs but somehow, she arrived at his door. Out of curtesy, she knocked twice before entering.

'Sienna.' He smiled at her as she peered through, and her stomach settled. It wasn't a smile with an underlying intention. For once.

She returned his smile and took a seat knowing that he would insist upon it if she didn't.

He studied her. 'You look a wreck.'

She lifted her eyebrows and let out a loose laugh. 'Thanks Damian.'

He frowned and leaned forward to get a better look at her. 'Is everything ok on the home front?'

She knew he meant well but she was tired of being interrogated. She tucked an oily strand of hair behind one ear and gave him a convincing nod. 'Yes, fine. You wanted to see me?'

He stood to his feet, walked to the door and closed it. Suddenly, the settled feeling was gone and she was nervous again.

'Tell me, was Nolan at school today?' He took a seat again at his desk.

'No, he wasn't. Why's that?'

He nodded slowly. 'I received an email from Miranda. She isn't happy with the special treatment Nolan's receiving.'

'Excuse me?'

'She also feels attacked.'

'Attacked?' She was definitely wide awake now, and fuming. This woman was unbelievable.

'She also doesn't believe Nolan qualifies for the sessions he's having with Anita. She's upset that we went ahead without her consent.'

She gripped onto the end of her hair, flung it over shoulder and slouched deeper into the chair. 'She feels attacked?'

'Feels although her parenting has been questioned.'

'If she's *even* his mother.'

'We can't assume otherwise and either way, that's irrelevant right now.'

She nodded. He knew of her concerns and speculations over the whole mysterious case.

'She said until she has our trust, Nolan won't be returning to school.'

Something inside of her snapped.

'Is she serious? Why now? Why not a week and a half ago when she first had a problem? She's already doing him a massive disfavor pulling him out half way through next term, and now she wants to take him out sooner? It sounds like she's threatened to me. Over what, I'm not sure. But there's something going on. I know you think I'm reading deeply into everything but something's not right Damian.' She inhaled, catching her anger as it exploded everywhere like flying debris. 'Did you reply? How did … what did you respond to that?'

He was smiling again, to her disbelief he was actually smiling. It was hardly a smiling matter.

What the hell was wrong with him?

'Well that's why I've got you here, I thought we could work on a response together.' He spun the screen around so it faced her and clicked on the reply button to the email.

She leaned in and scrolled over the foolishness of Miranda's words. She could feel his eyes on her as she squinted her eyes over what the woman had to say.

'Nah, that's not going to work, come here,' he said, laughing. He wiggled his fingers, gesturing her to join him on the other side of desk.

'It's ok, I can see from here.'

'You might be able to see Sienna, but you need to be able to read it. Come on, swivel your sexy self over here.'

It was basically an order, one that made her want to run for the door. What choice did she have? The issue meant more to her than his usual flirty behaviour. She stood and obediently wheeled her chair over, making sure there was an appropriate distance between them. She sat down for a full three seconds before he took her chair and pulled it in closer so their shoulders brushed together. Her heart began to pound the same way it had when she was alone with him last. She glanced her eyes towards the door, relieved that it was closed from potential snooping eyes. At the same time, she wished it wasn't so she had an open pathway to flee.

Why did she always find herself in positions like these?

She sent him a hurried smile, then focused her attention back to the screen. She could see from the corner of her eye that the email was the last thing on his mind.

'What are your thoughts? How do we best approach this?' She positioned her hands on the keyboard, ready for his input.

He inhaled and redirected his focus to the screen. 'I don't think there's much we can do other than agree with the woman. Like you said, Nolan won't be seeing out the school year, he'll be gone soon so we don't want to aggravate things or give her any reason to take him out sooner. We'll just have to take him off Anita's hands and keep a close eye on him.'

She nodded. 'I'm happy to work with him outside school hours, like I had been doing.'

He scrunched his nose. 'I'm not sure that's wise, she's made it clear she doesn't want Nolan having any one on one attention.'

'What difference does it make? She's never around, she wouldn't even know about it.' She flung her back against the chair. 'She doesn't know the first thing about her own child,' she murmured under her breath.

He hovered his hands over where hers were positioned over the keyboard, ready to type. 'Maybe I'll take the reins on this one since you're all worked up. I'm a little concerned where that could lead,' he joked.

'Couldn't do any more damage than the damage she's inflicting on her son.'

He lowered his hands onto hers. She flinched and sent her hands to her lap. Did he just try to hold her hands? What a creep.

'You're always on edge around me, Henderson,' he smirked.

'I'm on edge in general.'

'Anything I can help you with?' his voice deep, slow and seedy. She had to commend him for his persistence. He never gave up, that was for sure.

'I just need to learn how to switch off. Need to meditate or something.'

She could see that his mind was dancing.

He raised his eyebrows. 'Always turned on, are we?'

'Excuse me?'

She was done here. She needed to leave. This email wasn't going to happen. His hands were already off the keyboard, his fingers now drumming a galloping rhythm on his desk. His shoulder brushed against hers again, harder this time.

She pushed her chair back.

'You're always on, I haven't seen anyone as wired as you. You really don't know how to relax, do you?'

She shrugged, lost for words.

He placed two hands on her shoulders and began to work his strong fingers on the stringy muscles at the base of her neck. 'When was the last time you had a massage?'

'Damian … ' She shook his hands off her, but he only tightened his grip.

'It's ok, I might be able to release this giant knot you've got going on here,' he said seductively.

She cleared her throat. 'The email.'

'Yes.' He sent little squeezes down the sides of her arms now, from the top of her shoulders, right down to her forearms. 'Don't worry, we'll get it done. You need to relax first, we need to settle that overactive mind of yours so you're in a position to think more clearly.'

We?

The only thing that involved any form of inclusiveness was getting this email written.

'I appreciate the thought but I think you should stop.' The assertiveness of her tone surprised herself. She slapped his hands away and pushed her chair further back this time. It was the firmest she had ever been with him.

As ordered, he released his hands from her. The relief that washed over her was immediate. She couldn't look at him, couldn't meet his eye. She didn't need to, she could already sense his rejection.

He hesitated for a moment, as though he was about to respond, then started typing a reply. His eyes hazy, halved in sized compared to a moment ago. His fingers moved at a similar speed as her racing heart.

She stared as she watched, contemplating what to do next. There was a knock at the door. The door opened and Judy from reception poked her head in.

'Damian, your four o' clock has arrived.'

Sienna looked at the way he stared blankly at the woman.

'Gary Thornton,' she clarified.

'Right, Gary. Of course, I'll be there in two.'

Judy nodded before quietly shutting the door behind her.

He peered at the clock on the wall and turned to face Sienna. 'I'll be sure that the email gets sent to the Livingstons before I leave tonight. Thank you for your input, Sienna.' Just like that, he was all professional again.

She nodded, stood to her feel and swiveled it back to its position on the other side of the desk. 'Thank you for that, I appreciate it.'

His eyes were still focused on the screen. He didn't look at her, he didn't nod. She walked to the door, looking back at him as his fingers continue to tap away at the keyboard before she closed it behind her. She only hoped she hadn't made another enemy, it would be more than she could handle.

When would something go right? Anything. Was it really too much to ask?

Her past record so far told her that it was.

She returned to the classroom, exited her many unanswered emails, took her bag, turned off the classroom lights and made her way to her car. She was done. She was ready for the day to be over, even though home was the last place she wanted to be.

She wished she didn't associate seeing Patrick's car with such dread. But she couldn't help but experience the word in its entirety as she pulled up beside it. She glanced at the time. It had just gone four thirty. He didn't finish work until five.

Maybe he had finished early, desperate to come home and apologise.

Maybe she would find him on his knees begging for forgiveness as she opened the front door. Or maybe he would be in the kitchen, putting together an 'I'm sorry for being an asshole' dinner. Even now, she held onto that visual.

IT WASN'T UNTIL she reached the front door where she realised she was holding her breath. She darted her eyes to the left; the kitchen was empty. He wasn't in the lounge room either. She walked the corridor that led to the study. Sure enough, there he was, with his headphones securely in place, his fingers scurrying over the keys as little animation figures darted across the screen. Instead of saying hi, she dumped her handbag onto their bed, peeled off her shoes and sank into the mattress. The number of times she found herself on her back staring at the ceiling these days …

'You're home early.'

He was standing by the door, arms crossed over his chest, expressionless. Instead of his business attire, he was dressed in tracksuit pants and a polo.

'I was thinking the same thing.'

'I left the office early. Been off since lunch. I thought we could do dinner somewhere.'

'Are you sure you'll turn up this time?'

'Go to hell.'

She lifted her chin sharply towards the ceiling, sending the tears back where they came from.

'I've been trying to get in contact with you all day,' he said abruptly.

'I haven't checked my phone. I've been in parent teacher interviews, remember?'

'I just find it interesting that for someone who keeps going on about how she wants to make this work, can't seem to take the thirty seconds to send me a simple message.'

She stared at him. 'And I find it interesting that the day after you walk out on me, you're conveniently home at a decent hour,' she hissed back.

'I didn't walk out on you. And that's exactly right, I'm here now, aren't I?' He was raising his voice now.

She snorted. 'Well done, so you're here now, but not when I'm in a heap on the floor balling my eyes out after you corner me into a wall like I'm some prey you're hunting down.' She wiped her tears away, frustrated that she even had any at all. He didn't deserve her tears after the way he treated her last night. Or the many nights before that for that matter.

'I didn't corner you, don't be so dramatic.'

'You did. And then you left me there, clearly aware of how much I was hurting.'

'Oh, while you were hurting? Are you that oblivious to the pain you cause me?' he roared.

She sat up and jammed her legs crossed underneath her. She clenched her hands tightly onto the doona either side of her. 'Do you really have too much pride to apologise for the way you treated me last night?'

He threw his arms in the air at that and laughed. He actually laughed. 'Self-inflicted, my darling, nothing that you didn't put on yourself.'

She tightened her grip, feeling her palms quickly forming a sweat.

Darling?

'Where were you last night?' she demanded.

He shook his head and let out a malicious laugh. 'And again, she doesn't trust me.'

Who *was* he?

'You didn't come home so I think I have the right to question where you stayed.'

'Brad's. I stayed at Brad's!'

'Whoever that is!'

'Good mate from work!'

'Right, yeah, ok.'

'I don't need to justify myself to you.' He was already out the door.

'I'll keep that in mind if I ever feel like running away the same way you do when things get hard.'

'Whatever. Run along to Jacqui's then.'

'At least you'd know where I am!'

'Does it even matter?' He was back in the room, opening draws, yanking out socks at the same time he searched for his runners.

'Yes Patrick it does. Believe it or not, communication matters.'

He pulled on his socks and erratically tied his laces into a tight knot, three times over. Maybe even four.

'Oh, you want me to communicate? Well, in case you want to clock my whereabouts for the next forty-five minutes, I'll be out on a run somewhere between Steller and James Street! I might even need a breather at the second oval, the smaller one, you know? The one opposite the station? Am I communicating this clearly enough for you? Feel free to take notes.'

His sarcasm made her want to throw something at him. Something hard. She shifted her eyes around the room as she seriously contemplated the idea.

'Perfect! Off you go then!'

'Oh, don't you worry, I'm going!' He jammed his earphones in and disappeared out the door.

She sat there for a moment, trying hard to inhale a steady breath as her heart pounded violently. She peeled herself off the bed, almost stepping on his phone that laid charging as her feet found the floor. In the six years they had been dating, she had not once thought of checking up on him. The thought had never crossed her mind to do so. There had never been a need for it. But with Patrick gone, and the train wreck that was their relationship, made the temptation too powerful to ignore. Besides, maybe she would get an insight to their relationship from his perspective if she had some more information. Maybe it would help her better understand him, which couldn't be a bad thing, right?

Her heart drummed feverishly in her chest as she picked up the phone and talked herself into all the reasons why she should, despite her instincts screaming against it.

His phone buzzed, startling her as it flew out of her hands and landed on the floor with a loud thud. With panicked hands, she did a quick assessment of the phone making sure there were no cracks or scratches.

She was in the all clear.

Her tired eyes, now alert as ever, stared at the message. The name at the top instantly injected a cold serum into her blood steam.

Louisa.

Brad's girlfriend? The girl from the café?

Without clicking into it she was able to read the message.

Hang in there handsome.

I know you're going through a lot at the moment. I just want to remind you again that I'm here for you and look forward to

The front door slammed. She quickly positioned the phone back down where she found it, reached for a book on the bedside table, opened up to a random page and scrambled to the opposite side of the bed with it. Her pulse was working overtime, there was no way she would be able to hide the fitful rise and fall of her chest.

Patrick entered, his earphones still in place. Without a word, he bent over and took his phone off the charger, placing it in his zipper pocket. She glanced over at him trying hard to act cool, calm and collected as she sent him a stiff smile. He didn't smile back. Within seconds, the front door slammed again and she was left with an inquisitiveness that was eating her alive.

She threw the book down and stared up again at the ceiling, biting down hard on her tongue so she wouldn't cry. Why the hell was Brad's girlfriend sending him an endearing, comforting message like that? And what was she looking forward to? It was the part that stirred her the most. She got to her feet, found her phone from her handbag and turned it on for the first time that day.

Her intuition told her it was more than just a friendly text. If only he had returned a few seconds later she would have been able to read the whole thing. She squinted her eyes shut, trying to visualise the message as a whole. Even though she wasn't able to read it all, she remembered seeing a bunch of kisses on the end. But what words had come before that? Did Brad's girlfriend have a thing for her fiancé? If he was a good mate from work then it made sense that they would spend a bit of time together.

Her head spun with the possible scenarios. Was she just being paranoid? Was Patrick right? Had they really reached the stage in their strained relationship where she had trust issues? Was she that insecure?

Brad.

Until a few weeks ago she had never heard about a friend named Brad before. Ignoring the days' worth of missed calls and messages on her phone, she went onto Facebook and jumped onto Patrick's page. She found his friends list and scrolled through. There was a Ben, Brandon, Brody. But no Brad. Not everyone was on Facebook, right? Ethan wasn't.

Suddenly the possibility dawned upon her. What if there was no Brad? What if Patrick had stayed at this woman's house last night? But when she thought about the café, surely, he wouldn't have had the nerve to talk to the woman he was having an affair with, right in front her? She searched under L to try and locate a 'Louisa' on his friends list.

Nothing.

If only she knew her last name, maybe she would somehow be able to come across the short haired, blonde woman she had seen that day and find out if she was single or not. Her mind continued to race. What if Patrick's motivation to quit drinking was because of this woman? It made sense that he would want to hide his problem if he was trying to win her over?

This was ridiculous. She was reading into everything way too much. Patrick would never cheat on her.

She left Facebook and filtered through her phone notifications. Four messages and two missed calls. Most had come from Patrick the day before, with a text from Jacqui and Mia. She opened up the one from her sister, cursing herself for not calling her again. It had been weeks.

She had invited her to a wedding in Aringdale in two weeks' time. Lance had to fly to Sydney for work so she had invited her to be her plus one instead. The guy getting married was Tim Burton; a friend Mia went through school with that Sienna also knew. Tim and Mia had basically grown up together, his friendship group consisting of several guys she knew from her school days including…

Ethan.

Her heart skipped a beat. Would Ethan be there? The thought of seeing him again strangely filled her with anticipation.

She held her phone to her ear. After half a dozen rings Mia picked up.

'Hey sis, I got your text. Yes, I'd love to be your date to Tim's wedding. Count me in.'

Nineteen

'I CAN SEE YOU in this.'

Jacqui took out a long, soft pink, strapless, lace dress from the rack and held it up with a brilliant smile. 'It's stunning, elegant, sophisticated.' She ran her free hand along the spaghetti straps. 'It's a pretty, neutral colour that will compliment any pair of heels and accessories, showing off that stunning little figure of yours.'

Sienna rolled her eyes at her friend's sale pitch that she didn't want to admit, had actually convinced her to want to try it on. 'The only downside is that you may outshine the bride in it, and that could ruffle some feathers …' she started. 'Especially when you're technically not invited.'

Sienna laughed and took the dress from her. 'Well, that's hardly a downside as there's no chance of that happening.' She uncovered the tag from the back of the dress. 'But the price is definitely one.'

It was almost four hundred dollars.

Jacqui glanced at the tag and nodded thoughtfully. 'Let me go in half with you.'

'Let you go in what? You're not putting any money towards this dress, Jac.'

'I think you should try it on and let me make that decision for myself,' she said stubbornly, shoeing her into the change rooms. 'It's your birthday in a couple of months. Let's make it an early present.'

'Exactly, in a couple of months and that's still far too generous.'

'Shush. Just go and try it on.'

Minutes later she pulled back the curtain and took a glimpse of herself in the full-length mirror. As her friend anticipated, the dress was faultless. The thin straps sat perfectly on her dainty shoulders, complementing her petite body as it sat close, but not too tightly around her torso before gracefully draping to the floor. The pink lace sat delicately over the ivory satin underlay. The contrast was stunning.

She clasped her hands together. 'Oh my God. It's absolutely perfect,' gasped Jacqui, her face beaming.

Sienna smiled and span to the side. She was already in love with the details along the back of the dress, the way it closed over her back in a low V shape. 'I can't buy this.'

'Of course, you can.' Jacqui was already rummaging through her hand bag in search for her wallet.

'Patrick will kill me if I spent this much. Especially for a wedding he doesn't even know about or even going to. There's just no way—'

'You know what, I don't want to hear it,' she exploded. 'I hate how much control he has over you. When was the last time you went out and treated yourself?'

Sienna thought about that for a moment.

'Point made. You haven't. Not for years. I think you deserve this, and you will wear it again. It's a classic, it's timeless.'

Sienna ran her hands along the lace as she digested the comment. 'I guess you make a valid point—'

'Yes, I do. And didn't you say that Ethan will be there too?'

Her heart stopped. 'Yeah … so?'

'Do you think it's possible that you're hesitant to buy it because he'll get to see you looking gorgeous in it, and Patrick won't?'

Sienna shrugged, then shook her head. 'Didn't even cross my mind,' she lied.

'Have you heard from him lately?'

'Not for weeks.' She stepped back into the changing room feeling her heart drop. 'There's nothing going on, Jac.'

'I know, I know that. I guess I'm just furious at the way Patrick is treating you.'

'We don't know he's cheating.'

Jacqui sighed deeply. 'You haven't connected properly in years. How can you be so sure what he is and isn't doing?'

She had a point. But she couldn't just assume the worst. If Patrick knew all about Ethan, he'd probably assume the same thing. Besides, today wasn't about Patrick, it wasn't about Ethan either. For the first time it was about clearing her head from all of it and spending some quality time with her best friend.

'I'm going to change now.'

'This dress was made for you.'

Sienna laughed. 'I know.'

'Does that mean you're buying it?'

'Yes.' She closed the curtain.

'Good girl.'

She carefully peeled off the size six dress and changed into her baggy clothes. 'Jac?'

'Hmmm?'

'I need a milkshake and a burger. And I mean the biggest, fattiest one on the menu … with sweet potato chips on the side.'

She could hear a snort from the other side of the curtain.

'Let's do it. We'll have you back in no time.'

Sienna smiled. She didn't quite understand it, but suddenly her appetite was beginning to come back. It was time to get some meat on her bones.

Minutes later she laid the dress down on the counter and took her wallet from her bag. The retail assistant smiled warmly at her.

'This has already been taken care of.'

'What do you mean?'

The woman shifted her eyes towards Jac who was standing by the door with the cheekiest grin. 'You have yourself a beautiful friend over there.'

Sienna's eyes sprung with tears—different ones this time.

'I really do.' She thanked the woman and followed Jac out the door. 'You didn't! Let me pay you back for at least half of it. I won't let you spend that much on me!'

Her friend gave her shoulders a little squeeze. 'Don't stress, the dress was reduced. I wouldn't have done it if I couldn't afford it. I wanted to treat you.'

Sienna hugged her friend and planted a kiss on her cheek. 'What did I do to deserve you? You're amazing.'

'If only you knew how amazing you are, S.'

Just like that, tears splashed down her face.

SHE DEVOURED INTO her chicken and brie burger, refusing to ponder whether Patrick really was at the driving range like he said, or cozying up next to the pretty blonde. She refused to wonder if his weeks of being sober had any correlation with the length of his affair. As they continued to roam the city, she was desperate to know whether every time he was 'seeing someone' about his drinking problem, he was in fact, seeing her. She was tired of analysing every single detail. Especially when the more she thought about it, all the pieces coordinated together quite perfectly.

And there was nothing perfect about that.

LIKE ANY WELL thought out affair, she found him in the study. His phone securely next to him, rattling off every couple of minutes. Messages she could only imagine were from *her*.

She wanted to question him, wanted to ask who was demanding his attention. But the thought of his response, terrified her. What if this woman was exactly who he said she was? It would only add fuel to the fire and validate his accusation of her having trust issues. If the woman was indeed exactly who she thought she was—well—that would make everything real, very quickly.

She wasn't ready to deal with that. She'd rather deal with the idea of galvanising pain, than slowly suffer from the truth. Because if the truth was what she feared it to be, it would destroy her.

Maybe forever.

'Hey,' she said as she passed the study and went to their room. She removed the dress from the bag and carefully placed it on a hanger.

'Hey,' he barely responded from the other room.

'How was the driving range?' She felt her muscles clench as she asked.

'Yeah, good.'

'Who ended up joining you?'

His phone went off again. She squeezed her eyes shut.

Silence.

'Um. Brad and Jake.'

There was his name again, the Brad that didn't exist. Jake, well, that was someone she did know of. An old school friend of his she had met more than a dozen times over the years. Obviously, his work and school mates hung out all the time together now.

What a lie.

She slid the cupboard door shut, went to the kitchen and poured two glasses of cold water. She sliced a lime, placing a wedge into each glass and took it over to her cheating fiancé.

Ok, so maybe she didn't know that for sure.

She placed the glass down directly next to his phone. As soon as it touched his desk his phone buzzed again. Before she had the chance to read the name that lit the screen, it was in his hands, angled away from her the same way as it had on the day of the wedding expo.

'Someone's popular today.' She couldn't help herself.

His face tightened, but only for a moment. 'Yeah, I'm part of a group message with the boys. Can't keep up.'

She nodded, studying his reaction as he quickly exited the message and placed his phone on the desk, face down this time on the opposite side of him.

Furthest from her.

'How was your day?' She couldn't remember the last time he had asked her such thing. She wished it was genuine, wished he actually cared, but his question held neither of the above. It was a distraction, a tactic for the subject to change.

And she would go along with it.

'I had a nice day. We did lunch, I bought a dress.'

'That's nice.'

That's nice?

He was maneuvering his cursor over the animated figures that were flying over pixelated objects.

'Do you want to see it?'

'See what?' He didn't look at her.

'My dress.'

'Oh.'

He continued to click away. At the same time his phone went off again. This woman was bloody persistent. She had to give her that. Gritting her teeth, she disappeared into the bedroom, took the hanger from the cupboard and waltzed back into the study. She held it up for him. Eventually he hit pause on the game, removed his headphones and swiveled his chair around to take a look.

'It looks like a wedding dress.'

'No, it doesn't, it's pink.'

'If you say so,'

'I do,' she agreed. 'But it is for a wedding. Mia's asked me to take Lance's place for a wedding in Aringdale, weekend after next. He's away for work, so I said yes.'

'Did you now?'

'I did,' she said evenly.

'Cool.'

'Do you like it?'

He shrugged. 'Depends on how much you spent on it. But I don't know how I feel about you spending money without consoling with me first.'

She bit down hard on her tongue.

I'm not happy the way you failed to consider the consequences of your affair.

She didn't say it, of course.

'I didn't think to console with you because it was a gift. Jacqui bought it for me.'

'And why would she do that?'

'I don't know, she wanted to treat me.'

He snorted. 'Yeah, ok.'

If she bit down any harder her tongue would split into two. He spun back to face his screen and was already back into his stupid game, his headphones securely in place.

She returned to the room and hung the dress back up, visualising what it would be like seeing Ethan again in two weeks' time.

The thought alone gave her butterflies.

Would they be seated on the same table? Would their connection be palpable to everyone around them? Would Mia be able to detect from the outside all that she was feeling on the inside?

She located her laptop from under the bed, took it out and took it with her to the lounge room. The room furthest from Patrick's demanding phone.

Dinner could wait.

She stuck her earphones in, allowing the soothing sound of Ed Sheeran's voice to still her mind. She closed her eyes as she waited for her laptop to start up. She then spent the next forty-five minutes watching an old episode of *Gilmore Girls*. It was the final episode of the season where Luke organised a surprise going away party for Lorelai's daughter, Rory, before she leaves Stars Hallow to become a journalist. In the show, Lorelai and Luke had been friends for years, secretly liking each other but never having the courage or perhaps the realisation, to voice it. Their relationship trialed and tested over the course of many years, with even a broken engagement. But in the final episode Lorelai takes a moment to step away from the party and pours her heart out to Luke, declaring he was the one, that he had always be the one.

The entire time she watched the series conclude, all she could think about was how she was Lorelai, and Ethan was Luke. Ok, so their story was a little different. There had been nine years separating them, after all. But like the show, there had been a small town that connected them, a friendship that encouraged them and a history that shaped them.

Patrick didn't leave the study once. And she was grateful for it. She was even more grateful that her earphones cancelled out the buzz of any incoming messages coming from her. She clenched her face, waiting for the current of pain to pass.

It didn't. Instead, it surfaced there.

A man who would without fail, be by my side through all seasons of life.

She had never shared her list with Patrick. They had never created a mission statement or vow for their relationship. They had never taken the time to sit down together and with the end in mind, built the fundamentals to equip them for the journey ahead. Without that shared vision, of course they were setting themselves up to fail. Because as soon as they found themselves in a difficult season there would be no foundation to keep them standing. It all seemed common sense really. Yet, they had somehow overlooked the backbone of it.

What were they doing getting married when if she really thought about it, they had never shared a single, meaningful conversation? What was their three-year plan, five-year plan? What sort of life did they want to create? Did he even want to create life? She still had no idea if he wanted children or not. Would it be something she would be willing to compromise if he didn't? Or would they be able to somehow synergize?

Questions they should have worked through years ago. And now, it was too late. His actions made it clear that he was not motivated to work on things. Instead, all of his energy was being invested into this woman.

Louisa.

She never hated a name so much.

It was crazy to think that she had once shared her mission statement, her vow for her future husband, with Ethan. It was as though she had more wisdom as a teenager than she did now. Or maybe she had just been conditioned in a way that had protected her from a world of deception. She missed seeing a blank canvas through innocent eyes. Uncontaminated by years of choices, disappointments, setbacks and regret. The years unfold, a new colour painted with every season. But instead of these colours holding their shape, they begin to bleed, running into each other, forming a lone puddle at the base of the easel.

She took out a spiral bound notebook from the bottom draw of the coffee table. She missed the freedom of writing. It was one of the few things that made her soul feel alive, made her feel as though a canvas decorated with a rainbow of colours was possible, for her.

She took out a pen, and just like an artist, allowed her hand to colour with a freedom as her words spilt onto the page, creating an unexpected piece of art.

5th August 2019

Writing you letters used to be, to me, as natural as inhaling oxygen. Receiving letters from you was a time in my life I miss the most. It's been years since I wrote to you last, so I thought I'd send you one more.

I know over the years we have had a lot of miscommunication, a lot of missed opportunities as timing was never on our side. But one thing it didn't take from us is the rare friendship I know we will always have.

If timing has given us anything it would be the beauty of the seamless connection whenever we come together, closing the gap of every year that divided us.

If I'm honest with myself, I did take you for granted. I took us for granted and the depth of all that we shared. I hate myself for allowing those 9 years without you, to simply pass. I can't help but wonder what life would be like if I hadn't.

I can almost hear you assuring me that this wasn't all my fault, just like I can hear your voice every time my heart is stirred with a memory of us. No one has ever made me laugh as hard and as well, as you have. You made me feel as though anything was possible, Ethan. You made me believe that the sky was my limit and the space between was within my reach.

I have always loved you.

I loved you when I got you and Sadie together. I loved you when I was dating Brody. And I love you now.

I don't know what's going to happen, what the future holds. Life is uncertain like that. But I do know that I'll always love you.

That is one thing I am certain about.

Yours always,

Sienna

Twenty

'OKAY, I'M READY whenever you are.'

Mia stepped into the kitchen all dolled up. The sight of her sister was enough to make Sienna gasp.

'Oh my god, you couldn't look more beautiful!'

It was true, she looked like Audrey Hepburn the way her long dark hair swept into an elegant bun at the top of her head, her soft features giving off an uncanny likeness. She was dressed in a tiffany blue, A-line dress with complementing pearl coloured heels.

Mia's brown eyes glisten at the compliment, her lips curling to show off her perfect set of teeth. 'And you're a vision sis. That dress!' She gave her the once over and nodded slowly in approval. 'Who are you trying to impress?'

Sienna let out a nervous laugh and took her clutch from the counter. Inside, was the letter had she wrestled with the decision of taking with her. After turning it over in her hands more than a hundred times she decided it would see the light of day. With wrinkled edges from all the handling, she had shoved it inside the envelope and hadn't looked back. She still had no idea when she would give it to him, not knowing if they would have a moment alone. But as much as the idea made her stomach churn, it was something she needed to do. Something she felt she had to do in order to filter him from her heart.

Once and for all.

Her sister let the question slide, completely unaware of how close she was to hitting the nail on the head and gathered her things ready to leave.

Their morning together had been exactly what Sienna needed. Their father had cooked up a breakfast of sausage, eggs, French toast, tomato and avocado while their mum set up a little 'do it yourself' juice bar with an array of fruit and vegetables—fresh from the veggie garden. The single meal was enough to have fed her for a week. The quantity of food in one sitting was overwhelming, yet she was able to eat all of it guilt free. That in itself was freeing. She was able to laugh, joke and be herself without the fear of being condemned. Instead of being ignored or condemned for everything she said, her family embraced her, and loved her. They had been attentive to her every word.

She could have spent hours running around the house with little Bailey playing hide and seek and dancing like an idiot as the TV broke into songs from the Wiggles. Bailey would just stare at her with her little brown eyes, before jumping up and down in fits of giggles as her aunty amplified their every move. It was one of those moments where time really did stand still.

Maybe it was possible, after all.

No one asked about Patrick. No questions about wedding plans were mentioned when it would have been fitting, of all days, to bring it up seeing as they were going to one. Maybe after all these years they had finally drawn a conclusion, or maybe they thought she had. Either way, it was all a bit sad. But her heart that morning had been filled with far too much joy, allowing no room for such wasted emotion.

SIENNA DROVE THEM to the church. Being a small town, nothing was more than a fifteen-minute drive away. Being a city girl, she underestimated this and pulled up a good twenty minutes early. The choice of venue was beautiful. It was an old Catholic church octagonal in shape, with an arched wooden doorway and high-rise, stained-glass windows. Even though they were one of the few cars in the carpark, her eyes naturally scanned the premise for his. But thankfully for her own sanity, he hadn't arrived yet.

Her thumping heart could take a rest.

They got out of the car and miraculously, made their way over the giant cobblestones in their heels without twisting any ankles. They took the seven steps to the entrance and took a program before taking a seat somewhere in the middle rows of the wooden pews. Crossing a leg over the other and with her hands in her lap, she took in the splendor of the setup. There were white and pink peonies tied to the end of each pew with silver satin ribbon weaving each bouquet together. Running down the centre was a white carpet with an array of pink flower petals scattered all the way up to the platform. Vases bursting with peonies stood a metre high on either side, highlighted by fairy lights that dangled from the ceiling.

It truly was a magical sight.

As the church slowly filled Sienna found herself becoming more fidgety by the second. The number of times she turned her head back to see if he had arrived should have been more than enough for her sister to have questioned her. But Mia, being the extrovert that she was, had her back constantly turned chatting to every face that walked by, oblivious to it all.

Sienna swept her long golden curls over her shoulder and reached for her clutch. It was another one of those days she hadn't checked her phone. This time not because she didn't want to, but because it hadn't even crossed her mind. Even now it was a last resort, something to keep her mind off the man who would at any moment, enter through those wooden doors. The man, whether she admitted to or not, held her heart in a way no one else had.

No messages from Patrick. She wasn't surprised. If anything, she was surprised she felt ok. Surprised she wasn't filled with a shot of anxiety or that horrible ache. Instead she felt, *nothing.*

It was then she heard Mia call his name. Even with her back turned she could feel her sisters weight shift as she leaned over the back of the pew and reached out her arms to hug him. Her heart leapt into her mouth at the acknowledgement of his presence his cologne instantly gave away. With a smile resonating every fiber of energy inside of her, she turned. It was within these seconds of coming face to face with him, where every high came to a crashing low.

'Sienna.'

She knew him well enough to know that the smile he was flashing was underlined with shock. Panic even. The pain inside her spread like wild fire.

'Hi Ethan. It's good to see you.' Being as good at hiding her emotions as she was, she was able to offer him a convincing smile. Her eyes quickly took in the gorgeous woman by his side. She extended her hand and widened her smile. 'Hi, I'm Sienna.'

The woman had the most beautiful green eyes she had ever seen. Her dark hair fell flawlessly in soft waves over her toned, brown shoulders— so toned, it made her insides pang with envy. She had never looked that good, not even in her ballet days. This girl was basically a super model.

'Amber. It's nice to meet you.' The woman's smile wasn't as full. In fact, her expression was quite stricken. Was there a chance Ethan had mentioned to her who Sienna was? Or was the woman intuitive enough to detect some sort of history between them?

'Nice to meet you too,' Sienna said politely, unable to meet Ethan's eyes.

A few more words were spoken before Mia jumped into a conversation with another couple who had just arrived, leaving Sienna alone with them. There was a brief silence.

'I didn't know you'd be here.' Ethan laughed a little too casually. Amber inched closer to his side and reached for his hand. He took it.

She felt as though she had been shot. She flickered her eyes back up, connecting with his. She could almost literally feel the effects of the wound shot, spread wide across her chest.

'Neither did I! I'm taking Lance's place today. He's interstate for work. Tim was happy for me to be Mia's plus one,' she responded way too enthusiastically, like an animated character from a Disney film. Ethan must have thought so too the way his lips pursed together in a knowing smile.

There was another silence. Longer this time.

'I'm terrible. Sorry, I haven't introduced you two. Sienna this is Amber. Amber, Sienna.'

She could see that he was uncomfortable. She knew this the way he was flicking his nails together with his free hand. His body language stiff, visibly tense beside the pretty brunette who was practically cemented to his side.

'Yes…' Sienna smiled. 'We have done the introductions already.'

The woman looked up at him and squeezed his arm. 'Aringdale is very cute. It's been so special to see where Ethan grew up. Are you from here too?' She turned her eyes back at Sienna and smiled in a way that lit her entire face.

That stunning face that sat above those bloody toned shoulders.

'It is a cute little town', Sienna responded. 'I hope Ethan has been a good tour guide.' She refused to look at him, she simply couldn't.

She wouldn't take a second bullet.

She could feel him staring at her, but she couldn't meet his eyes. It would kill her. 'Yeah, I grew up here, but Melbourne is home,' she finally answered.

'Oh, so you're a city girl? Me too.'

She looked at Ethan again with adoring eyes and nuzzled into his arm. She was too short to get anywhere near his shoulder.

'Where in Melbourne are you from?' Sienna asked.

'Lilydale.'

That was when the bullet penetrated deeper.

Lilydale. It all made sense now.

'And you?'

'Kensington.'

'Beautiful suburb.'

'It is.'

She finally found the courage to look up, unable to read him as he stood immobile, like a stuffed mullet.

'That's where we met.' Amber wrapped her arm around him all possessive like. 'In Lilydale.'

Sienna swallowed hard. 'That's *lovely.*'

Silence again.

'Yeah, it all happened very quickly,' he finally jumped in, sounding defensive as though he owed her an explanation.

'Ohhhh, tell me more, let's hear the story,' she said, dying a little bit more inside.

It was like a drawn-out death—the worst kind. What was she doing? She didn't want to hear a word of it.

He was still staring at her, but she still refused to meet his eye.

'It was a windy night, had been hailing only moments before, but I wanted to get down to the beach for a run anyway. When I reached the shore, I spotted a woman running around in circles and knew she couldn't have been on a run like me. No running style could be that bad. When I got closer, I could see she was wrestling the wind with something.'

It sounded like some vomit from a Nicholas Sparks movie. Amber began to giggle. It felt like high school all over again.

Please, not again.

'It was my bookmark of all things. Sounds lame, but that thing is sentimental. I like to read by the water every night, no matter what the weather is doing. It's something I have always done since I've lived on the coast' she added. 'I must have looked so ridiculous.'

Ethan laughed. 'It was amusing to watch but I knew I had to step in at some point. You weren't even close to catching that thing.'

She slapped his arm playfully. 'Oh really? Exactly how long were you standing there watching me?'

'Long enough to see that you were struggling.' He let out a honk of a laugh—the one she was all well too familiar with.

That hit hard.

'That was a crazy night.'

Their eyes locked as the memory came to life and in perfect unison, turned to face Sienna.

Crazy night?

She didn't want to hear the details. She had heard enough.

She forced a smile. 'It sounds like something from the movies you two!'

Amber reached in for a kiss. He bent down to meet her lips.

She could barely breathe as she watched their faces come together.

'It kind of was. I'm a lucky girl.'

So, they were a couple.

Sienna finally met his eyes. 'Yes, you are. Ethan's a good egg.'

He gave her a weak smile in return. One she hadn't seen before.

Amber giggled some more. 'A good egg. I like that.'

As painful it was to be in such position, she couldn't help but like Amber. Part of her wanted to despise her, but she couldn't. She was the type of girl Sienna could see herself being friends with. And maybe one day, she would.

By now the church had filled and everyone had taken their seats. For the entire duration of the ceremony all she could think about was the two of them sitting directly behind her—stroking each other's hands growing more smitten with each other, encased in a setting that celebrated love.

She could barely concentrate as the priest welcomed everyone before delving into the story on how the happy couple met. She stared blankly at the stained-glass window with Mother Mary at the centre as the readings took place, and the vows were exchanged. Then there was the kiss that brought everyone to their feet in applause. She blinked back the tears as Tim and Casey slowly moved down the aisle as they became the newly 'Mr and Mrs Burton'. Tears that could have easily been mistaken for happiness as flower petals were thrown in the air like fireworks, hugs and kisses exchanged left, right and centre.

Why was she so upset anyway? Ethan didn't belong to her. He never would belong to her. She was just surprised that he had met someone so quickly. She just needed some time to adjust. To get used to the idea. That's all.

And by the end of the night, she would.

Drinks and canapes were arranged to be served at the Hills restaurant before the reception took place. Already she was dying for a drink. Alcohol would help prolong the numbness that plagued her body. She would rather feel nothing than feel the pain of her reality. She had already felt the effects brutally enough.

The crowd started filtering from their pews. She could see Ethan slide his arm around Amber's waist as they followed behind the train of guests. She and Mia followed closely behind. This allowed her to examine the picture of the two more closely. Amber was a slim woman, with curves in all the right places. Her mauve cocktail dress complimented her toned, perky bum that Sienna weirdly, couldn't help but appreciate. Even her strappy silver heels highlighted the line of her refined calves and petite ankles. The woman had good taste. Well, obviously. She was with Ethan after all—wasn't she?

Mia didn't seem to notice her silence as they drove to the reception venue. Thank god, because she couldn't find the energy to string a single sentence together. Instead, Mia had waffled on about something to do with Casey's dress malfunction and how it was a miracle that she got it back in time after it had arrived with all the wrong measurements. Sienna hardly heard a word but threw in a little laugh and nod where it seemed appropriate. Her assignment from this moment forward was getting through the rest of the evening with a convincing smile on her face, knowing that the four of them would most likely be sitting on the same table together like one big happy family.

Just fabulous.

She wouldn't give him the letter. Absolutely not. There was no chance that was going to happen. Now that she thought about it, the whole thing was a crazy idea. What was she trying to achieve by giving it to him anyway? What was she thinking declaring her feelings for him all over again? She had regretted it nine years ago and would be foolish to repeat her mistakes a second time. Especially now that she was an engaged woman. Other than leaving him confused, nothing could possibly come from it. Their friendship, if they still had one, would be as good as over.

Luckily, Mia had offered to be the designated driver for their trip home. For someone who rarely had an evening out when there was a toddler to consider, she was surprised that she had leaped at the opportunity. Maybe she was pregnant again. It was a possibility as she watched her sister head straight for the non-alcoholic wine when she would normally enjoy a drink or two. But when she had asked her about it, she had laughed it off and assured her that she wasn't.

As SOON AS they made their way through the front doors, she spotted them over at the bar with arms around each other, completely smitten. She watched them as Ethan introduced her to his old school friends. Friends they had in common during their school days.

Friends that had once predicted they would end up together.

His body language was more relaxed, far less rigid than it had been in the church, proving that he had felt awkward seeing her again. Especially with this new woman of his.

When did that happen anyway?

She didn't want to go anywhere near the bar. She didn't want to be placed in a position where she would have to engage in small talk with them whilst pretending like she was completely unaffected. She couldn't keep up the act anymore. Fortunately for her, waiters were circling the venue with wine. She took a glass and wandered over to the seating chart.

As she predicted, they were seated on the same table.

She drifted over to table nine, the one located closest to the dance floor. She hovered her eyes over the placement cards, cursing under her breath to find Ethan's name conveniently positioned next to hers. She reached over to swap his name with some lad named Will when Mia joined her.

'What are you doing?' She laughed, watching her.

Sienna jumped back a little. 'I just wanted to make sure Amber was seated next to her boyfriend.'

'You mean Ethan?'

'Yeah, Ethan. Very cute couple.' She plonked herself down and took another sip. A gulp, actually. 'I'm surprised she got an invite seeing their relationship is very … recent.'

Mia sat down too. 'Is it? Yeah, I don't know. It's nice to see him with someone though,' she said, watching them basically wrapped around each other at the bar.

'Yeah it is. Amber seems so *lovely*,' she said, following her sisters' gaze. This time, her smile genuine as she watched them laugh together in a way that filled her with envy.

'Do you two still talk?'

She took a giant gulp of her wine and tried not to cringe as she placed it back down. She shook her head. 'Not really anymore.'

'That's a shame. You two were so close as kids. I think at one point I even thought you guys might have ended up together. I think we all did.'

She almost choked on her wine as it hit the back of her throat.

Mia nodded. 'But I get it. It's hard to maintain friendships when one moves away. You probably would've grown out of each other anyway. Tim and I did. I was actually surprised I was invited at all. But hey, pretty grateful I'm here.' She leaned in and gave Sienna's shoulders a little shake. 'But even more grateful to have you here with me. I've really missed you.'

'Me too. I'm enjoying our bonding time.' Sienna took her arm that was wrapped around her neck and squeezed it. She was happy not to let it go.

It wasn't long until everyone began taking their seats. She could sense Ethan's hesitation from a mile away, and sure enough was the last to approach the table. Instead of sitting next to her, Amber took his seat, and he took hers. She wasn't sure what his intention was in doing this, but she figured he dreaded the idea of them sitting next to each other as much as she did. It wasn't all bad, the woman was unexpectedly up for a conversation, keen to know every detail of their childhood friendship. She didn't appear to be jealous, but Sienna could see that she was curious. That behind her spirited smile, Amber was aware there was something drawing them together.

Sienna filled her in on the basics, brushing over the heart of their friendship. She shared that their families were close, that they went to the same schools. She left out the bus rides, the letters and every-thing that eventually divided them. Ethan sat there basically immobile listening in as Sienna let the story unfold as platonically as she possibly could.

As the night went on, the two women couldn't stop talking. Amber was wonderful. She was intelligent, super down to earth, with a sense of humour that was actually similar to her own. As far as Sienna could tell, she was exactly Ethan's type and despite her deep sadness, she was happy for him. She actually was.

For both of them.

She was a physiotherapist, specialising with elite athletes. Being the beauty that she was, she could imagine all the attention she would get. She was probably in high demand with a waiting list of hot, muscly men dying to be treated by her. She could picture the woman giving Ethan massages with those skilled fingers of hers after a long, hard, physical day at work. Maybe she already had.

Ethan must have gone to the bar three or four times, bringing them back a new glass of wine before they had the chance to finish the previous one. Eventually he loosened up, obviously feeling as though it was safe to let them be and finally began chatting with the other guests at the table who up until that point had been ignored.

By the time speeches finished and all three courses had been devoured, it was time to hit the dance floor. She almost had to laugh at the expression on Ethan's face as Amber took her hand and spun her over to the dance floor. She had to swallow a chuckle when Amber chose her over Ethan even though they stood up at the exact same time. It certainly was an unforeseen, budding friendship. It wasn't long until Ethan intervened and took his girlfriend's hand, leading her into a jive across the other side of the dance floor, keeping one eye back at Sienna as they bounced around.

For an event that she was convinced would never end, the end of the night snuck up quicker than she anticipated. But by eleven o'clock she was emotionally drained and more than ready to go home. She was ready to pretend that a pretty woman by the name of Amber, with dark hair and green eyes, never existed.

SHE WAS WALKING to the car when Ethan approached her. Mia was finishing up the final rounds of goodbyes inside and Amber was in the bathroom. As soon as he called her name, her clutch flew from her hands and onto the asphalt. Her belongings spilt everywhere on its way down as the clasp broke open. With her head spinning she reached to the ground, stalling as the tightness of her dress locked her in position half way to the ground.

'Don't even think about it in that gorgeous dress of yours,' he laughed. He bent down and began collecting her things together.

Her heart leaped from her chest as he reached straight for the letter.

'It's really ok, I've got it.' She tried a second time. Again, the restrictiveness of her dress wrestled against the idea.

He picked up the envelope and turned it over. Slowly he stood and looked carefully at her, confusion filled his face. She tucked what was now loose curls behind her ear and sighed as she looked up at the stars that filled the clear, country sky.

'What's this?'

Through her intoxicated state she swore he looked almost …

Upset.

'It's nothing.' She snatched it from his hands. 'Thank you,' she responded more gently.

He let her take it, but his eyes didn't move off hers. 'I don't think it's nothing Sienna, it has my name on it.'

With quivering hands, she stuffed it back into her purse along with her lipstick, license and phone. She kept the key out and pointed it towards her car. It unlocked. 'Yes, I suppose it does. It's just a little letter. It's not important now.'

'It's not important *now*? What does that even mean?'

She shrugged, pretending she was wasn't bothered. She looked up the stars and kept her focus there for a while. It really was a perfect evening.

So still. If only her heart felt that way.

'What did you want to tell me?' He lowered his voice. 'You can talk to me.'

She shook her head. Bad idea that was, it only made her head spin more. 'No Ethan. I can't.'

She began walking towards the car. Faster this time. Just because her relationship was down the toilet didn't give her a right to flush his, too. She needed to leave now. Before she said something that she would regret tomorrow.

Where was Mia? What was taking her so long?

'Of course you can. You know that.'

Oh god, he was following her. She opened the passenger door and turned to face him. 'You told me to keep my distance. You said it was best for everyone.'

He grew quiet and lowered his head to his feet. She wondered what he was thinking.

'I'm still your friend S ... we're friends.'

She pursed her lips together and squeezed her eyes shut. They were the very words that had tormented her for half her life.

It was although it was 2010 again and they were in her St Kilda apartment, the scene was playing out a second time.

'Yes, we are. And as your friend ...you should know that I think Amber is amazing. She is really great, Ethan. You've done well.' She was grateful the darkness of the night meant he wouldn't see the tears that had made their way down her flushed cheeks.

He grew quiet. 'Thank you. Yeah, she is.' He placed his hand gently on her shoulder.

How was that a simple touch could give her such intense butterflies?

'How are you S? Are you doing ok, really?'

The question unlocked another round of tears. She let them fall this time.

It was fine, it was dark. He wouldn't see it.

'I'm well.' She inhaled. 'Patrick has stopped drinking.'

'Really?' his voice lifted.

If only it filled her with the same hope.

'That's so great ... I'm so glad to hear that. So, things are looking up then, yeah?'

She wouldn't tell him the truth. She wouldn't burden him with her problems any longer.

It was time to set him free.

'Yeah.' She managed a smile so big that her cheek bones lifted high enough to release the remaining tears from her eyes. 'Everything is unfolding the way it's supposed to.'

He released his hand, leaving her with a tingling sensation where it had rested on her shoulder. 'It's definitely a big step in the right direction. Looks like he's putting in some effort and fighting for you. You two will pull through, give it some time.'

She swallowed and looked up again at the stars, wondering if he actually even believed a word of it. She sure as hell didn't. If anything, time had proven that it only made things that much worse.

As soon as they arrived back at her sister's house, she quickly said goodnight and stepped outside onto the back patio. Breathing in, she found herself gasping as the cool air hit her lungs. She felt as though she was having some sort of panic attack.

Breathe.

She steadied herself against the railing and opened her clutch that was now dirtied from the ground. She took the letter out from the wrinkled envelope and without a second thought, tore it up into tiny pieces.

Pieces so tiny, they could have been mistaken for confetti.

Twenty-One

Whatever Damian responded back with in his email, it was worded well enough to bring Nolan back to school.

Following that afternoon, he had kept his distance, sharing very little information of Miranda's reply.

'She says she trusts that Nolan will participate in all classroom activities without any special attention,' he had told her in a very dry and matter-of-fact tone.

As she had feared, she had somehow hurt his pride and now he wouldn't even look at her. It felt as though her colleagues made up for the lost pair of eyes as they glared at her condescendingly. It was as though they had all been flies on the wall that day in his office. Perhaps there had been one after all of that. Instead of letting their ignorance inhibit her, she found it sad. If they spent their energy getting to know her instead of loathing her, things would be different and just maybe, her life would be more tolerable.

She doubted Damian would have said anything, but he hadn't needed to. Already people were noticing the way he dismissed her when she would usually hold his full attention. This generated even more whispers. She had never studied the theatre room table as thoroughly as she had that Monday afternoon during their faculty meeting.

Damian was going on about something to do with scope and sequence documents, but all she could focus on was the small gold nail sticking out from the edge of the table. It looked as though it had been there for years—now blunt on the end and building rust. How had she not sliced herself on it before? She made a mental note to report it, but by the time the meeting finished up it had slipped from her mind.

She had bigger things to think about. Curiosity had been eating at her for far too long.

She would keep trying.

Maybe Nolan would open up and share more than Miranda ever would. Sparking a conversation with him would be the easy part, they had broken down the wall of communication months ago. Going deeper was the tricky part.

Tuesday was lunch duty day. As usual, she found him in the locker breezeway sitting against the brick wall with his pile of library books. As usual, her heart crumbled at the sight of him hunched in the same position as every other lunch time; his skinny legs folded under his chin with his book rested on the ground beside him.

He looked up at her as she moved closer, the jingle of her keys around her neck having been a dead giveaway. His big brown eyes widened through his thick rims as his face lifted. 'Hello Miss Henderson.'

Always so polite.

'Hello Nolan. How's your reading going?'

'Well, thank you.' His smile broadened. 'I'm reading about the planets.' He turned the book around showing a page of pictures surrounded by tiny black text.

'That looks like it's a bit of a tricky book. Are you sure you're able to follow ok?'

He pulled out a dictionary from the middle of his tower of books. 'This thing is a life saver.'

'I'm impressed,' she said brightly. 'Any words you need help on?'

He shook his head. 'I think I've got them all covered, thank you.'

He flipped through the pages. 'What's your favorite planet Miss Henderson?'

She thought for a second. 'I think it would have to be Saturn. I think the ring system is very beautiful.'

'It's also huge,' he added thoughtfully. It's the second biggest planet after Jupiter, although colder than Jupiter. We'd freeze there.'

'Yes, we would certainly turn to ice cubes! What's your favourite planet, Nolan?'

'Mars. Definitely Mars.' He yanked up his sleeve slightly and took a sip of soup from the canister. 'Because the planet shows evidence that there may have been water there in the past. It has river valleys and channels in its surface which I find pretty fascinating. It also has the largest volcano in the solar system, Olympus Mons, which is about three times the size of Everest!'

She was impressed by the depth of his knowledge and use of vocabulary before being distracted by the purple mark imbedded in his left forearm. Without trying to be too obvious, she took a step out of the sunlight to inspect the print closer. If she didn't know any better, she would have passed it off as a fall. But the print held a peculiar shape, joining together the many dots in her head. This wasn't a bruise from the playground, or from some rough play in PE class. The blotchy mark looked like hand print. Could it be?

The prospect made her want to be sick.

'Nolan, what happened to your arm?'

He stopped talking then and followed her eyes. He rolled down his sleeve and wiped his mouth with it. 'I tripped over playing soccer.' He placed the book down and began taking hurried gulps of his soup. He barely swallowed before shoving the next heaped spoonful in.

'I didn't know you played soccer. When did you hurt yourself?' She tested him.

He shrugged, unable to meet her eye. 'Ummm … a couple of days ago. It's no big deal, it doesn't hurt that much.'

She kneeled down to his level and reached for his sleeve.

He jerked back abruptly. 'It's fine.'

This wasn't like Nolan.

'I just want to have a look at it. We might be able to put something on it to help it heal faster.'

'No, I'm fine Miss Henderson,' he reassured her. 'Please, I'm fine.'

She hated how panicked he sounded. He was hiding something. Were his parents hurting him? The nauseous feeling churned away in her stomach. Surely not. But there was no way of knowing for sure. It was clear Nolan wasn't going to tell her, even if it was the truth. If such speculation got back to Miranda, she would kick up a fuss and maybe even pull Nolan from the school. Then what?

He would disappear into the hands of a child abuser.

'Ok, its ok, I'll leave it.' She stood to her feet. 'Does your Aunt Lindsey play soccer with you?' She wasn't ready to leave this alone.

He took the planet book back out and turned to a random page, bouncing his knees as his legs folded under him in a cross position. 'Sometimes.'

For someone who liked to talk a lot, he suddenly had very little to say.

'Did she take you to the soccer at all when you were younger?' If he was still with a foster family then he wouldn't have had much of a history with his so called 'family'. Without reading the page he was on, he turned another.

'No.'

'What about your parents? Did they take you to any games?'

He shook his head.

Think.

She smoothed her lips together tightly. 'What were some of your favorite things you did as a family when you were little Nolan?' Far out, she was prying, and Nolan knew it.

He looked up at her and frowned. 'No offence Miss Henderson, but you're asking a lot of questions today.'

'I'm sorry I'm quizzing you so much,' she said with a little laugh. 'Your mum mentioned you're leaving us soon and would love to get to know you a little more before that happens.'

Suspicion darkened his face. 'Pardon?'

'Los Angeles? 'Surely this wasn't news to him. Had she just put her foot in it again?

He didn't respond, but instead studied the ground harder, longer this time.

'Nolan?'

It was then his little body began to tremble. What had she done? A little sob escaped. She regretted pushing him for answers. Seeing him broken in tears would never make it worth it.

She squatted down and lowered her bum onto the cold cement. 'I didn't mean to upset you, buddy. I shouldn't have asked you so many questions like that.'

They lapsed back into silence. He sniffed a little more before wiping his nose with his sleeve. She took a tissue from the first aid bag she had clipped around her hip. 'You know I'm always here for you Nolan. There's nothing you can say or do that would ever change that. Not even being on the other side of the world.' She didn't know if she was saying the right things, but his sobs seemed to be easing.

He uncovered his face from his arms and shook his head. 'You ... don't ... know,' he managed to spit out.

She crouched down closer to him. 'I promise you Nolan. You have my word. I'll always be here for you, you don't need to worry—'

'No, you don't understand.'

'What don't I understand?' She asked gently.

He didn't answer, but stared out ahead at the brick wall. She gently touched his arm. He yanked it back and muttered a groan.

'Nolan, I need to see this bruise.' She was firm now. She had to be. 'Nolan.'

He shook his head with little conviction, then reluctantly, pulled up his sleeve. What was uncovered was no accident. Up close the jagged bruise wrapped around his forearm formed a clear shape of a hand print.

Chills passed over her. 'Did someone do this to you?'

He wrinkled his nose, his bouncing knees accelerated in pace. He looked down again, wanting to formulate a lie. But she knew he wouldn't.

She drew a steady breath. 'Did your parents do this to you?' she lowered her voice. 'It's ok, you can talk to me, Nolan.'

He jerked his head up with wide eyes, his breathing dangerously strained. Just when she thought he was going to answer her, he scooped his books in his arms and bolted down the breezeway. He disappeared around the corner before she had a chance to get to her feet.

She was now convinced that her speculations this whole time were true.

SHE DIDN'T CARE that Damian wouldn't look at her. She had to report what she has seen. It was vital that he knew about it and to see the bruise for himself. But by the time the bell went, Nolan still hadn't returned to the classroom. She panicked. The last thing she wanted to do was to call someone to go out searching for him. But even if she did, she knew he wouldn't talk to anyone else. Thankfully one of the library staff saw her desperation and had offered to step in.

She was able to breathe again when she found him in the library, sitting in the same aisle as last time. It was almost as though he wanted to be found. He wasn't crying anymore, just rocking slowly forward and back, over and over again, staring out the window that overlooked the playground.

'I'll be ok. I just want to sit here for a while,' his voice vacant, emotionless.

She sat down next to him and crossed her legs to match him. She knew it wasn't the time to reopen the case. The file would stay closed.

For now.

The important thing was that he had someone there for him. It was what he needed and that was exactly what she would do.

'Ok.' She looked up at the books that were neatly ordered in the shelf. 'Any good ones?'

He followed her eyes then shrugged. 'Dunno.' He squinted his eyes, studying them more carefully. 'Actually … there could be one.' He stood to his feet and brushed his fingers along the National Geographic collection. He took out four or five books from the shelf and settled back down on the carpet beside her.

Then they spent the next forty minutes exploring Ancient Egypt together.

DAMIAN HAD SUDDENLY become much harder to hunt down. She found it amazing how he suddenly wasn't available for her. Instead of letting it be something to be concerned about, she was grateful for the extra breathing space. Although now wasn't the time for a game of hide and seek.

She needed to talk to him.

She knew better than to leave a note in his office. There was no way she would be doing that again. Instead, she spent a good half hour after the bell went, documenting the situation in a well thought out email. They would discuss the issue tomorrow. And it would be discussed. There would be some sort of investigation, an action plan. She would demand it.

This would not be left alone.

She was somewhat surprised to see that Patrick had left her a message. That he had randomly made the effort to let her know that there would be, yet again, another late night at work. By now it was expected that every late night would go without an explanation attached to it. Which was why she was amazed to be given one tonight. Amazed that after weeks of treating each other like strangers as they tiptoed around the house, that a text finally justified this particular absence. It was this single message that sparked the last drizzle of optimism that was left inside of her. At least it was communication. Was it the truth? She doubted it. But for every late night, she would tell herself over and over again that he was exactly where he said he was.

It was another day she had forgotten to eat. Her clothes barely fit her anymore as they hung off her disappearing frame. But with all the latest stressors, food was the last thing she thought about. But as soon as she stepped into the empty apartment, it was the first thing on her mind. Not because she was hungry, but because if she focused on anything else, she might collapse in a heap on the floor.

Focus on the task at hand.

It was all she had to do. If she did this, she would be ok. She opened the pantry hoping to be inspired by what was there. Curry powder, brown sugar, chicken stock—a whole bunch of staple ingredients. She hadn't done a full supermarket shop in over two weeks. Then she spotted the peanut butter and lemon juice, remembering she bought chicken breast the night before.

Satay chicken it would be.

She laid out the ingredients, collecting pots, pans and measuring cups. She could hear the sound of ambulances and police cars whizzing by below, sirens so loud as though they were coming from the very apartment next door. Noises like that filled their apartment on a regular basis, filling any space for silence. It was the price you paid living close to the city along with a chorus of wailing cats, barking dogs, beeping horns and the smashing of glass bottles from the streets below on a Saturday night. Not to mention the screaming matches that went on between the Indian couple on the floor above as she tried to sleep at night.

Complementary add-ons that fueled her anxiety.

No wonder her heart was constantly racing. Home was no longer a place where she could find peace and escape the hustle and bustle of life. It only followed her home. She remembered the feeling of peace every time she set foot in Aringdale. It was a place where she was able to breath, where her mind was free. A place where she made better sense of who she was, embracing everything she now neglected.

Here, she was always on the go, never having the time to stop, reflect or dream. The goal each day was to make it through, before waking up and repeating exactly that. As long as she was here, time would never stand still. Not like it had every time her heart relived the memories Aringdale gifted her with.

But there was no point dreaming about a life she couldn't have. She wasn't a dreamer anymore, she was a realist. And the realist in her reminded her that she had a secure, steady job at one of the best private schools in Melbourne. A position she had always told herself she would see out for at least another five years until she reached her ten-year long service leave. In those three months of leave they had plans to jet off and travel Europe and Asia. That had been the plan. Well, it had been the plan when she first took the job, when their relationship was fresh, young and full of aspiration. Even if the plan happened to change, they would still use those three months to do something life changing together.

What else was there? Well, there was Jacqui of course and ...

Well, that was more than enough. She had so much to be grateful for.

She wouldn't move back to Aringdale for something as pathetic as an escape from the stress this particular season saw her in. Even if it had been a prolonged season, spread across half a decade now.

It wouldn't always be this way. Life wouldn't always be this way. If she wanted an escape she could get on a plane and spend a week or two on a tropical island somewhere. She wouldn't have to give up her life for the sake of a steady pulse.

Before she got too carried away, she put on some music to drown her thoughts and allowed her body to dance. After all, wasn't music medicine for the soul? It sure felt that way as her feet led her through a series of movements around the kitchen floor.

SHE WASN'T SURE whether it was the dancing, the music or the sheer commitment she had towards the dish, but it turned out perfectly.

She was pretty proud how it all came together and, wow, it smelt delicious. She ate it quickly, unaware of how hungry she actually was until she took the first bite and demolished the whole thing within minutes. Patrick's full plate rested on the bench beside her empty one. Like all meals these days, she covered it with plastic wrap and placed it in the fridge where it would wait there for however long it would be until he came home.

It was an unseasonably warm night, and with Cortex Consulting only a fifteen minute drive away she suddenly had the urge to get it to him. Surely, he would appreciate the gesture after a long day at work. She wouldn't disturb him or stay for long. She would just merely drop it off then would be on her way back. Besides, it would keep her mind preoccupied for at least another forty minutes.

She changed into a comfortable pair of jeans, took the plate out from the fridge, and transferred the meal into an air tight container. Taking her keys, she locked the door and jogged down the stairs to the car park.

There weren't many people on the road at this time. Despite all of her bad luck that day, she managed to avoid all seven traffic lights along the way. Twice now she had had a good run to his work. Somehow that little victory made her feel all positive.

She slowed as she approached the building and leaned forward over the steering wheel to locate his black BMW. Like last time, all she could see were the two same cars belonging to the cleaners.

The familiar knot in her stomach returned.

She inhaled deeply, forcing her heart to settle as she gently lowered her foot down on the break and took a left turn down Watson Street—one of the four streets bordering the property. She was glad there were no cars behind her as she crawled at twenty kilometers per hour, looking like a crazy woman as her body lurched over the wheel in search for his car.

Nothing.

Well, there were several cars, but no black BMW.

She made another left into Duke Street and went around the back. She only had to drive about fifty metres before she spotted the familiar number plate. The knot in her stomach loosened and she was able to breathe again.

But as she approached closer, she could see silhouettes moving around inside the vehicle. She pulled over to the curb and turned off the engine. She wouldn't have any distractions. She made sure she was far enough from him where he wouldn't spot her, but close enough to see what was going on. She couldn't work out if what she was seeing was the back of one head, or two.

She didn't have to wait long.

Seconds later the shape split into two. She could see the outline of a profile, hovering inches away from the other one. There was more movement now, the two shapes coming together to form one, then breaking apart again.

She didn't need to watch them bob around in unison any longer. She knew exactly what was going on in there. She took the plastic container and fumbled out of the car. With trembling legs, she concentrated on placing one foot in front of the other as she stumbled across the road as though she was on ice, her eyes glued to the two shapes growing in detail as she drew near.

His window was up so she knocked on it calmly and forced a quivering smile through the rattling of her teeth. The window slowly gravitated down. There next to Patrick was the pretty woman from the café.

The one with the short, cropped, blonde hair.

She stared blankly at him, finding it strangely satisfying to witness the shock written bold all across his face. His eyes discoed with fear and all she could do was look on as she watched him quickly pale in colour. Her heart collapsed with an excruciating pain as her worst fears became a reality right before her eyes. Somehow, maybe through the adrenaline of the moment, she found a smile.

'I thought I'd surprise you and bring you dinner.'

Twenty-Two

S HE DIDN'T WAIT for a response.

She threw the container through the window, not caring if the satay spewed over him or his slutty companion as she bolted to her car. She could hear him calling out her name over and over again, but she didn't turn around. She couldn't bear the sight of him a moment longer. She needed to keep moving. She wouldn't stop, otherwise she would burst into tears and would never recover.

It took three or four jabs to get the key into the ignition as her shaky hands sent her entire body into a seizure of spasms. If she failed to look like a complete lunatic before, she did now as she pulled out from the side of the road, turning the car around without a single head check.

Drive. Just drive.

It was all she had to do.

Focus on the task at hand.

She was repeating the words over as she stared out at the horizon with tears streaming down her face. She couldn't go home. Not a chance. There was no way in hell she would step back into that apartment, not tonight.

Maybe not ever.

She just needed to keep driving. She could hear her phone demanding her attention from the passenger seat, but she ignored it. It continued to vibrate and she seriously considered throwing it out the window. She took it and threw it somewhere in the back of her car instead. Before she had time to process anything, she was making a turn onto the freeway and was following the big green signs to Aringdale. She didn't have anything on her other than the clothes on her back and hopefully, a working phone. She didn't even have her wallet. But she didn't care, she just had to drive. She glanced at her fuel gauge, it sat on half a tank. She would get there comfortably on that. She would be fine, she wouldn't need to stop for petrol. Not that she had a way to pay for it if she did.

She still couldn't believe it. She was still in shock over his deceitfulness, even though a big part of her had expected it. But even then, no one should ever expect the worst from their partner. How dare he mislead her to think that he was working late? How many of those nights had been spent in his car kissing this woman? She refused to refer to the woman by her actual name. Fine, so maybe she wasn't exactly shocked. She did know it had been going on for a while.

Really, she knew. She knew it the whole time. She should have trusted her intuition.

But how long was a while? How long had it been going on before she had seen her at Nancy Green's that day? If she was shocked about anything, it would be the way he conversed with his mistress in broad daylight in front of her like it was the most natural thing in the world. How was he even capable of such a convincing poker face? He was a clearly good actor. Which only made her wonder how long he had acted with her. How well did she know him anyway? There was probably a lot of things she didn't know about him. How much did he know about her? He never knew how much family meant to her, how she longed to dance or be part of that world again. He didn't know how much she despised her job ninety percent of the time, or how broken she was after losing Ethan. But obviously, she wouldn't voice that with him. He probably didn't even know who Ethan was. In the same way she didn't know who this other woman was, or how she captured his heart in a way she hadn't.

There were still so many questions. Was this woman really Brad's partner? Did Brad even exist? Or was she a coworker? Was she married? Did she care that Patrick practically was? Or did she not know? Maybe he had told her he was engaged, maybe he hadn't.

Maybe none of it even mattered.

Because no matter what the answer was, it wouldn't excuse a single second of it. Nor would it deteriorate the damage that had already been done. It would be easier to blame this woman, the affair, for what they had become. For shifting the blame onto an outsider who had never been accountable for the ruins of their relationship. The truth was, they had been broken for years. And like anything shiny and new, lust had found a thrilling escape from that.

The questions played over and over again in her head like a broken record. The more they looped, the less tears she had left to cry. Eventually the tears stopped building with every emotion overriding the previous one, making it almost impossible to know what to feel. She fell back into numbness. It was easier to cope that way. She couldn't undo what had been done.

What good would tears do when she had already cried a lifetime supply of them already?

EXACTLY TWO HOURS and six minutes later she pulled into Mia's driveway. According to the clock, it was almost nine thirty, but felt like it was midnight. The sun was well and truly down now, yet the stars lit the sky bright enough for her to catch her reflection in the rearview mirror. She barely recognised herself. She didn't know who the woman was as a gaunt face stared back at her. One with hollow cheekbones and dark circles framing a pair of lifeless eyes.

She had hit rock bottom.

There was no way in hell she was going to explain any of it to her parents. As far as she was aware, they still believed all the lies she had fed them over the years. But with Mia, she wouldn't have to. Because as soon as she knocked on that door, her sister would know.

She unfastened her seatbelt and reached her arm into the back seat, slapping her hand around in search for her phone. By now the battery had died and she didn't have a charger. Not that she really cared as she had no desire to read a single word Patrick had to say. She would call her coordinator on Mia's phone and leave a message until morning when she would call again. Relief teachers were called in all the time. She wasn't worried.

She somehow managed to get out of the car feeling the brisk country air serve as a remedy, calming her almost instantly. Being conscious that Bailey would be asleep by now, she knocked on the door ever so gently. A light turned on in the passageway and footsteps made their way towards her sooner than she expected. The door opened to find Mia's eyes wide as an owl, studying her. She probably looked as though she was dressed for Halloween with black smudges of mascara mixing in with her tear stained face.

'Sweetie, what are you doing here?' The look of shock liquified to one of empathy as Sienna's body began to shake uncontrollably.

What was happening to her?

'I couldn't go home … I needed to get away. Far away.' She took a breath, hoping the fresh air would calm her like before. But she couldn't stop shaking. She sighed deeply, literally feeling her heart breaking inside her chest. 'I'm sorry for just turning up like this. I would have called you, but my phone died and—'

Her sister threw her arms around her before she had a chance to finish her word vomit. 'Stop that talk. You're always welcome here, you know that.'

Her sister's hand swept up and down her shoulder blade in a comforting rub. 'What happened S?' She pulled back and took hold of her bony shoulders, trying to still her. 'My god, what happened? Are you ok? You're scaring me.'

Sienna shook her head as the scene took form inside her head all over again.

How could he do that to her? To them?

'Patrick's having an affair.'

Mia nodded slowly with a sense of knowing that she knew had been there all along. Her eyes narrowed and began to glaze over as if she too, was about to cry. 'That bastard.' She pulled her in close again. 'I knew he wasn't good for you. I feared it would only be a matter of time until that idiot did something irreversible.'

This wasn't helping, she was meant to be the calm, rational one.

'Mia, please, don't. He isn't as bad as you think he is—'

'What?' She pulled back again, her big brown eyes exuded with rage. 'Oh, come on, please don't tell me you're going to let him get away with this with just a little slap on the wrist. Sienna, without knowing any details, what he has done is unforgiveable.'

They got out from the cold and made their way down the hallway and into the living room. The TV screen held a still image from a familiar romcom movie.

Bridesmaids.

Of course it was. Out of all the movies out there, it had to be that one.

She didn't care, she wouldn't care. Not tonight. Not now. She wanted to end the conversation, curl up on the couch and watch something brain numbing in peace.

She sat down and stared at the screen. She didn't want to talk. She was done talking. Done thinking. Done analysing every single detail. But Mia was standing over her, clearly wanting answers. They were silent for a moment.

'Don't get me wrong. I'm mad. I'm so mad at him for what he's done. And yes, what he did deserves every horrible word under the sun, but that doesn't mean he should be labeled as that. Because he isn't that person. I know you don't believe me, but he isn't. Somehow, he lost his way over the years … the same way I have.'

She was crying again. But this time, for an entirely different reason. Because as soon as the words were spoken aloud, she realised the powerful truth they held. She realised that she was in fact, just as guilty as he was. She may never had cheated physically with Ethan, but emotionally, she had.

SHE BARELY SLEPT that night, even after forcing three melatonin tablets down her throat. They were meant to be some homeopathic sleep remedy but felt as though she had digested sugar tablets. She had found them in the bathroom cabinet at some ridiculous hour. But after waiting half an hour for them to kick in her legs were still as jittery as ever as she tossed and turned, destroying the bedding in the process.

Her body clock woke her up at seven. She had woken up freezing and exhausted with the doona hanging off the edge of the bed. Her eyes felt like sandbags, heavy from the lack of sleep. She wouldn't have had more than three hours. But all was forgotten as soon as she heard Bailey's little feet pitter pattering down the hall. She passed her door, clenching her pink bunny, oblivious of her auntie's visit until she made the double take. The way her face lit up said it all. She let out a little squeal and caved into Sienna's arms. It felt liberating to be loved, adored, wanted. She could have spent forever following her niece around the house as Bailey entertained her with anything her little hands came into contact with.

After playing dinner parties, taking her doll for a stroll in her pram and putting her body through a serious stamina test of horsy rides, Mia finally woke. She found them in the kitchen as Sienna prepared Bailey's breakfast of mashed banana on toast.

'Can I employ you as my full-time nanny?'

Sienna positioned Bailey's plate in front of her on the high chair and took a seat next to her. Her wiggling fingers danced with excitement before sinking into the banana. 'When do I start?' she asked, watching the banana go everywhere other than her mouth. 'She's so much fun. We've had a great morning together. Haven't we?' She kissed Bailey's forehead as she nuzzled her little body into her.

Mia laughed and wrapped her dressing gown around herself tighter. 'She loves her aunt Sienna, that's for sure. Don't you Bailey?'

Her brown eyes locked on hers as a sweet smile appeared on her little face. 'Wuv voo!' she managed through a mouth caked full of mushy banana.

They both exploded into laughter.

'I have a charger for your phone, if you want it.'

Sienna nodded as an upsurge of anxiety closed over her. 'Yeahhhhh. I should probably get onto that. I called work again this morning on your home phone and left another message but should probably confirm to see if it's all sorted.'

"I'm sure it's all fine. I left it in your room.' She opened the fridge door and took out condiments one by one. 'Well, while you sort that out I'll whip us up some French toast. You still eat that, yeah?' She eyed Sienna up and down, making a point that there wasn't much left of her.

'I haven't had it for years. I can't say I really have an appetite right now, but I'm sure that will change as soon as my teeth sink into that goodness. Thank you!'

'No worries. I think I have everything we need to make it.' Her head disappeared into the fridge. 'Ah damn. Out of eggs.' She rummaged a bit more. 'Oh god, I don't even have milk for my coffee.' She closed the fridge door, defeated. 'How did I manage that?'

Sienna jumped to her feet. 'What do you need? I'll go to the super-market now.'

'Are you sure? Hang on, let me give you some money.' She reached for her handbag.

Sienna waved it off, already making her way down the hallway. 'I do have my bank card. I forgot it was inside my phone cover. It's all good. Anything else you need?' she called out. She spotted the charger and plugged her phone in.

'I think that's it for now. Thanks sis, you're the best.' Mia called from the kitchen.

'Not a problem.'

She stared at her phone as she waited for it to start up. It finally came to life. Her heart clenched in anticipation at what messages would come through. After a minute or two her phone began to spasm uncontrollably. Nineteen messages, eight missed calls, three emails. She didn't even know where to begin.

So, she left it.

Instead, she ignored the ones starting with a repulsive P and clicked on the missed called messages. As expected, she received one from work. Janine—one of the receptionists had assured her absence had been taken care of with one of the regular relief teachers stepping in. She felt her body ease in an instant. It was all she gave herself permission to care about, her only concern right now. She was surprised to see a missed call from Damian but even more so to see it paired with a text.

> **It's unlike you to have a day off. Hope you're ok. Let me know if you need to take a couple more. We've got you covered.**

She couldn't help but smile. Even though he had hardly looked at her the past couple of days, he still cared enough to check in. Maybe everything wasn't as bad as she thought it was. And just maybe, she would be back at work tomorrow.

She changed out of Mia's pajamas and threw on her clothes from the day before. She slapped on some foundation and mascara, tied her hair into a knot on top of her head and was out the door. The super-market was only a ten-minute walk away, there was no need to take her car. She was happy to walk anyway. The fresh country air would do her good. She left her phone charging inside and took out her bank card. As far as she was concerned, she was happy to keep it there, unattended all day. She never expected she would feel so free without it. The longer she went without it, the longer life waiting for her could stay on hold.

It was cool out. She forgot just how cold the mornings were here. She enjoyed the quietness of her stroll, her vacant mind allowing room for her to take in the beauty that surrounded her. Peak hour here was nothing compared to the city. There were no hideous lines of cars banked up at the traffic lights, no one blasting their horns at each other. No sight of pedestrians dashing across a busy road rushing to catch public transport. It was calm, and peaceful. So peaceful she could meditate.

She could even hear the birds chirping as they danced from one tree to another. As she admired the flowers and smell of freshly cut grass along the pavement, she could actually see, hear and appreciate nature. It was enough to send a little spring to her step. Even though she had reached the lowest of lows, it was these little things that made her feel as though she wouldn't be there forever.

And she hadn't felt that way in a long time.

She entered the supermarket, feeling a gust of warmth welcoming her. She took her time, walking up and down every aisle, collecting a few extra things along the way. She decided that she would make a quiche for lunch, so she took an extra cart of eggs before filling her basket with everything else she needed. A chuckle escaped her lips as the 'Backstreet Boys' filled the building. Time really did stand still here. Even the playlist hadn't changed.

'Sienna Henderson, is it really you?'

She turned to the familiar voice behind her. 'Mrs. Teasdale,' she said smiling, acknowledging her old music teacher from her Mason Grammar days. One of the few teachers she adored, and also happened to be an old family friend.

The woman was exactly how she remembered her. Tall, slender, her barely greyed ginger hair was fastened back the same way to the side, held by a giant butterfly clip. Maybe it was even the same one? Surely not, how funny.

She chuckled. 'Oh please, don't make me sound older than I am.' She sent Sienna a look that assured her that the formalities could be dropped.

'Diane.' Sienna laughed, correcting herself. 'How are you? Are you still teaching?'

The woman put down her cart and placed one hand over the top of the other. Her posture so composed. 'Yes, indeed I am. Still at Mason Grammar teaching music. Although head of performing arts now and have been for the past six years, mind you,' she stated proudly. 'What about you? Are you still here? Wait a minute … what about all that ballet you were doing? Did you end up going down that path?'

A combination of sadness and regret punctured Sienna out of nowhere. She shook her head, spreading her lips into a faint smile even though the pain had taken a seat deep inside of her. 'I actually moved to Melbourne. I did try the dancing thing for a few years, although I fell into teaching. I teach a beautiful grade three class at Kings Cross.'

'Oh! I do know that school.' Diane's hands clasped together. 'It has a very good name for itself. Very reputable.'

Sienna nodded, finding it strange to hear that a school that caused her so much grief was painted in such light.

'So, you're not dancing at all then?'

'No, I left it behind.' She squirmed slightly whilst making sure her smile was still intact as she placed her food cart down.

'Was that difficult? When I think of you, I remember how much you adored it. How determined you were. It's all you ever talked about.'

It was although Diane could see beyond the façade, probing deeper to bring the girl she remembered, out.

'It was difficult at the time. I must admit, I do miss it and would have loved the opportunity to have done more with it. But there's a season for everything and who knows what the future holds,' she said stiffly with a laugh. Half laughing at herself at how generic she came across. She sounded as though she had recited a quote from somewhere, and in some ways, she had. She had rehearsed the response too many times to count.

Diane was still looking at her, her eyes indicating to her that she sensed more than Sienna was letting on.

'I don't know what position you're in at the moment Sienna, but I have a job prospect that could be perfect for you.'

Her heart quickened and suddenly the Backstreet Boys faded away completely. 'A job prospect?'

'Yes.' Diane smiled. 'Last year we launched a creative arts program at our school for students considering a career in the entertainment industry.'

The kindness in the woman's eyes made her want to check out her groceries and sit down and have a cup of tea with her.

'For the dance stream, it's a point eight teaching load. Other than theory components that need to be covered, there's flexibility on how you structure the classes, with a full scaled performance at the end of each semester. You'd be well looked after, a highly attractive salary with all travel compensated for, if you were to commute.'

She had her full attention. How could this all sound so perfect? Maybe it was the way Diane was selling it. The timing of the conversation alone sent chills down her spine.

'Our current dance teacher is heading off to the U.K at the end of the term so we will be advertising for someone for term four, onwards,' she continued. 'If you're interested, I can easily line up an interview for you and put in a good word, a strong reference.'

Sienna nodded slowly, a smile filling her face in a way it hadn't for months. She could see that Diane was finding it amusing the way she was standing there completely tongue-tied.

'Yeah? How does all of this sound to you? I know it's probably a lot to take in and I might be putting you on the spot a bit! I have to admit, I'm surprised we're here having this conversation, and having bumped into each other at all. But Sienna, as a student, you stuck out to me like a sore thumb. If your work ethic and drive is anything like it was all those years ago now, then this job I believe would be so perfect for you.'

Opportunities never presented themselves like this. Diane had a way of making it sound like the job was hers already. Surely there had to be a catch, things like this just didn't happen to her.

'Wow,' she inhaled. 'I didn't expect to run into you and to be presented with this!' She exhaled and tightened the knot of hair on top of her head. She wished she looked more presentable, but Diane didn't seem to think anything of her ratty appearance. 'Can I get back to you? Can I maybe grab an email address or number and have a think and get back to you? I have to be honest, it all sounds wonderful and I really appreciate that you think I would be a suitable candidate for the position.'

Diane waved her hand and nodded quickly, multiple times over. 'Of course, of course. I understand that completely. I'm just pleased that you are open to considering it.' She took hold of Sienna's shoulder and gave it a little shake. 'Ohhhhh, we'd be so lucky to have you, Sienna. We will be in touch soon. You know where to find me.'

She was such a kind-hearted woman—she always had been. Sienna could imagine her being a lot of fun to work with. The single encounter made her want to neglect all her commitments, throw away everything she had spent years building and say yes, right there and then.

They exchanged contact details and chatted for a few minutes more before the woman pulled her in for a hearty hug. With her head spinning, Sienna made her way to the self-serve check outs, keeping one hand hovering over the details warm inside her jean pocket. Maybe they would stay there, buried inside, maybe they wouldn't. She didn't know what was next, where she would go from here, or what tomorrow would bring. All she could do was hold onto this moment and the hope that came with it.

As soon as she reached the white picketed fence of her sister's house, she could hear the excited squeal from Bailey's lips seep through the cracks of the front door that had swung half open.

Maybe love was in fact, everywhere. It was within a baby's smile, through the kindness of woman offering a potential job opportunity, and proved itself over again through the unconditional love of a family.

Adjusting her grip, she jiggled the contents of groceries by her side and galloped down the pebbled path and up the uneven steps to the door. She could hear Bailey's squeal of excitement grow louder with every nearing footstep. She waited for a moment, then slowly peered her head inside to find her niece on her hands and knees beaming up at her with the same big brown, almond-shaped eyes they both shared. Immediately she was filled with an overwhelming sense of love and every wall around her heart liquified within a single beat.

This is what life was all about. This was home. And the truth was, Aringdale had never felt more like home.

Even after nine years.

To be continued in the sequel

HERE I STAND

Beneath the Clouds Series

ABOUT THE AUTHOR

Jessica is a 30-year-old primary school teacher, former fitness professional and dancer. She was born and raised in Bendigo, Victoria before moving to Melbourne in 2008. For as long as she can remember she has had a passion for storytelling—in all forms. From writing countless short stories as a child to later completing a creative writing course, written by one her favourite authors, Karen Kingsbury, Jessica was adamant to become a published author. 

NINE YEARS is the first book in the two-part series BENEATH THE CLOUDS.

jessleed.com
facebook.com/jessicaleedauthor
@jessicaleedauthor (Instagram)

ACKNOWLEDGEMENTS

Writing a book is harder than I thought but more rewarding than I could have ever imagined.

None of this would have been possible without my family. A special shout out to my incredible father who was responsible for the beautiful front cover and promotional images. Thank you for your enthusiasm and creativity in bringing these characters to life.

To my beautiful friend, Lauren—from the beginning I always envisioned you as my 'Sienna Henderson'. Thank you for kindly donating your time and for being a significant part of the production of this book. You have been such a joy to work with.

To the faithful Bernadette who hosted my book launch despite having a new born baby on her hands! You have such a heart for the community and for helping others. I am so grateful for you and for your generosity.

I'm eternally grateful for John who spent countless hours reading over this novel, being a big part of the design of the cover and for composing the most stunning piece of music 'Beneath the Clouds'. Your talent, heart and generosity blows me away. Thank you for being my biggest supporter and sharing my excitement about my dream of seeing my manuscript make its way to publication. Thank you for your unwavering belief in me and for being there through every detail of this journey.

Finally, to my wonderful readers, these pages would be closed without you. It is my hope that as the pages unfold you will be swept away on a journey that will move you in some way.